SHIFTING SANDS

Recent Titles by Anthea Fraser from Severn House

The Rona Parish Mysteries
(in order of appearance)

BROUGHT TO BOOK
JIGSAW
PERSON OR PERSONS UNKNOWN
A FAMILY CONCERN
ROGUE IN PORCELAIN
NEXT DOOR TO MURDER
UNFINISHED PORTRAIT

Other Titles

PRESENCE OF MIND
THE MACBETH PROPHECY
BREATH OF BRIMSTONE
MOTIVE FOR MURDER
DANGEROUS DECEPTION
PAST SHADOWS
FATHERS AND DAUGHTERS
THICKER THAN WATER
SHIFTING SANDS

SHIFTING SANDS

Anthea Fraser

This first world edition published 2011
in Great Britain and in the USA by
SEVERN HOUSE PUBLISHERS LTD of
9–15 High Street, Sutton, Surrey, England, SM1 1DF.
Trade paperback edition first published
in Great Britain and the USA 2011 by
SEVERN HOUSE PUBLISHERS LTD.

British Library Cataloguing in Publication Data

Fraser, Anthea.
  Shifting sands.
  1. Widows – Fiction. 2. Safaris – South Africa – Fiction.
  3. Journalists – Fiction. 4. Sudden death – Fiction.
  5. Suspense fiction.
  I. Title
  823.9'14-dc22

ISBN-13: 978-0-7278-8057-4 (cased)
ISBN-13: 978-1-84751-363-2 (trade paper)

All Severn House titles are printed on acid-free paper.

Severn House Publishers support The Forest Stewardship Council [FSC],
the leading international forest certification organisation. All our titles that
are printed on Greenpeace-approved FSC-certified paper carry the FSC logo.

MIX
Paper from
responsible sources
FSC
www.fsc.org   FSC® C018575

Typeset by Palimpsest Book Production Ltd.,
Falkirk, Stirlingshire, Scotland.
Printed and bound in Great Britain by
MPG Books Ltd., Bodmin, Cornwall.

ONE

Jonathan Farrell pushed back his chair and strode to the window, staring down at the street two floors below. It did little to lighten his mood. Pedestrians hurried by, doubtless with meetings to go to, appointments to keep. Cars swept past; even a dog, pausing at a lamp post, seemed to have a sense of purpose.

Unlike himself. He was bored, restless, and worried on a number of counts. Foremost at the moment was the fact that, as a freelance journalist, he'd had no work for the past two weeks, while his friend Steve, whose London flat he was presently sharing, was engaged on a lucrative assignment.

He turned from the window to make yet another mug of coffee. There was also, he reflected, spooning in the Instant, the question of how long he could impinge on Steve's hospitality. Incredibly, he'd already been here three months, and though Steve, good friend that he was, insisted it was no problem and he was glad of the company, Jonathan felt increasingly guilty. For one thing, his presence affected Steve's love life, despite his regularly absenting himself in the evenings, passing the time in a nearby pub or cinema in order to leave the flat free. But the time was fast approaching when, unless he bought or rented a flat of his own – which seemed altogether too final a step – he'd have to sort things out with Vicky.

It was undeniable that he missed her and the boys. True, he went down to Kent each weekend to take his sons out, but it was an unsatisfactory arrangement, necessitating brief and difficult meetings with his wife. And at nearly four and six, they were increasingly asking questions he found difficult to answer. Nor was it ideal that during these visits he'd stayed perforce with his mother, who strongly disapproved of his conduct. At least she'd now gone on holiday, and for the next couple of weekends he'd have the house to himself.

But that brought him to another concern. It was only ten months since his father, who'd never had a day's illness, dropped dead on the golf course, a fact Jonathan still had difficulty accepting, and as a much-needed break for their mother, he and his sister, Sophie, had arranged this holiday for her. It was the most damnable luck that her friend Beatrice, who was to have accompanied her, had broken her arm and had to drop out. Which meant that instead of the loving support they'd envisaged, Jonathan feared she might now be lonelier than if she'd stayed at home.

His mobile rang suddenly, startling him into spilling his coffee, and, hastily locating the phone, he saw the call was from *UK Today* and felt a surge of hope. 'Nick, hi! Got something for me?'

'Sorry, mate, not at the moment. Or, come to think of it, just maybe.'

'And what the hell does that mean?'

'Some bird just rang, asking for your number. Sounded foreign. You might want to give her a call. Could be something in it.'

'Name?'

'She wouldn't give it. Sounded pretty cagey to me.'

Jonathan frowned. 'When was this?'

'Just now. She was on a mobile.' He read out the number, and Jonathan jotted it down.

'Right. Thanks, Nick, and if anything comes up, let me know, won't you?'

'Will do.'

Ending the call, Jonathan picked up the pad and regarded it thoughtfully. A foreign girl who wouldn't leave her name? He felt a stirring of interest. As Nick said, there might be something in it, but even if there weren't, he couldn't afford not to follow it up. Feeling more positive than he had in a while, he punched out the number.

She sounded French, but could as easily be Belgian or Swiss. They arranged to meet in a café across town, though she again withheld her name, saying merely that she'd be wearing a blue jacket.

Jonathan arrived with minutes to spare and, turning into the doorway, cannoned into a young woman on her way out – a young woman in a blue jacket. Her eyes widened as she saw him and a flush spread over her cheeks.

He said quickly, 'I'm Jonathan Farrell. Didn't we arrange to meet?'

Her eyes dropped. 'Yes, I . . . I am sorry. I changed my mind.'

'Well, since I'm here, let's at least have coffee, and perhaps I can change it back again.'

She hesitated, but he took her arm and led her inside to a vacant table, studying her covertly as she settled in her seat opposite him. Mid-twenties, at a guess; short dark hair, with a feathery fringe that accentuated large eyes, now lowered as she let her handbag drop to the floor.

Straightening, she caught his gaze and gave an uncertain smile.

'You could start by telling me your name,' he suggested.

A pause, then: 'Elise.'

'Elise what?'

She made a small movement of her hand. 'That will do for now.'

Hiding his impatience, Jonathan signalled a waitress, checked his companion's preference, and placed the order.

'Look,' he reminded her as the girl moved away, 'it was you who requested this meeting.'

'You must forgive me.' She smiled, lifting her shoulders in a gesture essentially French. 'I used up all my courage to telephone your paper. When you were not there, I was . . . relieved.'

The accent was attractive, perhaps deceptively so. Because, Jonathan reminded himself, however hesitantly she spoke, she was *thinking* in her own language.

'Yet you left your number, and when I called, agreed to meet.'

'Yes.' Her voice was low, and she was avoiding his eyes.

Their coffee arrived: latte for her, espresso for himself. He needed the kick that Instant had failed to give him.

He tried again. 'You asked for me by name, right?'

She nodded. 'I have read . . . your articles.'

That was a surprise. 'You live over here?'

'Since two years. For my work.'

'Which is?'

A tremor crossed her face. 'In . . . the leisure industry.'

Which could mean anything, Jonathan thought irritably. She might even be a high-class hooker. He leaned back in his chair, his eyes on her face. 'So why did my articles make you want to speak to me?'

She stirred her drink. 'You . . . find out things.'

'And what do you want me to find out for you?'

She looked up quickly, glancing around as though to check they couldn't be overheard.

He waited expectantly, but all she said was, 'I am not sure.'

This was like drawing teeth, he thought in exasperation. The fact that he'd come more or less on spec showed how desperate he was. Instead of immediately galloping over here, he should have waited for her to ring again, and since she probably wouldn't have done, they'd both have saved time and trouble. In any event, he'd had enough of being messed around. He swallowed his coffee, burning his tongue in the process, and pushed back his chair.

'OK, you've changed your mind. Let's leave it at that. Enjoy your coffee. I'll settle up at the desk.'

'No!' She reached out, laying a detaining hand on his arm. 'Wait! I am . . . sorry!'

He paused, looking down at her. 'Five minutes. I'll give you five minutes to tell me what you want, then I'm off. OK?'

She seemed on the verge of tears, and he wondered uncharitably if it was an act. 'You do not understand.'

'Too right.' But he sat down again. 'Well?'

She took a sip of coffee and drew a deep breath. 'It . . . might be dangerous.'

'*Dangerous*? Dangerous for whom?'

'For me. And perhaps also for you.'

'Look, I don't take kindly to threats—'

'No, no!' She was shaking her head violently. 'But there are people who would not wish me to speak to you.'

He looked at her helplessly, convinced, despite himself, of her genuine distress. 'People you work for?'

'Yes.' It was barely audible.

'And they are . . .?'

'That, I cannot tell you.'

He slammed his hand on the table, making the cups dance. 'Then what the hell do you expect me to do?'

She had jumped at his outburst, and now met his eyes at last. 'This was not a good idea,' she said quietly. 'I am sorry to have wasted your time.'

He gazed at her in frustration. 'Is there *anything* you can tell me?'

She spread her hands helplessly. 'Not enough. I see that now.'

'Right.' He stood up abruptly. 'Then all I can do is wish you the best of luck.' And, leaving her sitting there, he paid the bill and walked out of the café without looking back.

Exactly what was the point of that? he asked himself angrily, striding down the street. A new line in pickups? A honeytrap of some kind? She'd told him less than nothing. Perhaps he should have waited and followed her when she left the café. But to what end? To see if she'd report back to someone?

He smiled grimly; he was letting his imagination run away with him. He'd write the whole thing off as a diversion that had whiled away a boring morning and could now be forgotten. And, as a first step, he'd treat himself to a pub lunch before renewing his search for work.

But dismissing Elise left the field clear for Vicky, and, as he ate, his earlier worries flooded back. When, he wondered miserably, had things begun to go wrong?

When they'd met, she'd been a subeditor on the Women's Page of a paper he occasionally worked for – bubbly, ambitious, full of ideas. She'd shared his excitement as his name became known and increasingly respected, and her pride in him continued through the first year of their marriage. Gradually though, as, more and more often, prearranged visits and outings fell foul of deadlines, she'd become disenchanted.

'I can't depend on you at all these days!' she'd complain. 'This meal has been planned for ages, and you know how hard it is, finding a date to suit everyone.'

And he'd apologize, insisting it was out of his hands, and, as a fellow journalist, she'd grudgingly accept it. But then the kids came along, she gave up work, and her understanding wore thin. He wasn't there for birthday parties, or, later, carol concerts, nativity plays and sports days, and his apologies no longer carried weight. That was when the rows began.

'If you wanted a nine-to-five husband,' he'd flung at her, 'you shouldn't have married me! You knew I'd never be that!'

'All I ask is that you show some interest in your children! They might as well not *have* a father, for all the time you spend with them!'

'If I was in the Forces, I'd be away for months on end!' he'd retorted. 'In fact, I'm home *more* than most dads!'

'But shut away in your study! They're not allowed to interrupt you, and you don't emerge till they're in bed!'

And so it had gone on, their words growing increasingly bitter and incriminatory, until the final row, when deliberately hurtful remarks were exchanged, and Vicky had finally flung his briefcase at him and told him to get out. And he had. And that was three months ago.

He pushed his plate away and ran his hands through his hair, still convinced she'd been totally unreasonable – but then, so had he! The realization sluiced over him like a cold shower, forcing him to admit for the first time that he'd often used his work to avoid helping out – at bath times, when the kids were invariably hyper and the bathroom was awash; on visits to the zoo, which bored him; and particularly at birthday parties – raucous occasions filled with boisterous, yelling little boys, which, frankly, he dreaded. Telling himself he couldn't afford time with his family, he'd retreated with his ready-made excuses, leaving Vicky to handle them alone.

The crux had come during the Easter holiday, when, rather than face a fruitless discussion as to when or if he'd be free, she'd taken the boys to her parents' for two weeks, leaving him to his lonely deadlines. Within weeks of their return, the split had come.

God, how could he have been so self-centred? No wonder she'd had enough of him! Well, these last months had brought home to him how much he missed them. He wanted his family back.

Like probing an aching tooth, he conjured up Vicky in his mind: her small, trim figure, the mass of unruly brown hair, her peals of laughter and ready smile – the last two considerably less frequent of late. Perhaps, this weekend, they could talk things through – if they hadn't already gone too far.

Closing his mind to the possibility, Jonathan reached for his phone and called Steve.

'Are you seeing Maddy this evening?' he asked without preamble.

'No, it's girls' night out. Why?'

'Fancy a curry, on me? Not a takeaway, a sit-down affair?'

'You know me, I always fancy a curry!'

'Great. I'll book at the Raj and Rani for eight o'clock.'

'Wow! You *are* pushing the boat out! Landed some work?'

'No such luck. It's by way of a cheering-up exercise.'

'I'm all for that, too. You've been a right miserable bugger lately!'

'Go back to work, before I change my mind! See you later.'

'See you,' Steve echoed, and broke the connection.

'And that was as far as I got,' Jonathan concluded as, seven hours later, he finished relating his morning's encounter. 'Intriguing, isn't it? I don't often come across mysterious French girls who warn me of danger.'

'She's probably a glorified office girl,' Steve commented, reaching for a poppadom, 'with a grudge against her boss. Or even an au pair. Does that count as the leisure business?'

'Not from what I've heard.' Jonathan leant back, looking across at him. 'So you're telling me that, although I'm badly in need of a story, I should forget it?'

'You've not much choice, unless she comes back to you.'

Which, though he'd reached the same conclusion himself, Jonathan found depressing.

'Look, something'll come up soon,' Steve added. 'I've almost finished my piece; perhaps we could do a joint one next? It's some time since we did, and we work well together.'

'We still need an angle.' Jonathan smiled ruefully. 'Sorry to be such a Jonah; I underwent a painful self-analysis over lunch, but the outcome is that I'm determined to make a go of it with Vicky. If she'll have me back.'

'Well, that's great news!'

'I thought I'd broach it this weekend. Apart from anything else, it's time you had the flat to yourself again.'

Steve smiled. 'As it happens, that would be of limited duration. Maddy and I are thinking of getting hitched.'

'That's wonderful, Steve!' Jonathan slapped him on the shoulder. 'Congratulations, old son!'

At thirty-six, Steve Forrester had seemed a confirmed bachelor, with two long-term relationships behind him. Jonathan liked his present girlfriend, who was a partner in a dental practice, though it had never occurred to him they might marry.

'Positively no pressure, though,' Steve added. 'She'll stay where she is until her flatmate emigrates in the new year. Then they'll sell it and divide the spoils.'

'A spring wedding, then?'

'Watch this space!' Steve raised his glass. 'So here's to you and Vicky getting back together, and Maddy and me staying that way!'

'I'll drink to that!' said Jonathan.

It was odd, Ma not being there when, on Friday evening, he let himself into her house, and again he felt anxious on her behalf. God knows when he could expect a postcard.

He looked about him. The house felt strangely silent; he couldn't remember when he'd last been alone in it. There was a faintly stuffy smell, due, no doubt, to closed windows in the September sunshine, and he went round opening a few.

His parents' room, as he still thought of it, was as tidy as usual and held a faint remembrance of his mother's scent, sharp and citrous. His father's silver-backed brushes still stood on the tallboy, and Jonathan felt a tightening in his chest. The unexpected death should have drawn himself and Vicky closer, but, sadly, it hadn't. He'd refused her attempts at comfort, preferring to keep his grief fiercely private, and knew she'd felt rebuffed. She'd been very fond of her father-in-law, but he'd been little help in her grieving.

He deposited his bag in his boyhood room, which he'd been allocated during these visits. The narrow bed was made up with clean sheets, and there were a couple of *Reader's Digest* magazines on the bedside table. Familiar books lined the shelves – paperbacks of Rex Stout and Raymond Chandler for the most part – and the walls bore traces of long-removed posters from his teenage years.

On his first visit, he'd automatically turned towards the guest room, but his mother redirected him, saying matter-of-factly, 'You're behaving like a schoolboy, so you might as well sleep there.' And she'd been right, damn it, though he'd only just acknowledged the fact.

Jonathan glanced at his watch. Eight thirty. The traffic had been slow coming out of London, typical for a Friday evening, and he'd not yet eaten. He knew an assortment of dishes awaited him in the freezer, but first he must touch base with Vicky, and his mouth went dry at the prospect. Returning downstairs, he poured himself a tumbler of whisky. Then, his heart beating uncomfortably, he picked up the phone.

'Vicky . . .'

'Hello, Jonathan.' Unlike his own, her voice sounded cool and calm.

'Just . . . clocking in. OK if I come round about ten in the morning?'

'Of course.'

'I was wondering if we might have a word before I take the boys out?'

A pause, then: 'I'm afraid I shan't be here; Doris will stay with them till you arrive.'

His preconceived plans collapsing around him, Jonathan hastily tried to regroup. 'Perhaps when I bring them back, then?'

'I don't think so, do you? There doesn't seem much to say.'

'On the contrary,' he said harshly, 'there's the hell of a lot! Vicky, I—'

'I can't talk now; Sally and Robert are here. The boys will be ready at ten o'clock. Goodbye, Jonathan.' And she put the phone down.

'Bloody hell!' he said aloud. Well, there was still Sunday. Having geared himself up to a discussion, he'd no intention of returning to London without one. But the delay had wrong-footed him, increasing the inevitable awkwardness, and there was no way he could shunt the boys out of the way without her cooperation.

He swallowed a mouthful of whisky, standing irresolutely in the middle of the sitting room. He'd thought it would be easier without his mother's disapproving presence, but he'd been wrong. If she were here, he might even have asked her advice.

She and Vicky were close, and it was no secret whose side she was on.

He looked round the room, suddenly filled with nostalgia. He'd known this house most of his life, but it was too big for one person, and once Ma was over the worst of her grief, it would make sense to put it on the market. But how many memories were tied up in it! Christmas dinners round the table in the dining room – Dad and Ma, himself and Sophie, and whichever relations happened to be staying over the holiday. Candlelight and Christmas trees and laughter. How long ago it all seemed.

It was from here that he'd left for boarding school and, later, university; here that he'd brought Vicky to introduce her to his parents, and from here he'd set out for his wedding.

His eyes fell on the Doulton figure on a side table, and another memory stirred. The day Tom had taken his first steps, he'd lurched against the table, knocking the ornament to the floor and breaking off its head. Jonathan had been mortified, but his parents took it in their stride. It had been repaired, and only a very close eye would discern the faint line on the neck.

He sighed, swallowed the last of his whisky, and went to forage in the freezer. Food should put paid to this reminiscing.

It was an hour later, as he'd finished eating and was watching the *News at Ten*, that the phone rang. He snatched it up. 'Vicky?'

A light laugh, then his sister's voice. 'Sorry, no!'

'Hi, Sophie. How are things?'

'Fine with us. More to the point, how are they with you?'

'OK, I suppose. I've just been wallowing in nostalgia, thinking how we'll miss this place if Ma decides to sell.'

'Bricks and mortar, Jon, that's all it is. She had a good flight, incidentally; no jet lag, but then there's only an hour's time difference.'

'Talk about breaking news! How the hell do you know that?'

'Tamsin just phoned and mentioned that she'd texted her.'

Tamsin, at present away at boarding school, was his thirteen-year-old niece, and, in Jonathan's opinion, a right little madam. 'So how's it going so far?'

'Well, you know Ma. She'd rather die than admit she wasn't enjoying herself, especially to us, when we talked her into going.'

'So what *did* she say?'

'That she went up Table Mountain and saw some funny creatures called rock rabbits.'

'Nothing earth-shattering, then.'

Sophie homed in on his opening query. 'Are you expecting Vicky to ring?'

Damn; he'd hoped she'd forgotten that. 'Not really, no.'

'You *have* spoken to her, since you arrived?'

'Yes, and arranged to pick up the boys tomorrow.'

'So why might it have been her on the phone?'

He sighed. 'If you must know, I'd suggested having a discussion, but she gave me short shrift. I hoped she might have changed her mind.'

There was a moment's silence. 'You want to go back, then?'

'In a word, yes.'

'You're going to change your wicked ways?'

'Oh, for God's sake, Sophie! I'm in no mood for flippancy.'

'Poor love, you do sound down. You must come and have a meal one evening.'

'Thanks,' he said. 'Was that why you rang?'

'Partly, and partly just to see how you are, rattling around in an empty house.'

'Not enjoying it much, to be frank. Still, there's a freezer-full of goodies, so at least I shan't starve.'

'Well, don't brood. Vicky hasn't been too happy since you left, so if you want to make up, come straight out and say so.'

'That was my intention, but she foiled it.'

'Then try again; you can't give up at the first hurdle. And I'll phone you during the week, when you're back in town.'

She rang off. Why hadn't *he* thought of texting Ma? Jonathan wondered. Probably because he seldom texted anyone, preferring a vocal exchange. Nonetheless, phone calls to South Africa would be prohibitive, and at least it was a means of making contact. Provided, that is, she had her mobile switched on, which she probably wouldn't have for most of the time. He'd give it a try in a day or two.

As he shelved that problem, more immediate ones returned, threatening to overwhelm him. Trouble was, he'd too much time on his hands. He'd be able to think more positively if he could only land some work.

For several more minutes he watched the images on the screen, muted when the phone rang, then he turned up the sound and settled down to watch the next programme.

A couple of hours later, drifting off to sleep, the last face that filled his mind was, surprisingly, not that of his wife or sons, but of the reticent, enigmatic Elise.

TWO

Reaching her hotel room, Anna Farrell dropped her handbag on the bed and ran her fingers through her hair. She was still considerably shaken – an unusual experience for one who prided herself on her self-control. Even when Miles had died so unexpectedly, she'd maintained her public persona, a rock to her children's grief, succumbing to tears only in the privacy of her bedroom.

Which was why, when Beatrice had dropped out of this holiday, and Jon and Sophie worried she'd be on her own, she'd shrugged off their concern. 'Of course I'll be all right, darlings,' she'd told them breezily. 'We'll be in a group, after all. I'll soon make friends.'

In fact, their group consisted mainly of couples, threesomes and foursomes, and though everyone was friendly enough, she was chary of encroaching. The only other single travellers – a young man of about twenty and two women, one young and one middle-aged – were, unfortunately, the people she least wanted to spend her holiday with. And to make matters worse, the tour manager, determined no one should be left out, was already herding the singles together. On today's coach trip, Anna had eluded her only by sitting next to the odd member of a three-some, a pleasant woman in her forties.

But all that, she could cope with. What had disturbed her was her totally unforeseen reaction when, over lunch, the background music suddenly switched to a tune she'd danced to with Miles, and, to her utter horror, her eyes had filled with tears. (What was it Noel Coward said, about the potency of cheap music?) She was pretty sure no one noticed, but it had taken all her control not to break down completely. And God knows what would have happened then. She'd remained on edge all afternoon, terrified some other trigger might set her off again. And it was only the third day of the holiday.

She moved to the dressing table and studied her reflection. To her relief, she looked much as usual – a tall, slim woman of

fifty-five, with short, silver-blonde hair curving towards her face
and grey eyes, mercifully untinged with red, staring back at her.

So far, so good. She drew a deep breath and went to have a
shower.

Her party had again gathered in the bar, and Anna, a smile plas-
tered to her face, ordered a gin and tonic and drifted to the nearest
group, which included the tour manager. One of the men smiled
at her.

'We've been asking Edda's help in putting names to people,'
he said. 'I don't think . . .?'

'Anna Farrell,' she supplied.

'Hi, Anna. I'm Harry Bell, this is my wife Susan, and our
friends Bill and Prue Dyson. We met in Australia four years ago
and have holidayed together ever since.'

Anna was grateful for the clarification; she hadn't yet managed
to identify everyone. 'I should have come with a friend,' she
explained carefully, 'but unfortunately she broke her arm two
weeks ago and had to cry off.'

'What bad luck – for both of you!'

'She insisted I write a detailed diary, to show her when I get
home.'

'I saw you making notes,' remarked the woman called Prue.

Anna smiled. 'I'm not sure how long I can keep it up!'

Other people came to join them, more names were exchanged,
and talk became general. But when the time came to go in for
dinner, the groups automatically reformed, leaving Anna to trail
somewhat disconsolately after them, unsure which table to join.

Edda, at the dining-room door, saw her hesitation. 'There's a
seat over there,' she said helpfully, indicating a table where the
other singles had already gathered, and, since she'd no choice,
Anna obediently complied. At the adjacent table, one of the men
who comprised a threesome caught her eye and half-smiled, and,
detecting a hint of sympathy, she flushed, hoping her lack of
enthusiasm hadn't been obvious.

The younger woman, Anna remembered, was Shelley, the
middle-aged one Jean, and the boy Tony. It soon became clear
Jean would dominate the conversation, added to which, she had
a high, affected voice that Anna found grating.

By the end of the first course, they'd learned that Jean came from Hampshire, that she usually holidayed with 'Iris', who'd unfortunately double-booked this year (lucky Iris!), that she had two dogs – a spaniel and a terrier, which she'd put into kennels and was already missing – and that she was glad it hadn't been too hot so far, because she came up in blisters in the heat. By the bored look on both Shelley's and Tony's faces, Anna deduced all this information was for her benefit and the others had already been regaled with it.

Glancing up as her plate was removed, she again met the eye of her neighbour, who humorously raised an eyebrow, and, suppressing a smile, she hastily looked away. Jean's voice droned on, fortunately requiring no response, until finally, as she paused for a sip of wine, Anna broke in quickly, 'And where do you come from, Shelley?'

Shelley started, her attention obviously having been wandering. 'Bournemouth,' she said.

'Lucky you! I spent a holiday there once. Do you work there too?'

'Yeah.'

'Doing what?'

'I'm a hotel receptionist.'

'That must be interesting, meeting new people all the time.'

'Yeah.'

Anna could only hope she was more forthcoming with her visitors. In desperation, she turned to Tony and, after some fairly laboured questioning, learned that he was taking a gap year after leaving college, and would then work in his father's car-hire business.

Throughout these exchanges, Jean had sat in silence, lips pressed together, and when Anna, running out of questions, paused, she immediately reclaimed the initiative, embarking on a story of one of her previous holidays with the redoubtable Iris.

The band had started to play, and Anna tensed, praying their choice of music wouldn't put her to the test. The meal seemed interminable, and when, at last, they'd finished their dessert, she immediately rose to her feet.

'We've an early start tomorrow, so I think I'll go straight up,' she said, pre-empting alternative suggestions. 'Goodnight, everyone.' And she walked quickly out of the dining room.

In the hall, however, someone touched her arm, and she turned quickly, fearing she'd been followed. But it was the woman from the next table who was smiling at her.

'We wondered if you'd care to join us for coffee?' she said.

'Oh, I—'

'Forgive me if I'm speaking out of turn, but we thought you looked in need of rescue!'

Anna smiled back. 'How dreadful of me, to have given that impression!'

'Not at all; we shouldn't have been eavesdropping. But you will join us?'

'Thank you, I'd like to.'

She was escorted to the bar, where the two men who made up the threesome stood at their approach.

'I'm Wendy Salter,' the woman continued. 'This is my husband, George, and our very good friend, Lewis Masters.'

'Anna Farrell.' She shook hands, unsure, from Wendy's vague gesture, which was her husband.

'Can we get you a coffee?'

'If they have decaffeinated, yes, please; anything stronger, and I shouldn't sleep.'

The coffee duly arrived, and there was a moment's brief silence. Then Wendy asked, 'Have you been to South Africa before?'

'No, but I've wanted to come for some time. It's very beautiful, isn't it?'

'Yes, indeed. Thank goodness for digital cameras, or Lord knows how many films I'd get through! Have you got one?'

'Yes, my . . . husband gave it to me, the Christmas before last.' *Careful!*

'But he wasn't able to come with you?'

Anna took a deep breath. 'Sadly, he died last year.'

'Oh, I'm so sorry! How tactless of me!'

'Not at all.' She smiled tightly. 'I should have come with a friend, but she had to cancel at the last minute.'

The conversation veered to less personal topics as they discussed previous holidays, the hotel, and the itinerary ahead of them. After the stresses of the meal, Anna found it pleasant to relax and enjoy the company of people her own age.

Wendy Salter was small and plump, her light-brown hair merging almost imperceptibly to grey, her eyes bright blue, and her round face breaking easily into smiles. Of the two men, her husband, George – whom Anna had now identified – was heavily built and jovial, while Lewis Masters, who'd smiled at her at dinner, proved harder to analyse. Dark-haired and dark-eyed, the grooves between his eyes suggested stress of some kind, and his movements were quick and decisive, almost, at times, impatient. What, Anna wondered, had brought these quite different personalities together?

It was almost eleven when they left the bar, and she was glad none of her dinner companions was around to note that she hadn't, after all, had an early night. Nor, when she finally reached her bed, did sleep come easily. Memories of the tune she'd heard at lunchtime replayed in her head, and, in its wake, Miles's face came sharply into focus, filling her mind with an image so familiar, so immediate, that she actually gasped with the pain of it.

A wave of desolation swept over her, and hot tears trickled down her cheeks into her pillow. She shouldn't have let Jon and Sophie talk her into this holiday. More to the point, she shouldn't have insisted on going ahead when Beatrice had to drop out. Now, she was going to be stuck with the three incompatible people she'd sat with at dinner, an odd-one-out who belonged nowhere.

Despairingly, she buried her face in her pillow and wept.

They left the hotel at eight the next morning, and as Anna boarded the coach, hoping she might somehow evade the 'singles', Wendy again came to her rescue, patting the seat beside her.

'Come and join me, Anna! The men are talking cricket, so I'm opting out!'

Anna slid in gratefully beside her. The morning was cool and dull, with the promise of rain in the air. Table Mountain, visible from the hotel, was wearing its 'table cloth', its top shrouded in mist.

'Let's hope it clears,' Wendy commented, 'or we won't be able to see any distance.'

Edda, the tour manager, was counting heads, and, having

checked all were present, she signalled to the driver and took up her microphone.

'As you know, today we'll be driving down the Cape Peninsula,' she began, and as she started to describe the countryside through which they'd be travelling, Anna, mindful of her duty, took out her notebook.

'Our first stop will be at Simon's Town,' Edda ended, 'where we'll see the jackass penguins on Boulder's Beach. They came by their name because their call sounds like the braying of a donkey.'

As, indeed, it did. The penguins themselves were very tame, getting under their feet as they walked, and it was difficult to gain a sufficient distance from them to take photographs. Anna was trying to get the right angle when Lewis Masters materialized beside her.

'Shall I take one of you with them?' he offered.

'Thanks.' She handed the camera over and posed rather self-consciously with a group of penguins. 'My grandchildren would love this! I'd always thought these were cold-weather birds; I hadn't expected to see them in South Africa.'

'No, and they're found in Australia too, which I find equally unlikely.'

'Somewhere else I've never been.'

It was time to return to the coach, and they walked back together, just behind George and Wendy.

'You mentioned grandchildren,' Lewis remarked. 'How many have you?'

'Three: a girl of thirteen and boys of four and six.'

'Do you see much of them?'

'More of the boys, since they live quite close. My granddaughter's at boarding school, but her home's in London.'

'And where's yours?'

'Westbridge, in Kent.'

'Ah, I know it; I've played golf there.'

'Really? It's quite a famous course, I believe. My husband was a member.'

She climbed ahead of him into the coach, pausing as she saw George seat himself beside his wife.

Wendy looked up with a smile. 'It seemed a pity to interrupt your conversation,' she said.

'May I join you, then?' Lewis asked after a moment.

'Of course.'

Anna seated herself with mixed feelings. She already felt she knew Wendy, but Lewis was an unknown quantity, and, remembering his reserve the previous evening, she hoped she wouldn't have to make conversation.

'Have you any grandchildren?' she asked as an opener.

'Sadly, no, nor any in prospect. My son has what is euphemistically known as a "partner" – in my youth the word was mistress – and marriage doesn't appear to figure in his plans. My daughter, on the other hand, is living with a prominent barrister fifteen years her senior.'

'Oh dear! Not married himself, I hope?'

'Not any longer, nor likely to chance it again.'

Anna nodded in understanding. 'I have to keep reminding myself we can't live our children's lives for them.'

He raised an eyebrow. 'But surely yours are happily settled?'

She hesitated, and he said quickly, 'Forgive me – that was unpardonably intrusive.'

'No more than my question about the barrister. Actually, my son left his wife a few months ago, though he comes back every weekend to take the boys out.'

'Hard on the children.'

'Yes.'

They lapsed into silence, and Anna gazed out of the window at the flower-studded bush on every side, making occasional notes on her pad. Too bad Beatrice wasn't here; she would so enjoy this.

In the row in front of them, George and Wendy conversed in low voices, and Harry and Susan, whom she'd spoken to in the bar, were across the aisle. Shelley and Tony had teamed up together, while Jean had attached herself to the woman with whom Anna herself had sat yesterday. Gradually, she was sorting out who everyone was.

It was a day that, for several reasons, she would never forget: climbing up to the lighthouse on Cape Point; the open-air café, where redwing starlings alighted on the table and begged for crumbs; sampling the local fish at lunch on the way back; ostriches in the field alongside the road, and herds of antelope in the distance.

By the end of it, it seemed incredible that she'd known Lewis and the Salters less than twenty-four hours, for during the course of it, she'd been seamlessly incorporated into their party, and they all took it for granted that, back at the hotel, she'd sit at their table for dinner. What a difference a day makes! she thought whimsically.

In fact, it set the pattern for those that followed, and Anna's reservations about the holiday fell away, freeing her to enjoy the daily wonders of landscape and animals. In view of the number of miles to be covered, early starts were the norm, but as a habitual early riser, they didn't bother her.

Each evening she wrote her diary, transcribing and enlarging on notes made during the day to record its events in more detail: a visit to an ostrich farm, where they'd watched feather dusters being made, hand-fed the birds, and taken it in turns to stand on the eggs – (*we were told an ostrich's brain would fit in a teaspoon!* she wrote); the mysteriously beautiful Cango Caves; the thrill of stroking a semi-tame cheetah and hearing it purr.

Throughout these crowded, exciting days, the members of the group came to know each other quite well, the ephemeral nature of their friendship allowing more openness than would have been the case at home. Even Jean, whom they'd originally been wary of, grew progressively less strident and, as a result, more agreeable.

As the week went on, Lewis began to alternate with Wendy in sitting next to Anna on the coach trips. He was an interesting and knowledgeable companion, but she quickly learned that he had a short fuse if anything went wrong – an extra-long wait for the coach, a dish at dinner that wasn't up to standard.

One evening, when she and Wendy were waiting for the men to bring drinks from the bar, Anna asked casually, 'How long have you and George known Lewis?'

'Oh, donkey's years,' she replied. 'He and George met at university, and he was best man at our wedding.'

'He's mentioned his children, but not his wife,' Anna said tentatively.

Wendy grimaced. 'Par for the course. They've been divorced for years now, but it was a wonder they stuck it as long as they did. Talk about opposites attracting! Granted, Lewis wouldn't be the easiest person to live with, but Myrtle was impossible.' She glanced at Anna. 'You might have heard of her – Myrtle Page? She was one of the top models of the seventies.'

Anna had a vague memory of an ultra-thin woman in outrageous clothes on the cover of *Vogue*.

'Of course, she's not done any modelling for years,' Wendy continued, 'but she still hits the headlines pretty regularly and makes life difficult for him. As if he's not got enough on his plate.'

'Such as?' Anna asked carefully, monitoring the progress of the men in the bar queue.

'Oh, business worries, as always. He's a complete workaholic, to such an extent that we became quite worried about him. He's not as tough as he thinks, so we scooped him up and insisted he came away with us. God knows when he last had a holiday.'

'I gather he's involved with some sort of hotel?'

Wendy gave a short laugh. 'Is that what he implied? Not quite accurate, but at least he's sticking to our rule of no business talk.'

'So what *does* he do?' Anna asked curiously.

'Only owns the Mandelyns Health Resorts Group.'

'*Owns* it? You mean those luxury health spas?' Anna stared at her in amazement.

'Yep. He started way back by opening a series of health clubs, and gradually expanded into spas. They have three now, and another in the offing, I gather, but it's thirty years since he opened the first one, and celebrations are planned for later in the year. Myrtle was the face of their Lasting Youth line for years.'

'Good heavens!' Anna sat back to digest the news. 'Didn't they have some breakthrough new treatment a few months ago? I seem to remember reading about it.'

'They're *always* having breakthrough new treatments!' Wendy said wryly.

Lewis and George returning with their drinks put an end to the conversation, but it left Anna regarding Lewis in a slightly different light.

It was now more often than not Lewis who sat with Anna on the coach and who remained at her side while sightseeing, helping her up steep steps and guiding her over rough terrain. On the odd occasions when Wendy replaced him, Anna surprised in

herself a fleeting disappointment, which she instantly suppressed.
Nonetheless, after months of grieving, his obvious interest was
balm to her bruised heart. He was, after all, an attractive man,
and she privately admitted that, were she unattached, she might
well reciprocate – before realizing with a start that she *was* unattached, and hastily dismissing the thought.

Today, we drove along the famous Garden Route, and Edda
pointed out indigenous trees, among them the prehistoric cycat,
which was around at the time of the dinosaurs. They look like
stunted palms, with wide, barky trunks. Edda says they're
sometimes called bread trees, because flour can be made from
them.

Beatrice would be interested in that; she was an inveterate
gardener. Anna paused and stared into space. As usual when
the time came to write her diary, she was too tired to concentrate and wanted only to slide into bed. But she'd promised
Beatrice, and in any case, what she wrote would be a vivid
reminder that would last her for life.

More immediately, though, it was now eleven thirty. They were
leaving at seven for the long drive to Port Elizabeth, and her case
must be outside her door by six thirty. She really should get
some sleep, despite the postcards waiting to be written. She'd
do them tomorrow, she promised herself.

They flew from Port Elizabeth to Durban, bidding farewell at the
airport to Ali, their Cape Muslim driver, and his Greyhound bus.
The driver who met them at Durban was a Zulu by the name of
Nelson. He proved more taciturn than his predecessor and, as
they later found, less willing to stop on demand when they came
upon a group of animals. Like the others, Anna missed Ali and
his unfailingly cheerful smile.

Edda, however, was still with them, deftly filling them in on
South African history and politics as they went, interspersed with
tales of black magic and the 'immortal' Rain Queen, matriarch
of the Nabado tribe.

Whether or not thanks to the latter, the rain finally caught up
with them in Durban, spoiling their visit to the Botanical Gardens
and the afternoon trip to the Valley of A Thousand Hills, which
was shrouded in mist. The tour was cut short, and they thankfully

returned to the warmth of the hotel, where, at last, Anna was able to bring her diary up to date and write her postcards.

Nor was the following day any better, and Durban's famous landmarks were viewed through a curtain of relentless rain. There was a general feeling of disappointment and fear that the bad weather might follow them when they left the next day.

That evening, as Anna transferred items from her daytime bag to a smaller one, her mobile fell on the bed, and, thinking to check its battery level, she switched it on.

Immediately, its red light started flashing, and, to her surprise, she discovered a batch of texts from her family, a reminder that she'd been so caught up in the holiday and her new friends that she'd spared them little thought for the last few days.

She sat down and read the messages one after the other – from Sophie, from Tamsin, from Jonathan, and separate ones from the boys – of the 'Dear Granny, I hope you are well' variety. Anna felt a surge of love for them all, and, although it meant being late for pre-dinner drinks, she briefly replied to each of them.

But, as in Cape Town, sleep later that evening proved elusive. Since receiving their texts, her family had remained very much in mind, most particularly Jonathan and Vicky and the wedge that had come between them. She accepted that she'd been hard on her son, alloting him his boyhood room when he came for the weekend, rather than the adult comfort of the guest room, and making no attempt to conceal her displeasure with him. But for some time she'd been increasingly aware of his inconsiderate behaviour towards his wife, and it upset her to see Vicky, who'd always been so bright and bouncy, subdued and prone to tears.

Vicky had been only sixteen when her mother died, and five years later, her father had remarried and gone to live in the south of France. Consequently, when she and Jonathan became engaged, Anna and Miles had evolved more into parents than parents-in-law, and since Miles's death, the two women had grown even closer. It was therefore, incongruously enough, in the arms of her mother-in-law that Vicky had sobbed brokenheartedly on Jonathan's departure.

What was it Lewis had said, back among the penguins? *Hard on the children.* And indeed it was: her heart ached to see the eagerness with which the little boys awaited their father's weekly visits.

In the darkness of her hotel room, Anna gave a frustrated sigh. She loved Jonathan dearly – of course she did – but that didn't stop her wanting to shake some sense into him.

This was getting her nowhere, she told herself firmly, and, pushing her problems aside, she determinedly closed her eyes and waited for sleep to come.

As luck would have it, the next morning, as they were leaving Durban, the sun finally came out, and their last view of the city was, at last, under blue skies.

The drive north was a constantly changing kaleidoscope of hills folding away into the distance, of pineapples growing by the roadside, banana plantations, and sugar canes stretching for mile after mile.

They stopped for lunch at the village of Shakaland, where they were shown a display of Zulu dancing. Anna was particularly intrigued by the grass circlets the girls wore on their heads to enable them to carry pots.

It was late afternoon when they arrived at the game reserve where they were to stay, and a further twenty minutes before they reached the Reception Centre. Anna was taken aback by the vastness of the area; she wasn't sure what she'd expected, but certainly not mile after mile of hilly shrubland covered with bushes and stunted trees. As the coach moved slowly along, Edda pointed out groups of game browsing in the relative cool of late afternoon – white rhino, giraffe, herds of zebra and even, in the distance, a solitary elephant.

The coach deposited them at the Centre, and there was a long wait while their accommodation was sorted out. It transpired that they'd been allotted individual huts, referred to as rondavels, that were spread over quite a wide area of the camp, and maps were handed out, on which the route to their own huts had been highlighted in pink.

Typically African in appearance, they were, however, comfortably equipped with baths or showers, a sitting area, and a kitchen where, had they been on a self-catering holiday, they could have cooked their meals. As they were not, and would be eating at the main Centre, they'd been warned in advance to bring torches to light their way back after supper.

That first evening, after a convivial meal in the crowded restaurant, it was an eerie sensation to leave the lighted Centre and set off in the dark along unfamiliar paths. Anna was glad of Harry and Susan's company, their hut lying in the same direction as hers.

Then, when they'd almost reached their destination, she came to a sudden halt.

The other two also stopped, looking at her questioningly. 'Something wrong?'

'I'm trying to think what I've done with my key,' Anna said worriedly. 'It was too big to fit into my bag, so I was carrying it separately. I must have put it on the table when I sat down to dinner. Oh God, it's probably still there! I'll have to go back.'

Harry immediately offered to accompany her, but she shook her head.

'It's very kind of you, but I wouldn't dream of it. I'll be fine – I know the way now.'

Before he could insist, she turned and started to hurry back, passing other groups, indistinguishable in the dark, making their way to their own huts. She alone was going in the opposite direction, and she began to worry that the restaurant might be closed by the time she reached it.

To her infinite relief, however, it was not, though it was now almost empty and none of her own party remained. She hurried to the table where she'd been sitting and thankfully retrieved the key, still lying where she'd left it. Now for the return journey – alone.

A notice in the hut had informed her that although an electri- fied fence surrounded the camp, this was not 'foolproof', and great care should be taken when returning to the rondavels in the dark. Her mouth dry, she hurried along the path illuminated by her torch, seemingly the only light in the whole African night.

At one point, a pair of eyes glowed red in its beam, and she stopped with a frightened gasp. But it was only a zebra, peacefully grazing. Anna skirted it and had reached the place where she'd left Harry and Susan when her torch suddenly went out, leaving her stranded in total darkness. She came to a halt, desperately shaking it and pressing the switch again and again, before being forced to accept that the battery had failed. Now, of all times!

Heart thumping, she waited impatiently for her eyes to acclimatize, glancing nervously about her for the odd marauding lion. Then, moving cautiously forward, she started along the path again, before once more coming to a stop. Beside her was a fork she didn't remember. Oh God, had she taken a wrong turning? Should she carry straight on, or change direction?

Some way down the fork, a light showed in one of the huts, throwing a pale patch on to the grass outside, and, drawn to it like a moth to a flame, Anna started towards it. Perhaps, if she knocked on the door, someone could lend her a torch to light her to her own hut.

She'd just reached it when a voice spoke suddenly from behind the curtains of the open window. Startled, she came to an abrupt stop, before, seconds later, recognizing it as Lewis's. With a wave of relief, she'd raised her hand to knock when something in his tone made her pause.

'God, that's awful!' he was saying. 'What happened?' There was a brief silence, and she realized he must be speaking on the phone. 'Just like that? It's . . . unbelievable.' A longer pause, then his voice sharpened. 'What the *hell* do you mean by that? Of *course* there's no connection! God, what are you thinking? . . . This *is* confined to the two of you, I trust? . . . You're positive? Then make damn sure it stays that way . . . Yes, yes, I know. You did right to phone me, but— All right. Yes. Yes, I will. Goodbye.'

Motionless by the door, Anna gave a little shiver, then, abandoning her intention, turned quietly back the way she had come. As she regained the fork, still puzzling over his words, she saw a wavering light coming towards her.

'Anna?' It was Harry's voice, and she released her breath. 'Is that you?'

'Oh, Harry, yes! My torch gave out, and I must have taken a wrong turning.'

He loomed up beside her, the planes of his face grotesquely lit by the upward light from his torch. 'I thought that might have happened. I was watching out for you and, when you didn't reappear, thought I'd better come and investigate.'

'That's very kind of you,' she said shakily.

'So what's your hut number?'

'Seventeen.'

'We're twenty. You're not far off – it's just along here.'

Minutes later, they reached her hut, and Harry waited while she opened the door and put on the light.

'OK?'

'Yes. I can't thank you enough for coming to look for me. I might have ended up as something's supper!'

He laughed. 'Any time! Sleep well.'

And, locking the door, Anna leant against it and drew a deep breath. She was safely back in her own space, but she couldn't help wishing she'd not overheard Lewis's oddly disturbing phone call.

THREE

While, across the world, Anna was standing on ostrich eggs and stroking cheetahs, her daughter's life back in London was considerably more prosaic.

Sophie Craig ran down the steps of the tube escalator and through the train doors just as they were closing, collapsing on to a seat with a sigh of relief. She was already late for her lunch date; there'd been a series of hold-ups at the studio, which were still unresolved.

Sophie ran a designer knitwear business, and while most garments were made to order and sold direct to the public, they also supplied a couple of boutiques who, at the beginning of each season, liked to order a small stock. This morning, there'd been some doubt as to whether the quantity requested could be delivered in the time required.

To be honest, she could have done without this lunch. Fond though she was of Imogen – they'd been friends since schooldays – at recent meetings there'd been hints of marital discord, which, since Roger was also a friend, Sophie found uncomfortable hearing.

Reaching her station, she threaded her way through the crowded underground and along the pavement to the restaurant. Imogen, of course, was already there and raised a hand to attract her attention.

'Sorry I'm late. A hiccup with an order.'

Imogen nodded. 'They're bringing wine. I know you don't normally drink at lunchtime, but I'm in dire need of it, so I hope you'll make an exception.'

'One glass, then; I must keep a clear head.' Sophie sat back, steeling herself for the latest diatribe. 'So why the need for alcohol?'

Imogen's eyes filled with tears, and Sophie leant quickly forward, taking her hand. 'Imo, what is it?'

'Aunt Em died suddenly at the weekend.'

'Oh, no! I *am* sorry – what happened?'

'We don't know – that's the awful part. We went to dinner last week, and she was fine. In fact, she was looking better than she had for years. Then –' she gave a hiccuping little gasp – 'Uncle found her dead in bed yesterday morning. There . . . has to be a post-mortem.'

'Oh, Imo!' Sophie had known Imogen's Aunt Em and her husband for most of her life, and also called them Aunt and Uncle. The couple were childless and had frequently taken the two girls on weekends away or, when they were younger, to the annual pantomime. 'How's Uncle Ted?'

'Distraught, as you can imagine. Unbelieving might be a better word – he can't seem to take it in. Mum and Dad are staying there for the moment.'

'I must write to him.'

The wine waiter was approaching, and Imogen hastily dried her eyes.

'Sorry to spring that on you,' she apologized as, having filled their glasses, he moved away. 'Particularly as it'll bring back your own loss.'

After a moment, Sophie said quietly, 'You'll let us know when the funeral is?'

'Of course; though what with the inquest and post-mortem, it won't be for a while.'

'It was probably something she's had for some time and not known about,' Sophie suggested, wondering, as she spoke, whether that would make it better or worse. 'She was younger than your mother, wasn't she?'

'Yes.' Imogen's voice rocked. 'Fifty-two last week. That's why we went to dinner.'

'Oh God, Imo, I'm so, so sorry.'

Imogen fished in her bag for a handkerchief. 'Let's change the subject, before we both end up in tears.' She drew a deep breath. 'So – how's my god-daughter?'

'Fine. We spoke about a week ago, and she told me she'd texted Ma. Which reminded me that I hadn't, so I hastily did so.'

'Of course – she's in South Africa, isn't she? How's it going?'

'Fine, as far as we know. You heard Beatrice Hardy had to drop out, after breaking her arm?'

'No! Your mother's never gone by herself?'

'No option. Jon and I were really worried, but she insisted she'd be all right, so she's not likely to admit it if she's not.' Sophie paused, then, crossing mental fingers, added, 'Apart from Aunt Em, how are things with you?'

'Much the same. Daisy's nagging to go on a school trip, and Roger's digging his heels in, pointing out she's already had one this year, and it's Jack's turn.' She flicked a glance at Sophie. 'Believe me, there are advantages in having only one: it halves your problems.'

Sophie smiled without commenting. Having become engaged, and then married, in the same year, she and Imogen had gone on to have their first (and, in Sophie's case, only) child within a month of each other. They'd confidently expected their daughters to become friends and follow the family tradition, but unfortunately the girls had disliked each other from babyhood, and after being sent to the same prep school with disastrous results, were now at separate boarding schools.

'So, of course,' Imogen continued tiredly, 'Daisy's in a strop and refusing to answer texts, and Jack's going round looking smug.'

'Were we so bolshie at thirteen?' Sophie asked.

'Very probably. What about Jonathan? Any developments there?'

Sophie shrugged. 'I think for two pins he'd go home, if Vicky'd have him.'

Imogen looked surprised. 'And won't she?'

'The last I heard, he was screwing up his courage to ask her.' She sipped her wine. 'Which reminds me, I said I'd invite him for a meal. I must do that. Like to come along?'

Imogen brightened. 'Thanks; it would be good to see him again.'

'I'll phone this evening and fix a date.'

The dinner was arranged for Thursday, and Angus Craig made the requested detour to the off-licence on his way home. Though normally he enjoyed hosting dinner parties, basking in the reflected glory of his wife's culinary skills, he had reservations about this one. The death of Imogen's aunt, not to mention the apparently difficult patch she and Roger were going through, did not augur for a light-hearted evening, even without Jonathan's agonizing over his wife and family.

Pity about Roger and Imo, though; he hoped they'd sort things out. Strange, now, to think that fifteen years ago, he'd met Sophie and Imogen the same evening and debated which to ask to dance. Perhaps because of that, he'd always had a soft spot for Imogen. With her large eyes and silky, caramel-coloured hair, she brought out his protective instincts; whereas Sophie, then as now, had little need of anyone's protection.

Roger had come on the scene soon after, and the four had remained close friends, though to the casual observer it might seem the Fates had their wires crossed; Roger, tall, blue-eyed and supremely confident, at first glance seemed more suited to Sophie, and Angus himself, sandy-haired, shorter and stockier, to Imogen.

But appearances could be deceptive, and there were no crossed wires. Both marriages – up to now, at least – had been happy, and he was inordinately proud of his wife, relishing the know-ledge that men's eyes followed her wherever she went. It wasn't only that she was lovely, with her silver-gold hair and perfect bone structure; she had a – he searched for the right word – a *bearing*, a presence, that commanded attention, aided by her unerring dress sense, so necessary in her line of work.

His musings had brought him to his gate, and as he went up the path he abandoned them with a feeling of relief, readying himself for the evening ahead.

Despite his reservations, the evening was going well, Angus reflected thankfully. There'd been no sign of strain among their guests, and in fact Roger invited everyone to a supper party in a month's time.

'Isn't that around your birthday?' Sophie asked, wrinkling her brow.

He laughed. 'Well spotted, but strictly no presents. Honestly. If you really feel you can't come empty-handed, make it a bottle of plonk we can all enjoy.'

Jonathan, too, seemed in good form, and as they sat over coffee and brandy, intrigued them with a story about a French girl who'd arranged to meet him, then got cold feet and clammed up.

'Anyway, she's history,' he finished. 'Steve and I are now working on something else.'

'Pity you'll never know her story, though,' Imogen commented.

Jonathan shrugged. 'Win some, lose some – that's how it goes.'

'I hear you've packed your mother off on safari,' Roger remarked, passing him the cream jug. 'Have you heard how she's getting on?'

'Only spasmodically. Ma finds texting somewhat laborious, bless her, partly because she insists on spelling everything out in full. Consequently her messages are brief and to the point. We gather she's with a good crowd and has met some pleasant people, but any descriptions of the veldt, charging rhinos or rogue elephants will have to wait till we see her.'

Later, as they prepared for bed, Angus asked if Jonathan had approached Vicky about his return to the fold.

'He's not had the chance,' Sophie told him. 'She's been out on his last couple of visits.'

'Delaying tactics?'

'Almost certainly. It's a pity Ma's not here, to put in a good word for him. Vicky listens to Ma.'

'Imo and Roger seemed OK, anyway.'

'Yes, thankfully. Perhaps Aunt Em's death put everything into perspective.'

'Do you know what the trouble was?' A rhetorical question; he knew that Sophie, though she bossed her friend mercilessly, wouldn't betray her confidence.

'Nothing drastic,' she said dismissively. 'Imo's a romantic and believes in happy-ever-after. If there's a hiccup, she's inclined to panic.'

She lifted the corner of the duvet and slid into bed. 'So you can stop speculating, and come and make love to me.'

'Yes, *ma'am*!' he said.

Roger and Imogen did not make love that night. He fell asleep straight away, but she lay for some time, staring into the darkness.

Why couldn't she take everything in her stride, as Sophie did? She and Angus had rows, Imogen knew, but Sophie remained unruffled. There'd be a brief spat, and then it was over, whereas when things were out of kilter between herself and Roger, the world rocked on its axis. And those times had become increasingly frequent.

Listening to his even breathing, she tried to analyse them. Mostly, they concerned the children; Roger maintained she was too lenient with them, which he blamed for both Daisy's spikiness and Jack's cheek. But then Roger's father was a headmaster, and he'd been brought up with stricter discipline than was usual nowadays. Consequently, she had on occasion been guilty of shielding the children from his anger, concealing Jack's regular detention after school and Daisy's equally regular requests for money, which she secretly supplied; and when, almost inevitably, such instances came to light, Roger, also inevitably, lost his temper.

'How are we ever going to teach them right from wrong, when you repeatedly undermine me?' he'd demand. 'We must present a united front, or they'll continue to play us off against each other.'

She knew, of course, that he was right. It was just that she couldn't resist the children's pleading, well practised though she knew it to be. But though Tamsin was as difficult as Daisy – which was some consolation – Sophie and Angus seemed as unfazed by it as by everything else.

It had been through Sophie's coming to her rescue in the playground that their friendship began. Though they'd started school together, Sophie had been spared the harassment routinely handed out to 'new girls', principally, Imogen suspected, because the possibility of it had never even occurred to her. Supremely self-confident, she treated everyone as her friend, thus disarming those who might have tried to belittle her, and that same assurance led her to face the bullies on Imogen's behalf, rather than herd with the favoured few. And to some extent, Imogen thought humbly, Sophie had been fighting her battles for her ever since.

'You should have more backbone, Imo,' she'd say. 'It's no use wilting at the first sign of opposition, then whining about it afterwards.'

Wilting and whining. Sophie had never been one to mince her words, but as usual she was right.

'Why do you let her boss you about like that?' Roger would ask in exasperation, but Imogen knew the bossing was without malice and in her own best interest. She and Sophie were opposites in many respects, but their friendship was a strong bond, important to both of them. If only, she thought again, she could be more like her.

And, having come full circle, Imogen turned on her side and at last went to sleep.

That weekend, instead of phoning to arrange when to collect the boys, Jonathan called at the house on Friday evening, taking Vicky by surprise.

Seeing him on the step, her eyes widened, but before she could speak, he said quickly, 'Could we have a word?'

Her instinctive glance towards the stairs confirmed that the boys were playing in their rooms, which, knowing their routine, he'd counted on.

'You're not wanting to take them out now?' she asked in confusion, moving aside as he came into the hall.

'No, but lately you've not been around when I've called, and we need to talk.'

Her eyes fell. 'As I said on the phone, Jonathan, there's nothing to talk about.'

He put a hand under her elbow and, not wanting to alert his sons to his presence, steered her gently into the sitting room and closed the door.

'And as *I* said on the phone, there's the hell of a lot, principally,' he continued, raising his voice above her protest, 'that I've been a selfish bastard, and I'm truly sorry.'

She stared at him, and he went on more quietly, 'Really, Vic, I've had time to think things over, and I'm only surprised you stuck it as long as you did. I've been as miserable as sin these last months, and believe me, things will be very different if you'll just let me come home.'

Her eyes filled with tears, but as he instinctively moved towards her, she held up a hand. 'No – wait. How do I know you're not just missing home comforts, and when you've been back a while, you'll revert to your old ways? They were pretty . . . ingrained.'

'I know I got away with it far too long, but that's over, I promise.' He paused. 'Look, we could have a trial period, if you like. I could even sleep in the spare room, if it would make things easier.'

'It'd be an interesting news item for show-and-tell, that's for sure.'

He answered her half-smile. 'Well, I'm certainly not pressing it; I'm just trying to say I won't rush things. We can take it as slowly as you like, but perhaps –' his eyes strayed to the bar unit – 'we could at least have a drink on it?'

Vicky wiped her eyes with the back of her hand. 'I think we might manage that,' she said.

Jonathan joined them for supper on Saturday, much to the boys' delight.

'Is your work in London finished, Daddy?' Tom enquired, eyes shining.

Work had been the cover story which, for the first month or two, both boys had accepted. Lately, though, they'd started asking why he stayed with Granny on his visits, and though his mother's recent bereavement provided an excuse, it was one he was increasingly uncomfortable with.

'Almost,' he replied guardedly.

Vicky came to his rescue. 'Perhaps, when Daddy takes you out next weekend, I could come too – make it a family outing.'

'Like it used to be,' Tim said, nodding with satisfaction.

'But much better!' Jonathan added, and, catching Vicky's eye, they exchanged a smile.

The world was suddenly a brighter place, and there was a spring in his step when he returned to London.

'I must say you're much better company,' Steve remarked a couple of days later as they ate their evening meal. 'The only thing that puzzles me is why you didn't make this move weeks ago.'

'Because I've only just realized how objectionable I've been,' Jonathan said frankly. 'Up till then, I was convinced Vicky was at least partly to blame.'

'So you're now a reformed character?' Steve's raised eyebrow expressed doubt.

'You'd better believe it. If things go wrong again, it will definitely be curtains. I can't risk that.'

His mobile cut off Steve's reply. The number showing was not one he recognized, and he frowned, resenting the interruption of his evening. 'Hello?' he said brusquely, then stiffened, signalling Steve to come and listen.

'This is Elise, Mr Farrell.' She paused, and when he made no comment, went on falteringly, 'I am sorry to trouble you again, but I need to speak with you after all, if you could please meet me?'

Jonathan and Steve raised their eyebrows at each other.

'I'm not sure that I can,' he said stiffly. 'I'm engaged on other work now.'

'But please, I implore you!' A note of urgency crept into her voice. 'I do not know where else to turn.'

'What guarantee have I you won't change your mind again and refuse to say anything?'

'I promise. Things are more . . . serious now.'

'For a start, will you tell me who you're working for?'

A pause, then: 'Yes.'

'So why is this time more important than last?'

There was a silence, and he thought she wasn't going to answer. Then she said in a half-whisper, 'People have died.'

Jonathan felt the frisson that presaged a good story. 'Your last chance, then,' he said. 'Tomorrow morning, eleven o'clock at the same place?'

'Oh thank you, thank you so much! I shall be there.' And she rang off.

'Well, what do you make of that?' he demanded as Steve returned to his seat.

'Worth looking into, at least.'

'Will you come with me?'

Steve gave a surprised laugh. 'Afraid she might proposition you?'

'Hardly. I'd just like to know what you make of her. If it really is a big story, as she seems to imply, we might even work on it together.'

Steve shook his head doubtfully.

'What? You still think she's taking me for a ride?'

'I don't know; she could be.'

'She didn't strike you as genuine?'

'Oh, she was fairly convincing, I grant you. The test will be if she turns up tomorrow and spills the beans.'

'Then you will come?'

'OK, but only to satisfy my curiosity.'

By ten to eleven the following morning, they were seated at a window table. At least, Jonathan told himself, they'd not met Elise in the doorway, fleeing the scene. But as the hand of his watch crept past eleven, he was convinced, suddenly, that she wasn't coming. It was illogical – she was not yet five minutes late – but the certainty grew.

'Let's order for ourselves, anyway,' he said, ignoring Steve's quick look as he called the waitress over. Damn the girl! he thought furiously; that was twice she'd made a fool of him. Steve, he knew, was concentrating on not saying 'I told you so'.

Their coffee came. At nearby tables, people met, chatted, left. By eleven thirty, conversation between the two of them had dried up.

'All right,' Jonathan said harshly. 'Say it.'

Steve moved uncomfortably. 'Perhaps she looked through the window, saw me with you, and panicked.'

'Why should she panic? You haven't got two heads.'

'She might have thought it was a trap of some kind.'

'If it's a trap,' Jonathan said drily, 'I'm the one who's been caught. I can't believe I allowed myself to be talked into it again, after what happened last time. But what the hell is she playing at, Steve? It's not the first of April. What possible good can be achieved by making a fool of me?'

'Relax!' Steve said easily. 'It's no big deal. For all we know, she might have a genuine reason for not coming.'

'And pigs might fly.'

They had just asked for their bill when her call came. Jonathan glanced at the screen and swore under his breath; the number showing was the same as the previous evening.

'I've a damn good mind not to answer it.'

'At least give her the chance to explain.'

He jabbed at the button, but before he could speak her voice reached him, hurried and barely audible.

'I am so sorry – please forgive me! I could not get away. I'm afraid they might suspect—' The next few words were drowned in a burst of static. Then a rapid whisper: 'I shall contact you.' And she ended the call. Jonathan had not spoken one word.

'So that,' he said heavily, 'is that. If I'd had the chance, I'd have told her not to bother. I've had enough of being messed around.'

'It didn't sound like a hoax,' Steve said consideringly.

Jonathan stared at him. 'Are you pleading devil's advocate?'

'No, I just . . .' He broke off, shrugging.

'Just what?'

'It's hard to explain. At first, I assumed she was out for publicity; but the last two calls – I don't know; I'm inclined to think there might be something in it.'

Jonathan sat back in his chair, regarding him sceptically. 'Well, you've changed your tune.'

'Perhaps she's fooled us both. The thing is . . .'

'What?'

'If you *don't* hear any more, we'll be left wondering.'

Jonathan frowned. 'So what do you suggest we do?'

'There's nothing we *can* do. You've no address for her, have you? Not even a last name. Just what *do* you know about her?'

'Let's see: she works in the leisure industry – whatever that means – and has been over here for around two years. She wants me to look into something nefarious – or at least, she *thinks* she does, but the people she works for wouldn't want her speaking to me. And, most importantly, she says people have died.' He frowned. 'What the hell did she mean by that?'

'God knows. Industrial espionage?'

Jonathan gave a snort. 'She's hardly the type.'

'Well, you've met her and I haven't. But what else could it be?'

Jonathan shrugged, staring down at his mobile.

'You could ring her back on that number,' Steve suggested.

Jonathan considered for a moment. 'Suppose it got her into trouble? She didn't seem free to talk.'

'You see!' Steve said triumphantly. 'You're beginning to wonder, aren't you?'

'Let's say I'm not prepared to risk it.'

'In which case, we're back to square one, having to wait till she contacts you.'

'Or writing it all off as a lesson in being gullible.'

Their bill was placed on the table, and Jonathan took out his wallet. 'Thanks for coming with me. At least you can see what I'm up against.'

'A handful of smoke,' Steve declaimed whimsically, 'that dissolves in the air when you try to grasp it.'

'And a colleague who's finally lost his marbles,' Jonathan retorted, pushing back his chair.

Sophie sat in the studio, the latest brochure on the desk in front of her. The immediate rush was over, orders had been despatched, and they could now sit back and await the next batch. In the meantime, she saw from her desk diary that it would soon be her nephews' birthday. Tom and Tim had been born on the same date two years apart, so shared a joint party. She lifted the phone and called her sister-in-law.

After they'd exchanged greetings, she said, 'I'm in search of suggestions for birthday presents.'

'Well, they've both made lists,' Vicky replied, 'but that's little help, since they range from a puppy – which is *not* on the cards at the moment – to vastly expensive toys seen on TV, which they'd doubtless tire of within a week.'

'Then I'll have to use my ingenuity, but as you know, I don't do boys. Will there be the usual joint party?'

'Yes, but it'll probably be the last. So far, they've been happy with friends for tea and a conjuror or entertainer of some kind. But next year Tom will be seven, and among his friends, tenpin bowling or the cinema are already taking over. I'm pretty sure he'll be wanting something similar, which might not appeal to Tim.'

'Better make the most of it this year, then!'

'Oh, and as Anna only arrives home on Sunday, we'll be holding it the following weekend, so she can be there. You're invited, of course, if you can bear it.'

Sophie hesitated. 'And . . . Jonathan?'

There was a pause. Then Vicky said, 'Haven't you spoken to him this week?'

'No?'

'Well, we reached a sort of truce at the weekend. He came for supper on Saturday.'

'Oh, Vicky, I *am* glad! He's been so miserable.'

'So have I, heaven knows. But he really wants to try again, so we're going for it. He'll come home for good the weekend of the party – and what's more, he's promised to help with it, which will be a first.'

'Excellent!'

'I was to blame too,' Vicky put in quickly. 'It'll require an effort from both of us, but I'm sure our marriage will be the stronger for it.'

As the call ended, Sophie sat back with a sigh of relief. By the sound of it, she could stop worrying about Jonathan – which just left Imogen.

She did so wish her friend would pull herself together. Though she'd been happy to support her during their schooldays, she'd assumed her task was finished once Imogen married. Now, though, with her marriage under strain, Imogen had turned back to her, putting her in an invidious position.

It was not as though she were a weak character, either, Sophie thought in exasperation. It was only when her self-confidence was challenged that she buckled – under teasing at school, and now criticism from Roger. All Sophie could do was continue her efforts to bolster it and hope she'd meet with more success than had so far been the case.

FOUR

The next morning, Harry and Susan emerged from their chalet as Anna was setting off for breakfast, and they walked together to the Centre.

'Thanks again for coming to my rescue,' Anna said. 'It wasn't too pleasant, finding myself suddenly alone in the dark.'

'No problem. Glad I found you!'

The renewed thanks put a satisfactory end to the episode, she thought with relief. She'd feared Harry might refer to it in front of Lewis, and she'd prefer him not to know she'd been wandering around after he'd returned to his chalet.

On arrival at the restaurant, they were directed to a table where several of their party were already seated, and it wasn't until they gathered by the jeeps for the game drive that Anna saw Lewis. He was standing slightly apart from the Salters, staring frowningly into space, but Wendy saw her approach and came forward to greet her. It was therefore natural, when they climbed into the jeep, for the two of them to sit together, for which Anna was grateful. Still feeling guilty about the overheard phone call, she was not yet ready to face Lewis.

They were fortunate on the drive; a group of elephants, slow and lumbering, crossed the path only a few yards in front of them, and a little farther on they came across a family of lions at a waterhole. Like the others, Anna had her camera on video, watching in enchantment as the male lifted his head to look across at them, water dripping from his muzzle. She had to keep reminding herself that these were not captive animals in zoo surroundings, but wild and free in their native habitat.

The day passed in a kaleidoscope of sounds, sights and smells that conjured up the very essence of Africa. Then, after an early dinner, they set off on the Night Drive, with Edda and the local guide holding spotlights on either side of the jeep. After a slow start, sighting only the ubiquitous impala and zebra, Edda pointed out a group of buffalo the other side of the river and, minutes later,

hyenas feeding off a carcase. Then, close at hand, a giraffe materialized beside the road, and a herd of wildebeest crossed just in
front of them in the full glare of the headlamps. Finally, a fitting
end, a large rhino loomed up within a few feet of the jeep.

It was only ten o'clock when they were deposited back at the
Centre, but it had been a long, tiring day, and another lay ahead
of them. In twos and threes, they started to make their way back
to their chalets.

Having replaced her torch battery, Anna was looking round
for Harry and Susan when Lewis came up to her.

'Walk you home, ma'am? I've not seen much of you today.'

'It was pretty frenetic, wasn't it?' Anna said lightly, falling
into step beside him.

'Overkill, perhaps, considering we'll be going through much
the same routine at Kruger.'

'Oh, I don't know; I want to see as much of the animals as I
can.'

He smiled in the dark, threading her free hand through his
arm. 'You're really enjoying it, aren't you?'

Involuntarily, her heart set up a panicky beat. For heaven's
sake! she thought impatiently; he's no idea you overheard him!
Though even as the thought crossed her mind, she knew that
wasn't the reason for the dryness of her mouth and the sudden
heat of her body.

She said, surprisingly calmly, 'Of course I am! Aren't you?'

'It's interesting, yes, but I'm not much of a one for holidays
– too busy thinking of what I could be doing at home.'

'Work, you mean?'

'Did Wendy tell you I'm a workaholic? She's right, I suppose.
I find difficulty delegating, convinced no one can do things as
well as I do.' She felt him glance at her. 'But yes, to answer
your question, I *am* enjoying it, mainly thanks to you.'

She gave an uncertain little laugh. God, where was everyone?
Surely someone must be coming in this direction? She daren't
turn round, but all was quiet behind them.

'It's difficult to admit, for a hard-bitten old cynic like me,' he
was continuing, in that new, low voice, 'but it was I who suggested
Wendy ask you to join us, back in Cape Town. And I can tell
you she and George have been pulling my leg ever since.'

'I've . . . enjoyed being with you all,' Anna said.

He continued as though she hadn't spoken. 'It was a blow to learn you'd been widowed. With no husband in tow, I was hoping you were divorced, like me. Wendy warned it might be too soon, but – well, by then the die was cast. I'm known for my quick decisions – in business it's a necessity – and the more time we've spent together, the more certain I've become. But now time's running out, so I have to know, Anna. Is there any chance at all for me? If not now, in the future sometime?'

God help her, how could she answer him? Of course she enjoyed being with him, but Miles had only—

He pulled her gently off the path and into the shadows of a rondavel.

'At least not an immediate "no",' he said softly. And then, without either of them seeming to move, he was holding her close and kissing her, and all logic and reason evaporated in a surge of longing as the blood coursed through her veins, and sensations she'd never expected to feel again flooded over her.

Only the sound of approaching voices pulled them apart, and they stood immobile as a group, chatting and laughing, passed by on the path, a mere ten feet from them. As their footsteps died away, Lewis said, not quite steadily, 'It's like being sixteen again!'

Anna stepped quickly away, the enormity of what had happened sluicing over her. Oh, God, God, God!

'Anna?' he said tentatively.

'I don't . . .' she began, and stopped.

'Look –' his voice was gentle – 'I took you by surprise, I appreciate that. Damn it, I took *myself* by surprise. But surely that doesn't alter how we feel?'

She lifted her hands helplessly, searching for the right words – but what were they?

He sighed. 'Let's leave it for the moment. You need time to think things over. If I've jumped the gun, I apologize. We can take it as slowly as you like, continue to meet back in the UK, perhaps, and see how things develop?'

He paused. 'I suspect you're feeling disloyal to your husband, but ask yourself if he'd really want you to spend the rest of your

life alone. We're both adults, Anna, free to do as we choose
without hurting anyone. Remember that.'

When she still didn't speak, he took her arm and led her back
to the path. 'What number is your chalet?'

'Seventeen.'

He took her hand, and they walked in silence along the path,
lit by his torch. Much to Anna's relief, they saw no one. When
they reached her hut, he waited while she fitted the key in the
lock with shaking fingers, then bent and kissed her cheek.

'Goodnight, my love,' he said.

Stumbling inside, Anna pushed the door shut and leant against
it, eyes closed, straining to hear his retreating footsteps. As they
died away, she walked slowly to the bed and, sinking down, put
her hands to her face, fingers splayed. Her heart was still knocking
painfully against her ribs. Anna Farrell, she thought mockingly,
known for her self-control, her cool detachment, her sangfroid!
Where were they now?

Until the previous year she'd been on firm ground emotionally,
sure of herself and those around her. But, after expecting to grow
old together, Miles had suddenly died, and that firm ground gave
way to sand, no longer supporting her. Now, ten months later,
the sands had shifted again.

One thing, at least, was certain: the screens she'd been carefully erecting throughout the holiday had been well and truly
demolished, forcing her to confront feelings that, unacknow-
ledged, had been welling up inside her.

But could this really be happening? Was it remotely possible
that she, Anna, widowed less than a year, could, after loving
one man all her life, have fallen for someone else – someone,
she reminded herself, about whom she knew next to nothing – in
the space of two and a half weeks? And the answer to that, she
thought unwillingly, had to be 'yes'. Hadn't she and Miles
become engaged within a month of their meeting? Like Lewis,
it seemed she also was prone to quick decisions.

But, as he'd guessed, it was Miles, dead for less than a year,
who was foremost in her mind – the only man she'd ever slept
with, and had never doubted would remain so.

She raised her head, taking a deep breath and trying to be
dispassionate. Lewis had as good as said he loved her. How did

she honestly feel about him? That he was attractive, there was no disputing, his occasional broodiness and flashes of temper adding to, rather than detracting from, that attraction. He was also an entertaining and interesting companion, and from the first she'd been flattered by his attention.

Thus far she could be rational. But there was no denying his embrace had lit fires in her reminiscent of the early days of her marriage, fires which, though remaining warm and comforting, had over the years lost their fierceness. Tonight, incredibly, she'd been consumed with all the excitement and impatience of her teens, and, as he'd reminded her, their time together was running out. The thought of not seeing him again suddenly appalled her.

We're both adults, he had said, *free to do as we choose without hurting anyone.* And he was right, she thought with a sudden lifting of spirits. Though this was happening sooner than she could have hoped, it offered a chance of happiness that might not come again, and she'd be a fool to turn it down. At least she'd agree to their continuing to meet, and if, when they knew each other better, they still wanted to be together, so be it. But one thing was clear: whatever her feelings for Lewis, now or in the future, he would never replace Miles. She hoped that Miles himself, wherever he was – not to mention her family – would understand that.

Anna awoke with a sense of excitement that took several seconds to identify. Then the memory of the walk back from the Centre rushed into her consciousness, filling her with a mixture of anxiety and anticipation. How would she and Lewis greet each other? What should she say to him? She realized with some embarrassment that, after her enthusiastic response, she'd been distinctly unforthcoming. Might he have regretted declaring himself? Think she wasn't interested? She would soon know.

She was grateful for Harry and Susan's company again on the way to breakfast, but again they were shown to a different table from Lewis and the Salters. In fact, in her first, quick glance round the restaurant, she hadn't spotted them.

They were moving on after breakfast, and having ensured that her case had been loaded into the hold, Anna climbed aboard the coach to see Wendy and George seated together, and Lewis in the row behind them. He immediately rose, eyes raking her face as he made way for her to sit by the window.

She smiled at him, including him in her general: 'Good morning!' and the tension in his jaw eased a little.

'All right?' he asked in a low voice as she settled herself.

'All right,' she confirmed. She would, she decided, wait for him to raise the subject that was foremost in their minds.

As they left the reserve, Edda took up the microphone, summarizing the day's itinerary. They were making for White River, or Wit Rivier, where they would spend two nights, and en route they would be skirting Swaziland, a country outside the South African Republic, ruled by King Mswati III. Anna noted it down, hoping she'd spelled His Majesty's name correctly.

As the day progressed, the panorama unfolded on all sides – acres of citrus fruits, multicoloured bougainvilleas, girls washing their laundry in the river. They stopped for lunch, and again to visit a market, reaching their hotel just after five-thirty. And still nothing of significance had passed between Anna and Lewis. She began to wonder if he intended to ignore what had happened, and felt a stab of panic. Logic, however, suggested he was waiting till their conversation could not be overheard by George and Wendy in the seats in front of them.

They were allocated their rooms, their cases were delivered, and Anna unpacked and had a leisurely bath. When, at the agreed time, she reached the bar, she was surprised to see that although Lewis was there, the Salters were not.

Having bought her drink, he led her to a table by the window. 'How long are you going to keep me in suspense?' he asked in a low voice.

She smiled, relief flooding over her. 'I was waiting for you to bring it up.'

'Well?'

'I'd . . . like us to go on seeing each other,' she said.

He reached under the table for her hand. 'Thank God!' he said.

There was no time for more, as they were joined by Wendy and George, and shortly after they all went in to dinner. Furthermore, since there would be a very early start in the morning, everyone went to their rooms directly it was over, ending the possibility of further discussion. Still, Lewis had his answer, and for the moment that was enough.

The wake-up call came at five o'clock, and they collected their packed breakfasts en route for the coach. Wendy smiled at Anna and patted her arm as they boarded, making her wonder if Lewis had reported developments, but it was too early for conversation, and many of the group seemed still half asleep.

They reached Kruger National Park at seven o'clock, and another magical day began, filled with an abundance of birds and animals for their cameras to capture. When they paused for a sandwich lunch, the temperature had climbed to 38°, and they were grateful of the chance to replenish the water bottles they carried with them. Feeding the blue starlings with crumbs, Anna thought back to the red-winged variety at the Cape of Good Hope, the first day she'd spent with Lewis and the Salters. How long ago it seemed!

They left the Park at three thirty, eight and a half hours after arriving, though it seemed much less. On reaching their hotel, several of them walked down to the river to take photographs, and Anna found Lewis at her side.

'Alone at last!' he declared, with mock fervour.

Anna smiled. 'Hardly!' She gestured at the members of the group all around them, chatting, taking photos, walking along the bank.

'At least we can talk without being overheard. I can't tell you what a relief it was to hear your decision last night.' He smiled wryly. 'I'm not used to having to wait for answers!'

'To take-over bids?' she teased.

He laughed. 'Scarcely that. God, Anna, I want to climb on the nearest rock and announce it to the world!'

She laid a quick hand on his arm. 'But of course you won't.'

He looked down at her, sobering. 'Well, not literally, no.'

'Seriously, Lewis, I don't want anyone to know. Not yet.'

But know what? she thought suddenly. Was he thinking long-term, or was it only sex he wanted? What exactly was he asking her to commit to, and for that matter, what did *she* want?

He was frowning, and she added tentatively, 'Do Wendy and George . . .?'

'I've not said anything, if that's what you mean, but I was certainly planning to, when we were all together.'

'I'd . . . be grateful if you didn't.'

'Why the hell not?'

'I'd like to wait at least till after the anniversary of my husband's death in November.'

There was a silence between them, while extraneous sounds continued to bombard them – the call of a bird across the water, laughter among one of the groups, a plane flying overhead. Then he said flatly, 'Of course. Stupid of me.'

'No, no it isn't,' she said quickly. 'It's just—'

'It's all right, Anna; I understand.'

But did he? she thought miserably.

'I'm sorry,' she said, and he nodded absently, gazing across the river as though his thoughts had already moved on. Was this how it would be between them, a walking on eggshells?

She felt suddenly close to tears. 'I think I'll go and have a shower before dinner,' she said, and, when his only reply was another nod, she turned and made her way quickly up the slope to the hotel.

Perhaps it was only in her imagination that dinner was difficult. Certainly, Wendy and George appeared to notice nothing amiss. She managed to keep up light, inconsequential chat, and if Lewis seemed quiet, this wasn't altogether unusual. Over the weeks, Wendy had referred several times to his 'moods'. 'Just ignore him!' she'd advised laughingly. 'He'll snap out of it!'

They were due to leave for Pretoria in the morning. 'It'll be the last full day of the holiday,' Wendy remarked sadly. 'I'll hate leaving South Africa, but we must all at least keep in touch.'

Anna's smile felt strained. 'Of course,' she said.

'Didn't you say you live in Westbridge? We're in Richmond, and Lewis is near Beechford, so we're within easy reach of each other. We must exchange email addresses.'

'You'll have to watch her!' George warned. 'She's never happy unless she's organizing something. Give her half a chance, and she'll be running your life for you!'

After the meal they had coffee together in the lounge, then Anna excused herself. 'I'd like to get most of the packing done tonight,' she explained. 'I'm not at my best at six in the morning!'

So yet again she was on a see-saw, she thought wryly as she made her way upstairs. Perhaps, after all, it was as well the holiday was coming to an end.

Lewis was sitting with George when Anna boarded the coach the next morning, and she perforce joined Wendy, unsure if she was relieved or disappointed.

'Another long drive ahead of us,' Wendy commented. 'It makes you realize how small the UK is, doesn't it? Have you been keeping up your notes for your friend?'

Anna realized guiltily that, for the last week or more, the thought of Beatrice had never entered her head. 'I've been keeping a diary of sorts,' she said evasively, 'and the photos will help fill in the gaps.'

Suppose Beatrice had been with her: would Lewis still have made his move?

Pretoria, when they reached it, was awash with purple jacaranda trees laden with blossom seeming to line every street. Edda drew their attention to the magnificent government buildings, replicas of those in Cape Town, and the duplicate statue of Castor and Pollox shaking hands, symbolising peace at last between the British and the Boers.

After lunch they went on a tour of the city, Edda enlarging on historical details she'd already given them, until Anna's head was swimming with facts and dates. It was after five when they finally checked into their hotel, and, hoping for a few minutes' relaxation, she lay on the bed and promptly fell asleep.

To her consternation, it was an hour later when she awoke, and time to prepare for the evening ahead. Standing under the reviving shower, she realized, with a mixture of feelings, that she'd not exchanged one word with Lewis all day.

It was to be their Farewell Dinner. Everyone gathered in the bar as usual, and several members of the group began exchanging email addresses, though Anna doubted if, once back in their normal routines, they'd bother to get in touch. Lewis was at the far end of the bar, seemingly being talked at by David Lincoln, known for liking the sound of his own voice.

'A word of warning,' Wendy murmured, sotto voce. 'Lewis is in one of his moods. He had a stand-up row in reception, over the delay in his case being brought to his room. I pretended not to be with him!'

Anna was silent, wondering guiltily if she were responsible for his bad humour.

'George says he was pretty uncommunicative all day,' Wendy continued. 'Trouble is, once a mood gets hold, it can take him days to shake it off. It must make him hell to live with. Fond of him as I am, I do wonder how Myrtle put up with him.'

'I thought you said it was she who was difficult to live with?' Anna reminded her, increasingly uneasy.

Wendy shrugged. 'Six of one and half a dozen of the other, I suppose. I know for a fact they had the most spectacular rows. Still,' she added, belatedly realizing she might have spoken out of turn, 'I'm sure he'll have mellowed with age!'

Since this was their last night, all twenty-two of them were seated at one long table, with Edda at its head, and the meal was punctuated by people repeatedly jumping up from their chairs to take photographs. Having escaped from David, Lewis was seated between Anna and Wendy, but his mood did not appear to have lightened, and he made little attempt at conversation. Adopting Wendy's advice of leaving him to get over it, Anna chatted to Harry Bell on her left and the couple directly opposite.

Mellowed by pre-dinner drinks and several glasses of wine, her eyes drifted round the table. She'd come to know quite a few of her companions over the last two and a half weeks, and felt a general fondness for them all, coupled with mild regret that she wouldn't be seeing them again. Even Jean, of the loud voice and decided opinions, had melded into the group, and seemed the happier for it.

Anna was brought out of her reverie by Lewis's raised voice. 'I can't eat this!' he was telling the waiter standing behind him. 'It's cold, and the vegetables are raw. Take it away and bring me something edible.'

There was a lull in conversation as heads strained to see what was happening. Anna kept her eyes firmly on her own plate as the unhappy waiter complied, and, a little hesitantly, everyone resumed eating, while Lewis stared at the empty space in front of him. Minutes later, another plate was put before him with a murmured apology.

However, after trying it, he again pushed it away. 'That's no better! Where's the head waiter?'

'Please don't make a scene, Lewis!' Wendy murmured.

'Let me handle this,' he replied curtly. 'It's a four-star hotel, for God's sake. They should know how food ought to be served.'

The head waiter materialized, soothing words were spoken in an undertone, and within minutes a third plate of food was produced, which, to the relief of everyone, appeared to be satisfactory. Normal service is resumed, Anna thought.

The meal wore on, and her earlier mellowness merged into a vague sadness, imagining the days ahead, the large, empty house awaiting her, and the ongoing problems with Jonathan and Vicky. No more African sunshine – it would soon be winter in the UK, with short, cold days and long, cold nights. They seemed to have been away far longer than seventeen days.

Lewis did at least speak to her as the meal progressed, and she wondered if he regretted his outburst. Probably not, since it seemed he was prone to them. As things stood, she reflected, their relationship – if it could be called such – looked unlikely to survive the next twenty-four hours, degenerating into the mildly derided category of holiday romance. And after Wendy's revealing comments, perhaps that was just as well.

Coffee was served, Lewis receiving a complimentary brandy with his, and someone made a short speech, thanking Edda for making the holiday so enjoyable and ending in a toast. In reply, Edda assured them they'd been a wonderful group and reminded them they still had the best part of a day left. Johannesburg being a mere thirty-five miles away, they could have a much-needed lie-in, and the morning was free to look round Pretoria in their own time and do some last-minute shopping. They'd be leaving for Jo'burg after lunch.

It was time to disperse. Small groups formed for last photographs, and people began to drift away. Leaving Lewis and George talking to the Bells, Anna and Wendy excused themselves

and took the lift to their rooms, Anna emerging at the first
floor and Wendy going on to the third.

Anna felt in her bag for her key and, rounding a corner, almost
collided with the young couple, Tony and Shelley, locked in an
embrace. They seemed oblivious to her, and she hurried on, a
lump in her throat. How did the song go? *Don't cry, young
lovers, whatever you do, don't cry because I'm alone.* And
something about having had a love of one's own. As she had,
she thought, oh, she had! She was overwhelmed by a wave of
longing for Miles, for, above all, the reassurance of being loved
and wanted.

Eyes blurred by tears, she let herself into her room, roundly
cursing herself for a fool. She'd come away to put her grief
into perspective, she reminded herself. Never in her wildest
dreams had she imagined that perspective would include another
man.

Her open case, from which she'd extracted only what was needed
for that evening, stood on the luggage rack. She stepped out of
her dress, folded it between layers of tissue paper, and laid it on
top, adding her evening bag and sandals. The maid had turned
down the bed, and her nightdress lay draped across the pillows.
She slipped it on and, going over to the dressing table, started to
brush her hair. Her last night in Africa, she thought; this time
tomorrow, she'd be on the overnight flight, the following one in
her own bed at home.

She went through to the bathroom, her mind busily darting
from one subject to another, rather than winding down to the
required sleep mode. No doubt the coffee was responsible, since
with all that was going on, she'd forgotten to ask for decaffeinated. But it was essential she should sleep, she thought worriedly,
because she certainly wouldn't on the plane home.

Returning to the bedroom, she drank a glass of the bottled
water provided and glanced half-heartedly at her notebook.
Since she didn't feel tired, perhaps she should try to bring it
up to date. She was about to pick it up when a tap on the door
startled her.

Wendy? she wondered, in bewilderment. Edda, about a change
in the arrangements? But surely not at – she glanced at her
bedside clock – twelve thirty? She looked round quickly for

her dressing gown, before remembering she'd not bothered to unpack it and it was somewhere in the depths of her case.

The tap sounded again. A little apprehensively, she walked across the room and looked through the peephole. Lewis's face, distorted by the glass, swam into view, clogging the breath in her throat. Very slowly she opened the door, registering that he was wearing a silk dressing-gown in dark red. For a heart-stopping moment they stared at each other. Then she moved to one side and he came into the room.

FIVE

After various delays, it was almost eleven before the flight took off, and Anna looked out of the window to catch a final glimpse of the lights of Johannesburg spread out below them. She was sharing a row with Charles and Jenny Ward, whom she'd not seen very much of during the holiday. Lewis and the Salters were about six rows behind her.

Lewis! She still couldn't get her head round what had happened the previous night. Coming as it did just as she'd decided they were going nowhere, she'd been caught unawares, swept up in and fully responding to the passion of his love-making. The final act of betrayal. How could she hope to explain it to her son and daughter?

To her embarrassment, she'd cried afterwards, and he had held her, stroking her hair and not asking questions, for which she was grateful. He left her at five o'clock, before anyone was stirring, and she'd fallen into a deep sleep that had lasted – with no wake-up call – until almost nine. But everyone had slept late that morning, and she reached the dining room at the same time as George and Wendy, Lewis joining them at their table ten minutes later. She'd expected to feel awkward in his presence, but he was so natural, so much the same as he'd been throughout the holiday, that she soon relaxed and determined to enjoy the final day.

The four of them had strolled together round Pretoria, where Anna bought T-shirts painted with African animals, extra gifts for Tom and Tim, whose birthdays fell the next week, and a canvas shopping bag, similarly decorated, for Tamsin. Then, after lunch, they'd set off for Johannesburg, and an 'introductory' tour they'd be unable to follow up – past the De Biers Finance House, the planetarium, and the university where Mandela first became involved with the ANC. So, finally, to the airport, and a leave-taking of Nelson, their Zulu driver, who'd been with them since Durban, and, of course, Edda. Anna knew she'd miss her lilting South African accent.

Jenny's voice broke into her remembering. 'It was a fantastic holiday, wasn't it? I didn't want it to end!'

'Unbelievable!' Anna agreed. In more ways than one, she thought ironically. But for her, a part of it wasn't over; she and Lewis had agreed to meet in London, for dinner and the theatre.

'I'm not sure how long I can withstand Wendy's questioning,' he'd said smilingly, that afternoon.

'You could always employ the well-tried "No Comment",' she'd suggested, and he'd laughed.

'I doubt if I'd get away with that!'

But that was his problem. For her part, she'd certainly no intention of letting slip any hint of what had happened to the family – at the very least, not for another five or six weeks, and possibly, if things didn't work out, ever.

'Have you far to travel from the airport?' Jenny was asking, and Anna wrenched her attention back.

'About an hour's drive. As it's the weekend, my son's able to meet me.'

'Lucky you! We have to catch a connecting flight to Manchester, then it's a half-hour train journey. We won't be home till late afternoon.'

'You'll be exhausted,' Anna said sympathetically.

'Yes; which is why I wish they'd hurry up and serve the meal, so we can settle down to sleep.'

Anna nodded and glanced out of the window again. But there was nothing to see now, nothing but the dark African night and her own face reflected against it. She sighed, without knowing why, and, as Jenny turned back to her husband, opened her book and began to read.

Jonathan said, 'So you're glad you went?'

'Of course I am! I wouldn't have missed it for the world! It's the most beautiful country, Jon. You'd love it.'

'And you've lots of photos?'

'Hundreds!'

'Well, as you know, it's the boys' party next weekend, and Sophie and Angus will be over. So afterwards, when we're able to relax, we can view them on the TV.'

'We'd still be there the next morning! How are you all? Thanks for the texts, by the way; I'm sorry I didn't reply to the later ones – things were a bit hectic.'

'As long as you enjoyed yourself.' He paused. 'Actually, Ma, I've some news of my own.'

'Oh?' She turned quickly to look at him.

'Vicky and I are going to give it another go.'

'Oh, Jonathan, that's wonderful! When did this happen?'

'Last weekend, but I'm not moving back till the party so that I can be with you today, see you settled in and everything. We thought you might feel a bit flat, having had constant company over the last few weeks, then suddenly alone in an empty house.'

She laid a hand over his on the steering wheel. 'That's sweet of you, but you shouldn't have delayed your plans for me.'

'We're going there for lunch – Vicky and the boys can't wait to see you – but we won't stay too long, because you're bound to be tired.'

And she was, Anna admitted to herself. 'It'll be lovely to see everyone, and your news is the best homecoming present ever!'

Wendy said reflectively, 'Do you think there was anything going on between Lewis and Anna?'

'"Going on"?' George repeated, with raised eyebrows.

'Well, we know Lewis well enough to see he was smitten, right from the start.'

'He's always had an eye for a pretty face.'

'Oh, come on! It was more than that.'

'My love, Lewis must have had dozens of women since Myrtle waltzed off. I doubt if he was serious about any of them.'

'You think it was just a holiday romance? I tried gently pumping Anna, but she wouldn't bite.'

'A gloriously mixed metaphor! But they're both free agents, and if they did get together, so what? It's one of those things we'll never know.'

Wendy smiled. 'I don't give up so easily. I think, in a week or two, I'll invite them both to lunch.'

George sighed theatrically, rolling his eyes to the ceiling. 'Here we go!' he said.

*   *   *

'Ma sounds in fine form,' Sophie reported, putting the phone down as Angus came into the room. 'She's taking her photos to the boys' party, so we can look at them on the TV screen.'

'The joys of digital!'

'She seems to have been in a good crowd – says they all got on well. It doesn't sound as if she missed Beatrice overmuch.'

'So you could have spared yourself all that worrying,' Angus commented, slipping an arm round her.

'Well, I did feel responsible, having talked her into going, and then Beatrice dropping out at the last minute.'

'You underestimated her, sweetie. Plenty of stamina, has our Anna.' He moved to the drinks cabinet. 'She'll be pleased Jon's back with Vicky.'

'Delighted, yes. She had lunch with them, and she'll be going on Wednesday for the birthday tea.'

Angus turned, glasses in hand. 'Wednesday? I thought it was Saturday?'

'The party is, but their birthday's Wednesday, and they're each having a friend to tea, plus Granny.'

'It'll be great to have Jonathan back in the fold,' Angus said contentedly. 'Let's hope everything's plain sailing from now on.'

'Beatrice!'

'Anna – you're back! How are you?'

'Fine, but more to the point, how are you? How's the arm?'

'An infernal nuisance, but mending nicely.'

'What about work? Are you able to manage?'

'Fortunately, I'd cleared the decks in preparation for the holiday, so there was nothing urgent. Thanks for the postcard, by the way. It made me green with envy!'

'It's come already? I thought it would take weeks! Actually, it was quite difficult to write, letting you know what we were doing, without rubbing in what you were missing.'

'I was joking, love – it struck just the right note. And talking of notes, did you keep them, like you promised?'

'I did, yes. When I get a chance, I'll transfer them to my PC and print them off for you. Some parts are more detailed than others, but the photos will flesh them out – and I warn you, I took hundreds!'

'So I should hope!' Beatrice paused. 'It wasn't too . . . difficult, being on your own?'

'Not really.' Anna took a deep breath and followed up with the phrase she'd prepared. 'I missed you, of course, but a very nice threesome took me under their wing, so I wasn't alone.'

'Honestly? I know you'd never tell the family if things hadn't worked out, but this is me you're talking to.'

'And my answer's the same. I missed you, but I had a wonderful time and didn't feel lonely.'

'Well, that's a relief. I felt awful, letting you down like that. So – when am I going to see you?'

'Next week some time? It's a bit hectic at the moment; there's a mountain of mail, email and telephone messages to sort through, not to mention holiday laundry. Added to which, I'm going to the boys' birthday tea on Wednesday and their party on Saturday, and as if that wasn't enough, I've a dental check-up on Thursday.'

Beatrice laughed. 'You've convinced me! How about next Tuesday? Come for supper?'

'Are you able to cook?' The question was twofold, since Beatrice's livelihood involved cookery.

'With difficulty, but don't worry – I shall cheat and order a takeaway.'

'Great idea – I'll look forward to it, after two and a half weeks of hotel food.'

'My heart bleeds for you! Why not stay the night, then you needn't worry about drinking? Lovely to have you back, Anna – look forward to seeing you!'

Anna was smiling as she put down the phone. She and Beatrice had met five years ago, at a local craft fair; Anna was helping Sophie on her stall, and Beatrice giving cookery demonstrations to launch her new book.

They became instant friends. Over coffee that first day, Anna learned that Beatrice was divorced and had a married son living in Canada. She'd taught cookery for some years, before branching out to more elaborate dishes, which she took delight in concocting and then detailing, fully illustrated, in a growing number of recipe books. She also catered for special functions – and, in fact, had offered her services free for Miles's sixtieth birthday party. Anna's friends still talked about it.

A couple of years older than herself, Beatrice radiated capability. Tall and broad-shouldered, the highlights in her brown hair were her sole concession to vanity, her large hands with their blunt, unpolished nails being innocent of rings, and her watch, unlike Anna's slim gold one, as big as a man's.

She had the habit of holding the gaze of whoever was addressing her, listening intently to every word, which some people found unnerving, but it was that air of single-minded concentration, alternating with a whimsical, half-amused smile, that, to Anna, best summed up her friend.

For her part, Beatrice had learned that Anna worked part-time as a translator, mostly of books and documents from French or Italian into English, an occupation she found enjoyable and stimulating, and, being self-employed, one to which she could devote as much or as little time as she chose.

Remembering that first meeting and their discussion of careers, Anna, who had not looked at a translation since Miles's death, knew that to return to work would be a significant step towards picking up her life again.

In the meantime, there were the tasks she'd outlined to Beatrice to attend to, and as a start, she would put the pile of old newspapers in the boot of her car, ready to drop off for recycling. They were on a shelf by the back door, and she was sorting them into a more manageable pile when a name leapt off the page at her.

Ex-model Myrtle Page, 57, was at the centre of a disturbance at the elite Amelia nightclub yesterday, when barman Reno Diaz, 30, complained that she slapped his face during an altercation over the price of drinks.

Page, former wife of business magnate Lewis Masters . . .

Anna's eyes moved unseeingly down the column before returning to the picture that accompanied it – a head and shoulders shot of a high-cheek-boned face, not conventionally pretty, but certainly arresting. Hair piled on top of her head, shoulders bare, her wide eyes met those of the photographer – and reading public – with a hint of amused challenge. A publicity photo, no doubt, and presumably not a recent one.

Had she glanced at this article before she went away? Anna wondered. If so, it hadn't registered, since back then she'd never heard of Lewis and only vaguely remembered Myrtle's heyday.

Carefully, she replaced the paper on the pile to be discarded and covered it with another. What was it Wendy had said? *She still hits the headlines pretty regularly and makes life difficult for him.*

Determinedly putting both Lewis and his ex-wife out of her mind, Anna scooped up the pile of newspapers and carried them out to the car.

On the Tuesday evening, Jonathan arrived back at the flat with several large parcels.

Steve eyed them curiously. 'Your sons' birthday presents?'

'Got it in one. Hamleys was going like a fair at lunchtime. Anyone would think it was Christmas!'

'So what did you get?'

Jonathan grinned. 'An electric railway, and before you say it, yes, it's partly for me! That's their joint present, and they'll each have something smaller, but Vicky's seeing to that, thank God.'

'You know,' Steve remarked, getting two cans of beer out of the fridge, 'I've got quite used to having you here. It'll seem odd, next week, being here on my own.'

'You've been a real pal,' Jonathan said gratefully. 'I don't know what I'd have done without you. We'll have a slap-up meal on Friday, if Maddy can spare you. As it happens, though, you won't have time to miss me next week; we're off to Manchester, aren't we, to interview Keith Perceval?'

'So we are. Did you book us in somewhere?'

'Yep, just the one night. We shouldn't need longer than that.' His mobile beeped in his pocket, and he took it out, frowning. 'Who the hell . . .?'

Steve glanced over at him, watching his expression change as he read the text.

'God, it's that woman again!' Jonathan said incredulously. 'How she has the nerve beats me!'

'Not the mysterious Elise?'

'The very same. And – I don't believe this – she's asking me to go to Manchester! She must be psychic!'

'You're kidding!'

'Listen to this: *Next week I must go to Manchester. I know this is much to ask, but I beg you to come there. I can no longer*

*put off what I must tell you, and I promise you it will be worth
your trouble.'*

They stared at each other. 'It beggars belief, doesn't it?'
Jonathan exclaimed. 'Each time I determine to put her right out
of my mind, up she pops again.'

'What will you do?'

'Well, I sure as eggs wouldn't charge up there just to see her.
But since, by a pure fluke, we'll be there anyway . . .'

'Not so much of the "we"!'

'Oh come on, we work together, remember?'

'So you're saying you'll agree to meet her?'

Jonathan reread the message. 'I must confess all this cloak-
and-dagger stuff has whetted my curiosity.' He looked up, coming
to a decision. 'Yes, damn it, I'll call her bluff one last time. Get
her to come to our hotel. If she doesn't turn up, we won't have
put ourselves out, and if she does, at least we'll know whether
or not it's worth following up.'

Anna checked the list on the kitchen notice board. Laundry –
done. Ironing – still to do. Dry cleaner's – outstanding. Holiday
notes for Beatrice – outstanding. Reply to bank letter
– outstanding.

She sighed. She seemed to have been working flat out for the
last couple of days, with very little to show for it. And now it
was time to set off for the boys' birthday tea. Their gifts lay
ready on the hall table, including the T-shirts bought in Pretoria,
and nostalgia tugged at her as she remembered buying them with
Lewis at her side. And in the same moment the phone rang.

She hesitated, wondering whether to leave it to the answerphone. She really should be leaving, but . . .

She lifted the phone. 'Hello?'

'Hello, sweetheart.'

A wave of heat washed over her. 'Lewis!' she said.

Cameron Masters gave a cursory tap on his father's door and,
his eyes on the papers in his hand, pushed it open and went in.

Lewis was seated at his desk, his chair swivelled round so that
his back was to the door, and Cameron, seeing he was on the
phone, prepared to wait. To his surprise, however, his father broke

off his conversation and, turning, waved him peremptorily out of the room.

As he hesitated, Lewis put his hand over the mouthpiece and said curtly, 'Wait outside, will you? And close the door behind you.'

His face flushing, Cameron turned on his heel and left the room, closing the door with exaggerated care. Dismissed like a bloody schoolboy! he thought angrily, but he was damned if he'd stand meekly waiting by the door. If it hadn't been imperative to have a word, he'd have left straight away and let his father stew. He'd an appointment in less than an hour, dammit.

By way of compromise, he poured himself a cup of water from the machine and drank it slowly, looking out of the window at the extensive grounds. It was warm for October, and several of the guests were wandering round in their towelling robes, glasses of juice in their hands.

What the hell had got into the old man? Cameron thought irritably. Come to think of it, he'd been unpredictable all week, ever since he got back from holiday. If this was the result a break had on him, it was as well they were few and far between.

The intercom rang on the receptionist's desk, and a moment later she called across, 'Your father will see you now, Cameron.'

Oh, will he? Cameron raised a hand in acknowledgement of the message, but continued to sip slowly at his water until he'd finished it. Then he tossed the paper cup in the bin and, holding himself in rein, walked back to Lewis's office and knocked loudly.

'Enter.'

He did so, and father and son stared at each other. Then Lewis said, 'At least you remembered to knock this time.'

'As I did before.'

'But didn't wait for an answer, which defeats the purpose.'

'I've come in before when you were on the phone, and it hasn't been a problem.'

'Well, this time it was.'

Cameron waited for further explanation and realized it wasn't forthcoming.

'So what is it you wanted?' Lewis prompted.

'The figures in from Sandersons don't tally with the estimates. I've had a word with Smithers, and he thinks they're trying it on.'

'Let me see them, then.'

Stiffly, Cameron crossed the room to his father's desk and laid down his folder. Lewis glanced up at him. 'And you can stop behaving like a jilted virgin. You don't have to know every damn thing I do.'

In spite of himself, Cameron's mouth twitched. 'Fair enough,' he said, and, differences dismissed, father and son bent together over the discrepant figures.

'Mrs Nash?'

Imogen frowned, trying to place the voice. 'Yes?'

'Good afternoon; this is Elizabeth Wright, at Broadfields.'

Daisy's headmistress, Imogen thought, confused. 'Yes, Miss Wright?'

'I've no wish to alarm you, but have you heard from Daisy in the last twenty-four hours?'

Imogen's heart set up an uneven thumping. 'No?' She heard her voice rise. 'Why?'

'I have to tell you she's not been seen since lunchtime, and we've been unable to establish where she is.'

Imogen glanced instinctively at the clock. Five fifteen. 'And you've only just realized?'

'Indeed not, but we didn't want to alarm you unnecessarily. A search has been conducted in and around the school and her friends questioned, but they were unable to throw any light on it. I wondered if perhaps she might have come home?'

Imogen's mouth was dry, and she moistened her lips. 'I haven't seen her. But surely she must have told someone or left a note, if she was intending to . . . run away?'

'It seems not.' The voice was clipped.

'Was she . . . upset about anything?'

'She'd been reprimanded for not handing in some work, but that's scarcely reason to disappear.'

The word rang fresh alarm bells. 'Disappear? Could someone have abducted her? Have there—?'

'Mrs Nash, please! I assure you Daisy hasn't been outside the grounds. We're very strict about that.'

'She seems to be outside them now,' Imogen said baldly.

'Yes, well that's what we're trying to ascertain. We've made enquiries at the railway and bus stations, but no one remembers seeing her.'

'Oh, God!' Imogen breathed.

'I'm sure there's nothing to worry about,' the headmistress assured her, less than convincingly.

'Have you informed the police?'

'We were waiting till I'd spoken to you, though I appreciate that if she *had* arrived home, you'd have informed us.'

'Naturally.'

'Then all I can do is . . .'

Imogen suddenly stopped listening, staring through the window at the car that had drawn up at their gate. A taxi, surely? Heart pounding, she waited, Miss Wright's voice rattling incomprehensibly in her ear as – oh, thank God! – her daughter emerged from the back, carrying her school satchel.

She broke into the woman's spiel. 'Miss Wright, she's just arrived now. I'm so sorry about this. I'll come back to you as soon as we've spoken to her.' And without waiting for a response, Imogen dropped the phone and ran out of the house.

'Daisy! What on *earth* do you think you're doing?'

Slightly shamefaced, the girl turned to her. 'Oh, there you are, Mum. Could you pay the taxi? I used the last of my cash on the train.'

Imogen stared at her, and Daisy, bracing herself, defiantly held her gaze. Laconically, the taxi driver held out a hand, breaking the spell.

'Go and get my bag. It's on the hall table.'

Dropping her satchel on the pavement, Daisy set off up the path. Not until the driver had been paid and driven off did Imogen turn again to her daughter, grabbing her by the arm.

'What the *hell* are you doing here?'

Daisy's mouth set in a sullen line that was depressingly familiar. 'I'm not going back,' she said.

'Oh yes, you are, young lady. Wait till your father hears about this.'

Daisy switched to pleading mode. 'Please don't make me, Mum! Everyone's been getting at me – I hate it there!'

'Is this all because you didn't do your prep?'

Daisy stared at her in astonishment. 'How—?'

'I've had Miss Wright on the phone, that's how. There's been a full-scale search of the school and grounds, enquiries made at the station – uselessly, as it turns out – and she was about to call the police.'

Daisy looked frightened. 'I didn't think—'

'You never do! That's the trouble!'

'You sound just like Daddy!' Daisy accused her, and burst into tears.

With an exasperated sigh, Imogen bent to retrieve the satchel and, still grasping her daughter's arm, led her back into the house.

'She thinks she can do exactly as she likes!' Roger stormed. He'd had a trying day at the office and, looking forward to the weekend, had arrived home in the middle of a scene between his wife and daughter, whom he'd thought safely at school. Now, having despatched Daisy to her room, he'd rounded on Imogen.

'You're far too lenient with her, I keep telling you that, giving her everything she asks for – money, clothes, whatever fancy takes her. God knows if the school will have her back, and then what would we do, with GCSEs within spitting distance?'

'I managed to soothe them down,' Imogen replied, 'but your shouting at her won't help.'

'On the contrary, I've not shouted enough! I'm sick and tired of having my authority flouted by the two of you going behind my back.'

'Roger, I don't! I'm only trying to keep the peace!'

'But at what cost?' He strode to the drinks cupboard and poured himself a straight whisky, downing it in one. 'I've had the hell of a week at work, and this is what I come home to!'

'So . . . what are we going to do?'

'Send her back, of course. If you're sure they'll take her.'

'But shouldn't we try to find out what's wrong? She must have been unhappy, to—'

'Nonsense! She's not used to discipline, that's the trouble, and when someone tries to enforce it, she promptly runs home to Mummy, who's sure to take her side.'

'That's not fair!' Imogen flared.

'It's you who aren't fair, Imogen, letting her think she can get away with this.'

'But I don't! I never said that, though I do think we should give her the chance—'

'She's had plenty of chances.' He ran his hand over his face. 'Look, I need some peace and quiet. The three of you go ahead and have dinner. I'm off to the golf club. I'll get something to eat there.'

And before she could marshal the words to protest, the front door had banged behind him. Imogen ran into the hall, about to call him back, but Jack was standing motionless on the stairs, looking down at her. How much had he heard?

She steadied her breath. 'Have you done your homework?'

He nodded, eyes wide.

'Then you can have half an hour on the computer before dinner.'

'Is Daddy coming back?' Jack asked, his voice trembling.

'Not for dinner.' She knew that wasn't what he meant, but didn't trust herself to elaborate. She turned abruptly into the kitchen, her mind seething, and promptly lifted the phone.

'Sophie? It's me. Is this a bad time?'

'Well, supper's under way, but it's ticking over for the moment. Is something wrong?'

'Daisy's arrived home out of the blue.'

There was a pause. Then Sophie said simply, 'Ah!'

'All hell's been let loose. The first I knew was a phone call from her headmistress saying she was missing, and I was panicking about that when a taxi drew up and out she stepped, cool as a cucumber, announcing that she's not going back.'

'Oh, Imo, I'm so sorry.'

'As you might imagine, Roger blew a fuse and has stormed off to the golf club, saying he'll eat there. Naturally he blames me for this.'

'But what happened exactly? Why did she come home?'

'Because, if you please, she was given detention for not handing in her prep. Honestly, Sophie, I could have scalped her! They were about to contact the police.'

'So what happens next?'

'Well, I phoned the school, of course, and after some sweet-talking on my part, they agreed she can stay here for the weekend while we try to drum some sense into her, and they'll expect her back on Monday. It was made clear, though, that she wouldn't escape punishment for this, and quite right too. My concern is how we can persuade her to go back, if she digs her heels in. We can't drag her there, kicking and screaming; and suppose she runs away again, and next time doesn't come home?'

'Obviously your first priority is to get to the bottom of what happened. It must be more than detention, surely? Is she being bullied, do you think?'

The word catapulted Imogen back to her own schooldays – shivering in the playground until Sophie came to her rescue. 'God, I hope not,' she said.

Over the wire, she heard a voice in the background, and Sophie replied, 'Five minutes.' Then, to Imogen, 'Sorry, love, I'll have to go. I suggest you and Roger sit down with her and talk things through as calmly as you can. I'm sure you'll sort something out.'

She rang off. Imogen slowly put the phone down and, closing her eyes, leaned with both hands on the counter. Calm, reasonable Sophie. Then, straightening her shoulders, she began to prepare dinner.

SIX

Anna had forgotten how noisy twelve excited little boys could be, and by the time a succession of parents had arrived to collect their offspring, she was ready to collapse at the kitchen table with a cup of tea. The memory of Miles here with them last year – a point that had carefully not been mentioned – was an added strain. Her grandsons, she'd noted with a tug of the heart, were wearing their South African T-shirts, Tom's sporting a rhino and Tim's a cheetah. At least they both appeared to fit.

'It went off very well, didn't it?' she said.

Jonathan passed her the milk jug. 'Yes; and that's it, thank God, for another year.'

'Vicky was saying this might be the last ever,' Sophie remarked, putting the remains of the birthday cake in a tin and pressing down the lid. 'She thinks Tom will want a treat next year.'

'Then I'm even more grateful it was postponed till I was back,' Anna commented. 'These milestones are precious.'

'You did bring your camera, didn't you?' Angus asked, coming into the kitchen with a tray of debris. 'We're looking forward to a slide show later.'

'Yes, it's in my bag. I've not had the chance to look at them myself yet. No doubt they'll bring back all kinds of things I've forgotten.'

How many photos had she taken of Lewis? Anna wondered, with a spurt of anxiety. Not enough, she hoped, to give rise to comment, helped by the fact that it had been the end of the holiday before anything really developed between them.

Had it not been for his phone call on Wednesday, she might have thought, back in these familiar surroundings, that it had all been a dream. Did she seem any different to her family? she wondered. Could they sense she was keeping a secret? Watching them all as Jonathan took out the vacuum cleaner and the girls began stacking the dishwasher, she wondered a little wildly how they'd react if she suddenly announced that while she was away, she'd met another man and gone to bed with him. Furthermore, she was meeting him in London next week, when she would doubtless do so again.

Would they be appalled? Shocked, even disgusted? Or glad for her? She doubted the latter – not so soon after Miles's death.

'Anna?' Angus repeated, raising his voice slightly and bringing her back from her reverie. 'Would you like another cup?'

'Oh sorry – I was miles away. Yes, please, but is there nothing I can do to help?'

'Everything's under control,' Jonathan assured her. 'Thank God for paper plates and cups! It's only the serving dishes that need seeing to, and most of them go in the dishwasher. If you'd like to relax somewhere more comfortable, Vicky's restored order in the sitting room.'

Anna shook her head. 'I want to be in the thick of it, even if I am only an observer.'

'That'll be the day!' Jonathan teased, and, as he passed, dropped a kiss on the top of her head. He had brought her here, but Sophie and Angus would drive her home, since, as of today, he was moving back with his family.

Sophie, having finished at the sink, brought her mug of tea over and sat across from her mother. 'There's one sad bit of news you mightn't have heard,' she said. 'Imogen's Aunt Em has died. It's her funeral on Monday.'

'Oh, no!' Anna exclaimed. 'I *am* sorry. She was younger than I am, surely? What happened?'

'No one seems to know. She was fine the previous week at her birthday dinner, then Uncle Ted found her dead in bed. There was a post-mortem, but I don't know the result. I haven't liked to ask Imo. She was very upset.'

'I'm sure she was. I must write to her and her mother.' Anna had met Emily Broadbent on only a few occasions, but she'd been very good to Sophie when she was younger, including her in treats with Imogen and referring to her as her adopted niece.

'What time is the funeral?' she added.

Sophie laid a quick hand on her arm. 'You don't have to go, Ma – it's too soon. I'll represent the family.'

Yes, Anna thought, full of guilt, it *was* too soon for her to attend a funeral – for that matter, it always would be – but it was also too soon to have slept with someone else. She knew her daughter's sympathy would have been tempered, had she known about *that*.

The clearing up was completed, the boys were eventually packed off to bed, the adults settled down to supper, and the questions about South Africa began.

'You've hardly told us anything,' Vicky chided gently. 'All you said in your texts was that you were enjoying yourself and were in a good group.'

'I know, I'm sorry. But when you're travelling hundreds of miles, and seldom spend more than one night in the same bed, there's no time to go into detail. I'll talk you through the photos when we've finished eating.'

'But it really wasn't the disaster we feared, Beatrice dropping out like that?'

Anna shook her head. 'Poor love, she was so disappointed, but I'm ashamed to say I barely missed her. I'm going round next week, armed with the photos and the notes she asked me to make for her.'

'Did you bring the notes with you?' Jonathan asked.

'It never occurred to me, but in any case they're still on scrappy bits of paper; I'll have to type them up and print them before next week.'

'What was the best part of the holiday?' Sophie enquired.

Anna thought for a moment, censoring her memories. 'It was all wonderful, but I suppose seeing the animals free to roam where they liked. I know things here are better than they used to be, but they're still confined to some degree. And, of course, the scenery was spectacular.'

'Perhaps we should go and sample it ourselves!' Angus said with a grin.

'I strongly recommend it. Tamsin would love it. How is she, by the way? She was my most faithful correspondent and didn't seem at all fazed by my lack of response.'

It was Sophie who replied. 'She's fine. It'll be half-term in a couple of weeks, and she's asked if she can bring one of her friends back for the week. Actually, it'll be a help, because they'll be able to amuse themselves without calling on me the whole time.'

'Are you busy at the moment, work-wise?'

'So-so. Any time now, people will start thinking about Christmas presents and parties, and then it will really take off.'

'Heavens!' Vicky exclaimed. 'Don't talk about Christmas! It's only the beginning of October, and there's Hallowe'en and Guy Fawkes to get through first!'

It was nine o'clock before they were all settled in the sitting room, and as Anna's photos came up on the TV screen, she was momentarily startled both by their size and clarity. The camera had faithfully reproduced details she'd not noticed at the time – the pattern on Ali's shirt as he leant against the coach, the afternoon shadows lying across the pavement.

'Jolly good camera, Ma,' Jonathan said appreciatively. 'Is that the one Dad gave you?'

Anna nodded, transported back to the start of the holiday. 'That's our driver, Ali, and Edda, the tour manager. She really was excellent – so well informed, and able to answer every question thrown at her.'

The picture changed, giving way in turn to Cape Town's parliament buildings, the strange little creatures up Table Mountain, the view from Signal Hill. All this, Anna thought as she identified each shot to her family, before she'd exchanged so much as a word with Lewis or the Salters. Then, suddenly, there she was herself on Boulder's Beach, surrounded by penguins and smiling a little self-consciously. Behind her, she could see Jean bending towards a group of birds, camera poised, and, farther away, Harry snapping Susan, while beyond them all the Atlantic Ocean lay grey beneath an overcast sky. The photograph Lewis had taken.

Anna's face grew hot, but everyone's attention was on the screen as they exclaimed over the tameness of the penguins, and, her embarrassment unnoticed, she thankfully moved on to the redwing starlings at Cape Point.

As the slide show continued, Anna sometimes had difficulty identifying the precise scene before them, one view of the rolling veldt and grazing animals being much like another. And sometimes a picture recalled an occasion she'd forgotten, such as the enforced stop when Prue left her camera on the coach, and they had to wait while she and Bill hurried back to retrieve it. She'd taken the opportunity to zoom in on the exotic splendour of the flowers growing alongside the path – strelitzia, protea, flame lilies, nemesia – and their glowing, vibrant colours recalled for her the heat of the African sun.

'They were growing *wild*?' Sophie asked incredulously. 'What I'd give to have those in my garden!'

Next came the group photo they'd posed for outside Cango Caves, each of them taking turns to be photographer. That was Anna's first on-screen glimpse of Lewis, half hidden towards the back of the group, but thereafter he featured in more shots, usually with either George or Wendy, and Anna felt obliged to explain that this was the threesome who had befriended her.

After an hour and a half, with many pictures still to go, they called a halt.

'To be continued,' Angus said firmly. 'It's getting late, and I want to enjoy the viewing session without falling asleep! Anna, I charge you with remembering where we've got up to.'

'That's easy,' she replied, 'the arrival at the game park. It's a good place to stop; I took dozens of photos on the two safaris, and a lot will be poor quality and need deleting.'

'It's been lovely to see it all,' Vicky said, stretching. 'I feel I've been on holiday myself!'

Goodbyes and thanks were exchanged, and as Angus reversed down the drive and turned out of the gateway, Anna's last glimpse was of Vicky and Jonathan framed in the doorway, his arm across her shoulders. It made a perfect end to the evening.

Imogen said, 'Daisy's pleading to be allowed to stay over for the funeral.'

Roger snorted. 'Opportunistic little minx!'

'Oh, I don't know; she was fond of Aunt Em.'

He put down his paper. 'Really? What was it she said, when you told her she'd died? "Well, she was quite old, wasn't she?"'

Imogen bit her lip, regretting having reported the conversation. 'All the same—'

'*No!*' Roger interrupted forcefully. 'It's simply an excuse to delay going back, and she's in no position to beg for favours. How do you think Miss Thing would react, if you asked for an extra day's leave? A great-aunt isn't considered a close relative.'

'She was almost in tears . . .'

'I'll bet she was,' Roger said grimly. 'That child could always turn on the waterworks when it suited her.'

'You're being rather harsh,' Imogen protested. 'We could put her on the train straight after the service—'

Roger slapped his hand on the arm of his chair. 'For God's sake, Imogen, what part of "No" don't you understand? I'll put her on the early train myself, on the way to work. End of conversation.' And he purposefully turned back to his paper.

Imogen stared at him helplessly. He was right, she knew, but Daisy's tear-stained face had tugged at her heart. She did so wish she and Roger could reach an amicable compromise over the children, without every discussion ending in a full-scale argument, which she always lost. She wondered miserably how Sophie would have handled the matter – and accepted that, awkward though Tamsin could be on occasion, her parents seemed to have no problem dealing with her.

She sighed and left the room, bumping into Daisy in the hall.

'Well? What did he say?'

'That you must go back on the early train.'

'But *Mummy*!' Daisy wailed, the tears starting again. 'I want to say goodbye to Aunt Em! I've never been to a funeral!'

'That's quite enough!' Imogen snapped, noting the surprise on her daughter's face. 'You shouldn't have been home in the first place, then the question wouldn't have arisen. Jack's not going,' she added. 'He'll be at school as usual. Now, go and wash your face, and make the most of your last afternoon at home.'

Daisy glared at her, the tears drying on her face. Then she turned and flounced upstairs. Imogen waited for the inevitable bang of her bedroom door, then went into the kitchen and switched on the kettle. She almost wished she could catch the early train herself; she was dreading the funeral and the distress of people she loved, her mother and Uncle Ted chief among them. I wish it was this time tomorrow, she thought childishly.

'Imo?'

She spun round to see Roger in the doorway, a sheepish look on his face.

'I'm sorry I shouted just now. I know you're upset about Aunt Em, and I should have been more understanding. Oh, sweetie . . .' As tears spilled down her cheeks, he moved forward and took her in his arms.

'You will be there, won't you?' she whispered against his chest. 'You'll be able to get off work?'

'Of course I'll be there.'

'She shouldn't have died, Roger. Not for a long time.'

'I know, I know.'

'And she looked so *well* at the dinner.'

'At least she didn't suffer,' Roger said, and thought how trite it sounded. But it seemed to provide some comfort, because Imogen nodded and moved slightly away.

'I'm sorry, too,' she said in a low voice, wiping her eyes, 'for not being strict enough with the children.'

'It's not a question of being strict, sweetie, so much as not letting them take advantage.'

She nodded, looking so contrite and miserable that he felt a stab of guilt, and, taking her face between his hands, kissed her more thoroughly than he had in some time.

'Better now?' he asked as they eventually moved apart.

'Much better!' she said.

Beatrice Hardy lived on the outskirts of a village some ten miles from Westbridge – a twenty-minute drive through winding country lanes. It was dusk by the time Anna arrived, and she was grateful not to be driving home that night. She had, in fact, stayed over on a couple of occasions in the months since Miles died; Beatrice had been a good friend during that time, not fussing or oversolicitous, but there when Anna needed her.

Hers was the first in a row of six cottages on the outskirts of the village, and, since the gates stood open, Anna drove in and parked on the drive. She was extracting her overnight bag when the front door opened and Beatrice came out to greet her. Her arm, Anna saw with a surge of sympathy, was still in its cast, supported by a sling.

'Oh, Bea, it is good to see you!' she exclaimed, hugging her with care. 'How are you managing, really?'

'Not without difficulty,' Beatrice admitted. 'It's the incapacity that's so frustrating. Dressing myself is a major challenge, and I still need help with that. Fortunately, my next-door neighbour is a registered nurse, and she's been nothing short of marvellous. In fact, the whole village has been fantastic, phoning to see if I needed anything, bringing round cakes and casseroles. I've been quite overwhelmed.'

'Now I feel guiltier than ever, swanning off to South Africa.'

Beatrice laughed. 'Don't be ridiculous! Anyway, the cast comes off next week, then things will be a lot easier.'

They went together into the house.

'Your room's ready for you, thanks to Maggie,' Beatrice said, 'but leave your case in the hall for now, and come and have a drink.' Maggie was Beatrice's cleaner, who had been with her for years.

Anna followed her into the small, low-ceilinged room that doubled as both sitting and dining room. The similarly sized room across the hall was Beatrice's workroom, where she photographed her dishes and typed out the texts of her recipe books. At the back of the house, walls had been knocked down to make a large, state-of-the-art kitchen, where she did her cooking and taught a succession of students who, after leaving catering college, came on to her for specialist training. In addition to their daily instruction, they researched ingredients for her new recipes and acted as sous chefs, all the while absorbing more than they realized of her expertise and invariably emerging as imaginative chefs in their own right. Several had gone on to work in prestigious hotels up and down the country, a source of great pride to Beatrice.

She nodded towards an array of bottles and glasses on a low table. 'Help yourself, Anna, and a large G&T for me, please. Incidentally, the students wouldn't let me order a takeaway, insisting my reputation was at stake! They've prepared supper, bless them, as they have most evenings – a large chilli, so I hope you're hungry. It only requires reheating. Now,' she continued, seating herself in her usual chair, 'I want to hear all about the holiday, and I mean all!'

Anna poured the drinks as requested and handed Beatrice hers. 'I've typed out the notes I made, which I hope will give a flavour of it, particularly in conjunction with the photos.'

'Thanks, I'll enjoy reading those in bed, but in the meantime, give me a verbal account. You say you were with a good crowd?'

So, yet again, Anna gave brief thumbnail sketches of the various members of the group, referring to Lewis only as one of the threesome with whom she'd teamed up. Beatrice listened intently, inserting questions about the different hotels, the type of food they served, the varying temperatures as they moved about the country.

'Shall we have the first photo session now?' she suggested. 'Then we can have a break for supper, and another batch afterwards.'

Setting everything up, Anna had a moment of anxiety. It was possible Beatrice's eyes and ears would prove sharper than those of her family. She must be careful to give nothing away.

As requested, she identified everyone as they appeared on the screen, holding her breath as the first, full image of Lewis stared enigmatically out at them.

'Lewis Masters,' Beatrice repeated thoughtfully. 'He looks a moody devil. Attractive, though.' She shot a glance at Anna. 'What was he like, really?'

Willing herself not to colour, Anna smiled non-committally. 'You got it in one – moody but attractive!'

Beatrice said no more, and Anna hoped she'd satisfied her. A succession of photos followed – of Tony standing on a couple of ostrich eggs, arms extended to maintain his balance; of Zulu rickshaw boys in Durban; of zebras and giraffes and elephants.

After half an hour or so, Beatrice commented, 'They're wonderful photos, Anna; I almost feel I'm there. Let's have a break now, though. Would you mind switching on the oven? Sorry to make you sing for your supper.'

'It's the least I can do. I see the table's ready laid and the wine opened.'

'Oh, I've got advance preparation down to a fine art, I can tell you!'

'When I've lit the oven, I'll take my case up,' Anna said, 'and freshen up before we eat.' She also wanted to extract the gift she'd brought back for Beatrice – a pewter butter knife with a carved cheetah handle.

Up in her room, she unpacked her night things and toiletries, noting that either Maggie or the students had put a vase of late roses on the dressing table. She washed quickly at the little hand basin, reapplied make-up and brushed her hair, but her mind was elsewhere.

Seeing Lewis's photographs had unsettled her, and she suddenly regretted agreeing to meet him. After all, it was the magic of the holiday that had brought them together, and meeting in less exotic surroundings could lead to disappointment. It was foolish to prolong their liaison beyond its natural end, which, surely, had been that last day in Pretoria. Better to keep the memories intact and untarnished. She'd phone him tomorrow and make her excuses.

Picking up the gift-wrapped butter knife, she ran back downstairs, unsure whether or not she felt better for having reached that decision.

However, back home the next day, Anna repeatedly put off making the call. Several times she got as far as lifting the phone and starting to punch in the number, only to drop it back on its stand, telling herself Lewis would be at work – or at lunch – or perhaps visiting suppliers – and would resent the interruption. They weren't scheduled to meet till Friday – time enough to contact him. And, she remembered with a sense of relief, he'd told her he'd be away on business the earlier part of the week. Definitely too busy for personal calls.

Thankfully, she postponed taking action.

Jonathan and Steve had arranged to fly up to Manchester on the Wednesday afternoon, to allow comfortable time for their appointment the following morning.

'You texted our friend, I presume?' Steve enquired, fastening his seat belt.

'Yep. Brief and to the point. *Bar of Commodore Hotel, six thirty, Wednesday sixteenth.* And her reply was equally succinct: *I shall be there.* If she doesn't turn up – which, after previous experience, I'm quite prepared for – well, we'd doubtless be in the bar anyway, so it's no skin off our noses. We'll give her an hour or so, and then go in to dinner.'

'I hope she does come,' Steve remarked. 'All this on-off stuff has got me guessing. What does she look like?'

'French,' said Jonathan unhelpfully. Then, at his friend's

expression: 'Large dark eyes, fringe, nice figure. The accent adds *je ne sais quoi*, if you'll forgive the expression.'

'Intriguing,' Steve commented, and, opening his newspaper, he let the subject drop.

Six fifteen saw them both established at a table in the bar, glasses of whisky in front of them.

'I wonder what she wants to tell you,' Steve mused. 'Must be pretty serious, for her to keep coming back.'

'It had better be good, after all this shilly-shallying.'

As six thirty approached, they fell silent, their eyes on the entrance to the bar. But no small, dark girl with a fringe appeared. Jonathan could feel his irritation building, and when, at six thirty-five, his mobile bleeped, he swore under his breath.

'For God's sake, not *again*!' Impatiently, he flipped it open and read the text.

'Well?' Steve demanded. 'What's her excuse this time?'

'No excuse, actually,' Jonathan said slowly. 'She's on her way, but she'd prefer not to meet in a public place, and suggests coming to my room.'

'Oi, oi! She won't be pleased to see me!'

'Nonsense; she sounds really nervous, Steve.' He started texting.

'What are you doing?'

'Giving her the room number.' Jonathan closed the phone and rose to his feet. 'Come on. Bring your drink with you.'

They took the lift in silence and walked along the corridor to Jonathan's room. Once inside, he moved the two armchairs to face each other and brought over an upright chair. Then they stood waiting, unable to settle, until, six or seven minutes later, there was a tap on the door. Jonathan strode to open it, face-to-face at last with the elusive Elise.

'Come in,' he said briefly.

She stepped into the room, coming to a halt as she saw they were not alone.

'This is my colleague, Steve Forrester,' Jonathan said quickly. 'It's all right – we work together. You can speak freely in front of him.' He turned to Steve. 'Steve, this is Elise . . .?'

'Du Pré,' she murmured.

They nodded cautiously at each other, and Jonathan waved her to a chair.

'It is so good of you to come here,' she began, but Jonathan cut her short.

'Actually, you're not the reason we're in Manchester; we have a business meeting tomorrow. Now, can I get you a drink?' He indicated the minibar.

She eyed their glasses on the table. 'Thank you. Whatever you drink.'

He poured her a whisky, and he and Steve seated themselves.

'So,' Jonathan continued, 'you've finally decided to tell me what's worrying you?'

Her eyes fell. 'I think I must. Though I feel – *infidèle*?' She paused helplessly.

'Disloyal?' Steve hazarded, and she threw him a grateful glance.

'Disloyal – yes. It is hard for me to do this. I love my job, and I like the people I work with. They have been good to me.'

Jonathan leaned forward, his glass between his hands. 'And who are they, exactly?'

She took a deep breath before looking up and meeting his eyes. 'I work for the Mandelyns Group.'

He stared at her blankly, and it was Steve who, after a minute, said, 'You mean the health farm people?'

She nodded. 'I am . . . *assistante personnelle* to one of the owners.'

'How many resorts do they have?'

'Three at present, but we are here to consider a fourth.'

'Go on,' Jonathan prompted.

'You may not know, but as well as the resorts, we have a range of beauty products and treatments. For some years now, work has been continuing on a revolutionary new one. Its tests were completed at the end of last year, and it was introduced in the spring.'

'And?'

Elise hesitated. 'It is difficult to explain, but it is a special treatment – very expensive. For ladies . . . *d'un certain age*, you understand?'

'We understand,' Jonathan said, for both of them.

'It works in a similar way to Botox – you have heard of that?'
They nodded.

'And, like Botox, it is a bacterial toxin that must be rigidly controlled.'

'A toxin?' Jonathan repeated, surprised. Then, remembering, his voice sharpened. 'And people have died?'

After a moment, she nodded.

'Women who had taken this . . . treatment?'

She nodded again. 'At first it seemed . . . a terrible coincidence. But when it happened again, and then again—'

'For God's sake,' Steve interrupted harshly, 'how many of your clients have died?'

She raised her shoulders in a shrug. 'Four? Five? These are the names I recognize.'

The two men sat back in their chairs and stared at each other.

'And how many in total have had the treatment?'

Elise spread her hands. 'Oh, many, many more. Several dozen, at the least, which is why I tried to tell myself there is no connection. But if even *one* has died as a result, surely something should be done?'

'What raised your suspicions in the first place?'

'I read in the paper of someone's death – a member of Parliament, who was a regular client and had been at Mandelyns Woodcot a few weeks earlier. But I did not know then that she had received the treatment; I was just sad she died too young.'

'Did the paper say what caused her death?'

'A heart attack, I think.'

'And the next thing?'

'Maria Lang died – the actress? You must have heard. She, too, was a regular visitor, at Mandelyns Foxfield, where I work.'

'The treatment was on offer at all the resorts?'

Elise nodded. 'In her case, it was put down to a mystery virus. Then, by chance, I heard of a third. But you see, all these ladies lived in different areas, and different causes were given for their deaths, so no connection was made. But I knew they had one thing in common, and that was Mandelyns. I began to be afraid, and after that, I started to read the death columns.'

She looked up. 'It was easy to check, because many of our guests are celebrities. But still I did not believe—'

'You found the names of more clients?'

'A couple, yes. They were all of much the same age, so it seemed likely they had been offered the new treatment.'

'Surely there must have been post-mortems, if the deaths were unexpected?' Steve put in.

'In some cases, yes. There was talk of congenital defects, allergic reactions. But, you see, rashes, swelling, irregular heartbeat – all these symptoms could be side effects of the treatment.'

Jonathan frowned. 'Have you spoken to your boss about this?'

'I tried, but he became very angry. He insists there is *absolutely* no connection, and I must never suggest such a thing, or they take me to court.' She looked at them, her large eyes brimming with tears.

'So you want us to look into it. But we need a lot more to go on, you know.'

'Of course.' Her voice scarcely audible, she seemed to be fighting an internal battle. 'Records are kept of all our clients,' she went on more firmly, 'and a star is put against the names of those who receive the new treatment, so they may be monitored for reactions and results.'

'What kind of results?'

She shrugged. 'In their appearance, their fitness, their . . . *jeunesse*.'

'You have access to this folder?'

She shook her head. 'Though available to all the resorts, its access is restricted to the management and those in charge of the treatment.'

'Then how—?'

'I . . . was able to discover the password.'

'And you took copies?'

'Yes, on a USB memory stick.' She gave a little shiver. 'All the time, I was afraid someone would see me.'

Steve leaned forward eagerly. 'You have it with you?'

Elise raised both hands with a little grimace. 'I regret, no.' And, at his exclamation, hurried on. 'It is in the safe in my room. I intended to retrieve it after breakfast, but my boss needed to see me, and then we must go out and there is no time. *Malheureusement*, we were late back this evening, and if, on top of this, I delayed further by going to my room, you would think that once again I let you down and go out somewhere. I dared not risk that.'

Steve sat back with a gesture of impatience. 'Then how the hell—?'

Ignoring him, she turned to Jonathan. 'As I say, it is in my room – number four-o-six – in an envelope addressed to you. It is a double room, so I am issued with two keys.' She opened her bag and handed him a plastic key card, and he registered the name of her hotel. 'Tomorrow, we shall again be out all day. You will go and collect it?'

Jonathan stared at her. 'You want me to go to your hotel room and open your safe? Suppose a chambermaid comes in? I'd be arrested!'

She leant forward urgently. 'You go around midday and no one will come. The cleaners have all finished, and the guests will be either out or at lunch. It is a good time.'

'Where is the safe?'

'Inside the cupboard; the combination is forty-eight, seventy-two.' She looked from one doubtful face to the other. 'You will do this, yes? You will take the drive and look into the deaths?'

'You could be mistaken, you know,' Jonathan said slowly. 'It might be coincidence after all.'

'I pray that it is. But I must know for sure, or I go crazy.' She stood up abruptly, placing her empty glass on the table. 'I must go. I am expected back for dinner.'

'And if we do find something? We can contact you on your mobile?'

She shook her head quickly. 'There must be no further contact between us. I have given you all I have, and it is vital this information is not traced to me.' She paused, considering. 'If, however, it is essential that you speak with me for some reason, you must telephone in the evening, when I shall be home and alone.'

'Understood.'

She held out her hand, and Jonathan took it. 'I do so hope I am mistaken,' she said.

'We'll do our best to find out.'

'I don't know about you, but I could do with another drink,' Steve commented as Jonathan returned from seeing her out.

'My God, what a hornets' nest! Do you think there's anything in it?'

Jonathan opened the minibar. 'God knows. We'll have a better idea when we see the records, though I don't fancy having to break into her room to get them.'

'Hardly breaking in, when you have the key.'

'All the same, I wish I'd suggested waiting till we get back to London. She could have posted it to us, for God's sake.'

Steve took the glass handed to him, raising it in a silent toast. 'I have the feeling she can't wait to get shot of it. Our flight's at two thirty, isn't it? There'll just be time to collect it at midday, as she suggested.'

'You go then, since you're so keen.'

Steve shook his head. 'Oh no, this is your baby. You were her contact, and the envelope's addressed to you. That might be a saving grace, if someone *does* see you.'

'Thanks,' Jonathan said drily. 'That makes me feel a whole lot better.'

Steve laughed. 'Oh, come on! This could be the hell of a story – Mandelyns-gate!'

'We could also be sued for millions if we get it wrong. Still, there's no point in any more speculating till we know what we're looking at, so –' he drained his glass – 'let's get the hell out of here and go down to dinner.'

SEVEN

Anna's procrastination was in vain, for that evening Lewis phoned her.

'Lewis!' she exclaimed, wooden spoon in hand.

'You sound surprised to hear me!'

'I . . . thought you were away,' she said stupidly.

'But not incommunicado!'

'No, no, of course not.'

'Are you all right, love? You sound a little strained.'

'I'm fine. Just in the middle of preparing supper, actually.'

'Well, I'm sorry to interrupt you,' he said a little stiffly. He paused, and when she made no comment, continued, 'God, Anna, I can't wait to see you, especially after the week I'm having. Negotiations are proving trickier than expected up here.'

'I'm . . . sorry to hear that.'

'I did make it clear, didn't I, that the invitation's not limited to Friday? It's the weekend, after all; we might as well make the most of it – theatre, dinner, drive out somewhere – whatever takes our fancy. I've a comfortable *pied-à-terre* that makes an excellent base.'

The weekend? She caught her breath – but who was she fooling? She'd known all along what his invitation had implied. Memories of the night in Pretoria flooded back, and with them an intense longing for him.

She took a moment to ensure her voice was steady. 'Thank you, that sounds great.'

'I must go, my love; we're meeting in the bar before dinner. See you Friday.' And he rang off. For a moment longer she held the phone to her ear. Then, with a little smile, she replaced it on its stand and went to check the oven.

The meeting with Keith Perceval went well the next morning. He was the owner of a small manufacturing company that was struggling for existence and being constantly elbowed aside by the big boys. Perceval's grandfather had started the business after being decorated for valour in the First World War, and various members of the family had since achieved prominence – by winning a medal in the 1960 Olympics, by rescuing a family from a burning house, by swimming the English Channel.

Steve had caught a brief interview with him on television and thought both he and his company warranted further coverage. Family stories were always of interest, and with luck, an in-depth article in one of the nationals might also help the firm's commercial prospects.

Perceval was a hard-headed businessman in his fifties, proud of his northern roots and of what his family had achieved. His two sons worked with him in the business, extending the history of the firm over four generations, and after conducting them round the factory and introducing them to some of his men, he was happy enough to supply them with anecdotes, photographs and previous newspaper coverage of his illustrious forebears. He also passed on a few more leads to follow up, and the meeting ended with expressions of goodwill all round.

It was eleven fifteen when Jonathan and Steve emerged from his office and took a taxi back to their hotel, to finish packing and be out of their rooms, as required, by midday. Having checked the address of Elise's hotel, they agreed that Steve should take both bags to a nearby café, where, having accomplished his mission, Jonathan would join him for a snack lunch before making their way to the airport.

'Wish me luck,' Jonathan said as they parted outside the designated rendezvous.

'You'll be OK; you should be back in fifteen minutes tops. Remember the combination?'

Jonathan nodded. 'Right, here goes.'

He crossed the road and walked briskly along the opposite pavement to the hotel entrance. Steve watched him go inside, then, an overnight bag in each hand, went into the café and secured a corner table.

In the foyer, Jonathan paused briefly, looking for the bank of lifts, then made his way swiftly over to them, hoping he'd be the only occupant; on leaving the lift, he'd be unsure which way to turn, and had no wish to be seen hesitating.

His luck held, and he was conducted swiftly to the fourth floor, but as the doors opened and he moved forward, he found himself face-to-face with someone about to enter it. Jonathan hesitated, startled by the unexpected encounter, and the man smiled and stood to one side, gesturing for him to exit.

With a nod of thanks, Jonathan did so, the lift doors closed behind him, and the lift began to descend. He released his breath. Had the guy been a minute or two later, he might have seen him furtively entering Elise's bedroom. He could even be a member of the Mandelyns' negotiating team. It was a narrow escape.

A board on the wall opposite showed arrows pointing in the direction of the rooms, and Jonathan set off towards 406. A swift glance up and down the corridor showed it to be empty. Taking the key card from his pocket, he slipped it into the slot, turned the handle, and quickly let himself in, closing the door behind him.

The room smelled faintly of the scent Elise wore. He stood for a moment, looking around. The double bed had been made, so there was little likelihood of an inadvertent visit from the chambermaid. His eyes passed rapidly over dressing table, chairs, tea-making equipment, trouser press, before alighting on the fitted cupboard.

Repeating the combination under his breath, he opened the double doors – and stood staring in disbelief. The safe was there all right, on a shelf, as Elise had said. But its door stood open – and it was empty. God! he thought in a panic. Now what?

The right-hand half of the cupboard was a hanging space, where a couple of dresses and a jacket hung on a rail. Roughly, he pushed them aside, but no second safe was hiding behind them.

He looked feverishly round the room. The only other furniture with doors was the minibar, and without hope he pulled it open. As expected, all it contained was an array of miniatures and bags of nuts.

In desperation, he returned to the cupboard and felt around inside the safe. No envelope had been caught behind the door, and, knocking aside a pair of shoes, it was clear nothing had fallen to the floor.

The damn girl had changed her mind again! The least she

could have done was let him know, spare him this heart-stopping expedition. He turned, raking the room with his eyes. The only place he'd not looked was the en suite, and there wasn't likely to be a safe in there. Nonetheless, on the principle of leaving no stone unturned, he pushed open the door and received his second, brain-numbing shock. For Elise lay crumpled in the bath like a rag doll, her eyes staring sightlessly up at him and an ugly brown stain marring the whiteness of her blouse.

Bile in his throat, sudden sweat drenching his body, Jonathan struggled to take in the situation. Unbelievably, Elise was dead, had obviously been murdered, and – a stab of panic – his fingerprints were all over the bedroom!

Galvanized into action, he fumbled for a handkerchief and began rubbing frenziedly at all the surfaces he could remember touching – the minibar, the inside of the safe, the door handles. And all the while a mantra repeated itself over and over inside his head. *Don't let anyone come! Don't let anyone come!*

He should phone the police, he thought confusedly. But how to explain his presence in the murder room? No, he had to get out of here and back to Steve as quickly as possible.

Sheathing the doorknob with his handkerchief, he carefully turned it, easing the door open inch by inch until he could look out and satisfy himself no one was in sight. Then, heart hammering, he stepped into the corridor, pulled the door shut with his handkerchief, and walked rapidly away. Bypassing the lift, he took the stairs, hurtling down floor after floor, accepting that, though still nauseous and desperate to stop off at the restrooms, he couldn't afford the delay. Elise might be found at any minute, and the man by the lift could describe him.

Outside at last, gulping in the fresh air, he set off at a shambling run for the café where he'd left Steve fifteen minutes earlier. Legs like straw, a persistent stitch in his side, he pushed his way inside, and, though vaguely aware of his friend's raised hand, made straight for the sign reading Toilets. He reached the cubicle with seconds to spare and, kneeling on the tiled floor, vomited long and painfully.

Eventually, shaking, he sat back on his heels and wiped his mouth before rising unsteadily to his feet and sluicing his face under the cold tap. Nothing seemed real, nothing except that broken body in the bath, the blind eyes looking pleadingly up at him. How could they ever have doubted her?

As he emerged from the men's room, Steve was making his way towards him.

'Jon – are you OK? You look ghastly! Come and sit down.'

In a daze, he allowed himself to be led to the table.

'What happened?' Steve demanded urgently. 'Did you get the envelope? No one saw you, did they?'

Jonathan lowered himself gingerly on to a chair. 'No,' he said, 'I didn't get the envelope. The safe was empty.'

Steve's exclamation was lost as he added tonelessly, 'And Elise's body was lying in the bath.'

Steve gazed at him, aghast. 'She's *dead*?'

Jonathan glanced round. 'Keep your voice down, for God's sake!'

'But – I don't understand. Had she drowned or something?'

He shook his head impatiently. 'There was no water – she was fully dressed.' He ran a hand over his hair, made himself say it. 'She'd been stabbed, I think. That, or shot. There was a brown stain on her blouse.'

Steve paled. 'You'd better start at the beginning. Was her door open, or did you have to use the key?'

'It was locked, but before I even got there, I came face-to-face with a guy at the lift. He wouldn't have any difficulty describing me.'

'Nor you him, presumably.'

'God, you think—? No, he couldn't have done it: the blood on her blouse was dry.'

Steve bit his lip. 'Then, by the same token, neither could you. And since she must have died some time earlier, the police won't be asking about strangers around at midday. Come to that, in a hotel, who can tell who's a stranger? Forget the guy – he's not important. So, go on. You used her key to open the door. Then what?'

Trying to make sense of it as he did so, Jonathan stumbled through an account of his search and eventual discovery. As he came to an end, they both sat in silence, wondering with a sense of helplessness what they should do now.

'Ready to order?' asked a voice above them, and both men, lost in their private concerns, jumped.

Steve glanced at his empty beer glass. His appetite had vanished, and one look at Jonathan showed he was incapable of eating. 'We'll just have two whiskies, please,' he said.

The waitress frowned. 'We only serve alcohol with food.'

'Please! We'd be very grateful. My friend isn't feeling too well.' A glance at Jonathan's face was corroboration enough.

'In the circumstances, then,' she allowed grudgingly, and moved away.

Jonathan said, 'We should phone the police. Anonymously, of course.'

'No point,' Steve replied briskly. 'She's up here with colleagues, don't forget. She'll soon be missed, and someone will go to look for her. They might have already found her.'

He leant forward, putting his hand on Jonathan's arm. 'Look, Jon, it would have been different if she'd still been alive, but as things stand there's absolutely no reason for us to get involved. Nothing we do can help her now. OK, she told us various things, but without the memory stick we've no way of proving them, and we can't go shooting our mouths off, accusing her colleagues of God knows what.'

Jonathan wiped a hand across his face. 'Why the hell didn't she tell me before? Then this might never have happened.' A worrying thought struck him. 'God, Steve, it's just occurred to me: whoever killed her must have that envelope with my name on it! My address too, for all I know.'

'Hell's bells! Though, come to think of it, she didn't have your address, did she?'

'She had the newspaper's.'

'Well, you're safe there. They wouldn't pass it on.'

Jonathan wasn't reassured. 'But since it's obvious I've been in contact with her, whoever it is might think I know more than I do.'

Their whiskies arrived, plonked unceremoniously on the table in front of them. Steve nodded their thanks, while Jonathan sipped cautiously at his, hoping he wouldn't have to make a rapid return to the men's room. Fortunately, it seemed to settle his stomach and he began to feel marginally better.

'It must mean she was on to something, mustn't it?' he said.

'It would certainly appear so.'

'If only she'd brought the bloody thing with her last night! Then I'd never have gone near her hotel, let alone found her body.'

'She'd still be dead, though. Thank God we didn't meet her in the bar. Her photo's bound to be in the local paper, and someone might have remembered seeing us with her.' Steve studied his friend for a moment. 'Why do you keep looking at the door?'

Jonathan shrugged. 'Nerves, I suppose. I'll be glad when I'm safely on that plane, I can tell you.'

'Then let's go. No point hanging around here, and you'll be able to relax at the airport.'

The flight passed uneventfully, and in little more than an hour Steve was manoeuvring his car out of the airport car park.

As they emerged on to the M4, Jonathan commented, 'I'd better give Vicky a ring; she asked me to let her know what time I'd be home. God knows what I'm going to tell her, though; if I say too much, she could be in danger herself.'

'I hadn't thought of that,' Steve admitted. 'Same applies to Maddy, I suppose, though obviously I'm not as involved as you are. We'd better get our story straight before we see them.'

Jonathan took out his mobile, but as he switched it on, the phone bleeped, indicating receipt of a text, and the next instant he startled Steve by exclaiming forcefully, 'Oh, my God!'

'What?'

'It's from Elise! Sent this morning at eight forty-one. *Dare not keep item any longer, so am posting it to you. Will explain later. E.*' He spun to face Steve. 'So the killer *didn't* get the envelope, and he *doesn't* know my name! God, that's a relief!'

'But if she sent that at eight forty-one, why the *hell* didn't you get it sooner?' Steve demanded explosively, overtaking a pantechnicon.

Jonathan thought back. 'It would have been around the time we were arriving at Perceval's. I'd have turned the phone off ready for the meeting, and what with the rush to pack our things and dash out again, I never switched it back on. It would have had to be off for the flight anyway, and it wasn't as though I was expecting anything.'

'You do realize you could have saved yourself all that trauma?'

Jonathan nodded soberly. 'She must have sent it to the paper. Come to think of it, it could have travelled in a mailbag on our plane!'

'Well, at least we'll find out what it was all about,' Steve said philosophically.

That evening, Anna had another phone call from Lewis.

'Anna, I'm so very sorry but I might not be able to make tomorrow. Something pretty ghastly has happened, and for the moment I'm stuck in Manchester.'

She felt a shaft of alarm. 'What is it, Lewis? What's happened?'

'A member of our staff has been found dead, and the police want to speak to us.'

She struggled to understand. 'That's terrible, of course, but . . . why the police? How did he die?'

There was a pause, then Lewis said flatly, 'It was a she, and she was murdered.'

'*Murdered*?' Horror rang in Anna's voice. 'How?'

'She was stabbed in her hotel room.' And, at her gasp, he added, 'I know, it's . . . unbelievable. None of us can quite take it in. I can't go into it all now, but obviously we have to account for our movements, and so on. Fortunately, we were together most of the time.'

'But I don't understand! Was it a robbery gone wrong?'

'At this stage, no one knows. Look, sweetheart, I have to go – they're waiting for me. I'll be in touch as soon as I can.' And he rang off.

Anna stood stock-still, the phone in her hand. *Murdered*? Someone who worked for Lewis? And an unwelcome memory came of the conversation she'd overheard in the game park. It could be that Lewis Masters was a dangerous man to know.

*   *   *

The two detectives settled themselves and regarded him blandly. Then the more senior – Pringle, was it? – cleared his throat.

'Now, Mr Masters, what position did you say Ms du Pré held in your organization?'

'She was my son's personal assistant.'

'And could you explain again what brought you and your colleagues to Manchester?'

Lewis bit back his irritation. He'd done nothing *but* explain for the last two hours, but it was unwise to antagonize the police.

'My Group is hoping to purchase a new health resort, and we've been looking over some possibilities.'

'What was the victim's role in the process?'

'In the early stages, we aim to obtain as wide a view as possible of the assets or otherwise of the resorts we're considering. Women, as you'll appreciate, have different values and notice details a man might miss. Their opinions are an important part of our deliberations.'

Pringle studied some notes in front of him. 'She accompanied you on these expeditions earlier in the week?'

'Of course.'

'And how did she seem, sir?'

Lewis wished to hell he'd discussed this with Cameron, but they'd had little privacy since the girl's body was found. He thought back. 'With hindsight, a little tense,' he said slowly.

'How so?'

'Hard to put a finger on it. A bit jumpy, perhaps. Nothing dramatic.'

'Did she get on well with other members of the team?'

'As far as I know. You'd have to ask them.'

'I'm asking you, Mr Masters.'

Again, Lewis held himself in check. 'Then if I have to express an opinion, it would be a qualified yes.'

'Qualified?'

'Being French set her slightly apart; I sensed reserve on both sides.'

Pringle exchanged a glance with his colleague, the significance of which was lost on Lewis. 'There were six of you engaged in this – exploratory visit?'

'That's right: myself, my son, our Managing Director, and our three PAs, the women, as I've explained, for their different perspective.'

'And you visited one of these places yesterday?'

Lewis nodded.

'Where would that have been?'

'The Forest of Bowland. We're also looking at possibilities in Cheshire and Derbyshire, which is why Manchester seemed a good base.'

'And during yesterday's trip, did Ms du Pré seem in good spirits?'

Lewis considered. 'On reflection, she was slightly on edge. We were running late, and I had the impression she was anxious to get back to Manchester.'

'For a date, possibly?'

Lewis looked surprised. 'I can't think with whom, and she was with us at dinner.'

'What did you all do, when you arrived back at your hotel?'

'As I said, it was rather later than we'd envisaged – about six fifteen, I believe. I can only speak for myself, but I imagine we all went to our rooms, to relax for a while before dinner.'

'Where, you say, Ms du Pré joined you.'

'Correct.'

Pringle pursed his lips thoughtfully. 'And how did she seem then?'

'A little flushed, but otherwise much as usual.'

'She was also at breakfast this morning?'

'Only briefly. It was a buffet, and as we were all at separate tables, I didn't see her myself. My PA told me later she had only a cup of coffee and left before finishing it. Consequently, she wasn't surprised by the text.'

'Ah yes, the text. Received by your son, I believe?'

'That's right. Asking to be excused from today's visit, due to not feeling well.'

'And you thought no more of it?'

Lewis frowned. 'Why should I? She'd been flushed and a little overwrought; this offered an explanation.'

'Right.' Pringle toyed with his ballpoint, upending and righting it in a monotonous rhythm. 'So Ms du Pré left the dining room at about what time?'

'You'd have to check with Mrs Standish, my PA.'

'Who were you yourself sitting with?'

'My son briefly, but none of us lingered; we all had things to do before setting off for the day.'

'What time did *you* leave the dining room, Mr Masters?'

Lewis pursed his lips. 'Probably around eight forty-five. We were leaving for Chester at nine fifteen.'

'You went straight to your room?'

'Yes.' Lewis's tone was clipped.

'Did you see or speak to any of your group before you all assembled in the lobby at nine fifteen?'

'No, but that's hardly surprising; our rooms are on different floors.' Lewis paused, and added with heavy irony, 'The chambermaid will vouch for me; she was finishing my room as I arrived.'

Pringle nodded, and Lewis had the uneasy suspicion this had already been checked. Fair enough; in a hotel of strangers, those who knew the girl were obvious suspects.

'The text, then: were you with your son when he received it?'

'No; he told us about it when he joined us.' Lewis stirred. 'Look, Sergeant, I appreciate you have to go into all this, but surely it's obvious that someone went to her room after we'd left? We know she was alive at ten past nine, the time on the text, and we left the hotel at quarter past. It doesn't leave us much time to do the deed!' He gave a crooked smile.

Pringle didn't return it. 'You're assuming, sir, that it was Ms du Pré who sent it.'

Lewis was taken aback. 'But surely . . .?'

'Wouldn't it have been more usual in the circumstances to have telephoned, apologized personally? More polite, even, considering she was addressing her employer?' He let Lewis take in the implications before adding, 'A text, though, is nice and anonymous, isn't it, sir?'

Lewis said incredulously, 'You're saying her killer sent it? That she was already dead at ten past nine?'

'I'm saying nothing of the sort, sir,' Pringle contradicted smoothly. 'Merely that at this stage, nothing can be ruled out. Now, let us move on to your return to the hotel this evening. What was the first you heard of her death?'

With difficulty, Lewis wrenched his mind from unconsidered possibilities. 'As soon as we arrived back, the manager called me into his office and broke the news. A chambermaid had found her, when she went to turn down the bed. But you know all that – your men were already there.'

'Indeed.' There was a moment's pause. 'The safe was open and empty, so it would seem her killer was looking for something. Have you any idea what that might be?'

Lewis said drily, 'No, but the empty safe seems to indicate that he found it.'

The detective looked up, and for a long moment the men held each other's eyes. Then, abruptly, Pringle changed tack. 'The name and address of her next of kin, Mr Masters; presumably you can supply them?'

'Not personally, but they'll be on file at head office.'

'Had she any relatives in this country?'

'Not to my knowledge.'

'Then perhaps you'd arrange for her details to be sent to me as soon as possible. In the meantime, there's one further thing I must ask of you.'

Lewis waited.

'Due to the lack of relatives, it will be necessary for you to identify the body.'

Lewis stared at him. 'But there's no doubt, surely? I mean, she was found in her own room, and—'

'It's a legal requirement, Mr Masters. It won't take long: the mortuary's just next door. DC Smith will accompany you. After that, you'll be free to leave, though I shall need to see you again in the morning.'

At his cue, the constable, who'd remained silent throughout the interview, rose and opened the door for him, and Lewis, a cold feeling in the pit of his stomach, had no option but to go through it.

It was on the news that night. Anna, hands clasped tightly in her lap, gazed at the screen, unable to relate the only-too-familiar sight of police tapes and men in white suits with Lewis and his colleagues. At least his name wasn't mentioned; if he'd not phoned her, she'd have had no idea of his involvement. For that matter, the girl's name, which he'd not told her, had also been withheld, presumably to give the police time to contact her family, poor souls.

A woman of twenty-five. Whoever could have wanted to kill her? And in view of her death, Anna told herself, it was unforgivably selfish of her to mind so much about not seeing Lewis tomorrow.

With a sigh, she switched off the set and went up to bed. It would have astonished her to know that her son had been watching the same report with an even more personal interest.

It was eleven o'clock, and the five of them were in Lewis's suite. While the others discussed their interviews with the police, Lewis himself was trying to dispel the image of the girl in the morgue, which had burned itself on to his retinas.

Forcing it to the back of his mind, he rose to refill their glasses. 'The police wondered if she met someone when we got back last night,' he said. 'Did anyone see her before dinner?'

Everyone shook their heads.

'It would make sense,' Mike Chadwick, the Managing Director, put in. 'If it was a date of some kind, the guy might even have come back and spent the night with her.'

'Perhaps that's why she cried off today – to be with him,' his PA, Tina Martin, suggested. 'Then things could have turned nasty, and he killed her.'

'And perhaps we should rein in our imaginations,' Lewis said drily. He returned to his chair and took a sip of his drink. 'When the police asked for details, I realized how little I know about the girl. Did she ever mention a boyfriend, Cameron?'

'Not to me; we didn't discuss personal matters.'

'So what do you know about her?'

'Only that she was a damn good PA. Her home was near Paris – or at least, her parents still live there. She came over shortly before joining us, two years ago.'

'And lived near the resort, I presume?'

'Yes, she rented a bungalow in the village.'

'Did she share it with anyone?'

'I've no idea. No one from the Group, anyway. God, Father,

I've been through all this with the police!'

'Sorry.' Lewis turned from his son's drawn face to the two PAs. 'Anything you can add?'

They both shook their heads, and he suddenly hit the arm of his chair, startling them.

'What *bloody* timing! If she had to get herself killed, why now, for God's sake? We'll be lumbered with just the sort of publicity we don't need, and the negotiations could be seriously jeopardized. Not to mention casting a cloud over the anniversary weekend.'

He broke off, aware of their shocked faces, and wiped a hand across his own.

'Sorry,' he muttered. 'Put it down to stress. Obviously, I didn't mean that.'

But he had, and they knew it. Stress might account for his blurting it out, but it had been in his mind ever since the discovery of the body. He looked up, catching Yvonne Standish's eye, and she gave him a sympathetic smile.

Dear Yvonne! he thought fondly; in her fifties and divorced, she'd been his PA for over ten years, and her loyalty and efficiency were second to none. Lewis was aware she was in love with him, and the idea of sleeping with her had crossed his mind more than once. But now he'd met Anna; it was sheer bad luck that tonight, when sex would have been the ideal antidote, she was two hundred miles away.

He glanced back at Yvonne. Temptation was strong, but he suppressed it. Had Anna been one of his passing liaisons, he might have succumbed; but his relationship with her was on another plane, and he wasn't going to compromise it.

Cameron was saying, 'How long do you think they'll keep us here?'

'It's my son's school concert tomorrow,' Mike added. 'I'll be for it if I'm not home in time.'

'I shouldn't think it'll be much longer,' Yvonne said in her quiet voice. 'They've taken our addresses, so they can contact us at home if they need to. With luck, we should get away tomorrow.'

In which case, he could still meet Anna. Feeling slightly more cheerful, Lewis stood up. 'In the meantime, I think we should try to get some sleep. I'll see you all in the morning. Goodnight, everyone.'

As he closed the door behind them, he glanced at his watch. Eleven thirty. Too late to phone her. He'd ring first thing in the morning, ask her to hold the weekend after all. Despite the traumas of the day, something might yet be salvaged.

EIGHT

After a restless night, Jonathan came awake to the ringing of his mobile, and, befuddled with sleep, fumbled to locate it before it woke Vicky. The bedside clock pointed to six thirty. Who the hell . . .?

'Yes? . . . Hello? . . . This is Jonathan Farrell; who's calling? Do you know what time it is?'

There was silence, then a click as the line was disconnected.

'Well, thanks a bunch!' he muttered.

'Who was it?' Vicky asked sleepily from the bed.

'Some insomniac, dialling the wrong number.'

'Come back to bed, then.'

And, still grumbling, he did so.

Two hours later, he phoned the paper from Steve's flat.

'Hi. Jonathan Farrell here. Did a letter arrive for me this morning, by any chance?'

'If it did, it'll be forwarded,' a laconic voice told him.

'I know that; I just want to confirm it's actually arrived?'

'Hang on, I'll put you through.'

Jonathan glanced over his shoulder at Steve, standing rigidly behind him. 'They're checking,' he said.

'Sorry, mate.' Another voice. 'Nothing here for Farrell.'

Jonathan frowned. 'But there *must* be! It was posted yesterday morning, in Manchester.'

'Sorry,' the voice repeated.

'The post *has* arrived, I take it?'

'Yep, been sorted.' A pause. 'Perhaps it was sent second class?'

'I very much doubt it. Look, could you check again? It might be a package rather than a letter.'

A heavy sigh came over the wire, followed by a brief pause, then: 'Still nothing. Give us a call tomorrow.'

'OK, thanks.'

He put down the phone and stared wordlessly at his friend.

'Let's just think this through, before we panic,' Steve said. 'She wouldn't have had time to go out and find a postbox, so either there was one in the hotel lobby or she handed it to the receptionist.' He paused thoughtfully. 'Did she say she was *going* to post it, or already had?'

Jonathan clicked on Messages. 'Her actual words were "*am posting it to you*", which could mean either. Why?'

'Just wondering if something – or someone – prevented her from doing so.'

'Oh God!' Jonathan said tonelessly. 'So we're back to the killer possibly having it.'

'On the other hand, the hotel mail mightn't have been collected, or the receptionist forgot to post it, in which case it'll turn up eventually. What's clear, though, is that without it, our hands are tied and there's absolutely nothing we can do.'

'And if it *doesn't* turn up, she'll have died for nothing.'

'If that's why she was killed. For all we know, it could have been a lovers' tiff.'

'You're surely not saying this is all one big coincidence?'

'God, Jon, I don't know what I'm saying. I've not been mixed up in murder before, and I can't say I like it.'

'Ought we to contact the police, do you think?'

'And tell them what? That you found her? That's all the info you can give them, apart from the fact that you left the scene as fast as your legs could carry you, having probably removed the killer's fingerprints as well as your own.'

Jonathan groaned. 'I never thought of that.'

They sat in gloomy silence for several minutes. Then Jonathan said urgently, 'There must be *something* we can do. We owe her that much. Let's go over again what we know – or at least what she told us.'

'Which boils down to very little. To wit – one: the resort was trying out a new beauty treatment, after, presumably, it had passed the required tests. Two: it was aimed at older women with plenty of money. Three: several dozen underwent the treatment, and of those possibly four or five died shortly afterwards. Four: when she mentioned her suspicions to her boss, she was given short shrift and told to keep her mouth shut. Five: she somehow obtained copies of these women's notes and copied them on to a memory stick. Which is now missing. And that's the sum total.'

'So,' Jonathan said, 'without the memory stick, the only evidence is at the resorts themselves. We'll have to infiltrate somehow and root around ourselves.'

'*Infiltrate*? Are you mad? It might have escaped your notice, but neither of us is a woman of a certain age. If we start asking about beauty treatments, it'll certainly start tongues wagging!'

'There might be another way,' Jonathan said slowly.

'I'd be interested to know how.'

'OK, a guy wouldn't stand much chance of snooping, but a woman might, even if she wasn't of a certain age.'

Steve frowned. 'What are you getting at?'

'I was wondering if perhaps Maddy—'

'No way!' Steve interrupted. 'You can stop right there. I'm not sending Maddy into the lion's den on a wild goose chase.'

'Lions and geese! An interesting combination.'

'Seriously, Jon—'

'Look,' Jonathan interrupted in his turn, 'I'm just thinking aloud – bear with me. Suppose Maddy goes for one of these pampering weekends, either to Woodcot, was it, or the one where Elise worked. Obviously, she wouldn't be eligible for the treatment, but she could cosy up to some elderly women and see what transpires.'

'And suppose she arouses suspicion?'

'Why should she? There's absolutely nothing to connect her to Elise, and I bet they gossip all the time about the treatments they're having. She could say she's read about some fantastic product – even that some elderly relative had it – and has whoever she's talking to tried it?'

'No,' Steve said again, but less dogmatically.

'Suppose we let Maddy decide? She might welcome a weekend at a luxury place like that – facials and massages and all the rest of it.'

'Oh, I don't doubt she would, and if she knew there was some mystery attached, she'd be even keener. I'm the one who wouldn't be happy.'

There was a brief silence, then Jonathan said, 'Well, of course it's up to you, but God knows what else we can do.'

'It might still come tomorrow.'

'No, I think we have to accept that something prevented her posting it, or it would have been there by now.' He looked at his watch. 'In which case, it's time we stopped faffing around and got down to work on the Perceval piece.'

'Yep,' Steve said absent-mindedly.

Jonathan waited, sensing a change of heart.

'I suppose there's no harm in at least filling Maddy in,' Steve offered tentatively.

'None at all. And, of course, I'll have to tell Vicky; I was too shattered to go into details yesterday.'

'You'll stay up here for the rest of the day, though?'

'Yep, but to coin a phrase, thank God it's Friday. It's been quite a week.'

'I might see if Maddy can join us for lunch, so we can explain the position. It'd be better if you were there as well.'

'Excellent idea,' said Jonathan.

As expected, Maddy was only too ready to fall in with the suggestion.

'I've always wanted to go to one of those places,' she said enthusiastically, 'but I could never afford it.'

The men exchanged glances. 'It would be on expenses, of course,' Jonathan said smoothly. 'After all, it's part of the research on what could well be a scoop.'

'Then I'd be even more delighted! And what, exactly, do I have to do while I'm there?'

'You might change your mind when you hear,' Steve warned.

'I doubt it! Try me.'

But her pleasure faded as they told her about Elise, her suspicions, and her violent death.

'God, that's *terrible*!' she exclaimed. 'Poor girl! She certainly didn't deserve that.'

'We won't hold you to it, if you feel differently now,' Jonathan said, mentally crossing his fingers.

Maddy shook her head. 'No; you need to get to the bottom of this, and obviously only a woman can do it. I could suss out the layout, then pretend to lose my way and end up in an office with filing cabinets.'

Steve opened his mouth to protest, then closed it again.

'I wonder if they have any vacancies next weekend?' she mused.

'They'll have plenty, if they keep killing off their clients,' Steve said grimly. 'You must promise me not to take any risks, and if there's the slightest hint that anyone's watching you too closely, let me know at once and I'll come straight down and fetch you.'

'Don't worry, I'll be careful,' she assured him.

In the event, Lewis waited until he'd checked with the police before phoning Anna. He was informed that there were a few more points to go over, but they should be free to leave after lunch, in time for the flight on which they were originally booked. However, they were asked not to leave the country and warned that they'd be visited by their local police on their return home – a reminder than none of them had an alibi for the time between eight thirty, when Elise left the restaurant, and nine fifteen, when they gathered in the lobby.

'So if you're still free,' Lewis told Anna, 'we can have our weekend after all.'

'That's great.' She paused. 'It was on the news last night; I suppose there are no developments?'

'No, the investigation's still in its early stages. Personally, I find it quite impossible to take in – it's so totally bizarre.'

'But surely it was a bungled robbery?' Though according to this morning's paper, the estimated time of death was between eight thirty and ten thirty in the morning, an unusual – and risky – time for an opportunist thief to try his luck.

Lewis met her off the train, and they took a taxi to his flat in Kensington.

'I never use the car when I'm in town,' he told her.

In fact, in those first minutes Anna was grateful for the driver's presence; after two weeks apart, she felt awkward meeting Lewis again, and the prospect of the weekend ahead filled her with an equal mixture of anticipation and apprehension.

He had described the flat as 'comfortable'; opulent might have been a better word. Having nodded to the concierge and taken the lift to the top floor, she found that the rooms were large and airy, comprising not only two en suite bedrooms and a large, elegant living area, but also a room complete with long mahogany table and eight chairs, which Lewis referred to as the boardroom.

'We have senior management meetings every quarter,' he explained, 'and it's easier for everyone to meet here. Also, it's sometimes more convenient to see suppliers or our advertising people in London, rather than down in Surrey.'

'Do you live here most of the time, then?' Anna asked. Despite the elegance of the furnishings, there were few personal touches.

He shook his head. 'Only if I have business in town, or an evening engagement up here. Otherwise, I'm at my self-contained flat at Mandelyns Court, the Group headquarters.'

'Two flats but no house?' Anna asked, with raised eyebrows.

'Why should I need a house, when there's only me? I handed over the family home to my wife when we separated, though she sold it soon afterwards.'

'Now –' his tone changed, indicating that the topic was closed – 'I suggest you unpack anything you might need for this evening, then we'll have a drink and some canapés before we go out. That should keep us going until dinner after the show.'

Oliver Beresford, whom Lewis referred to as his son-out-law, closed the front door softly, then smiled when he saw the line of light under the door of the sitting room. He'd told her not to wait up, but was glad that she had.

He pushed open the door. Lydia was curled up on the sofa in her dressing gown, head resting against a cushion and eyes closed, while the television, unwatched, bleated in its corner. He crossed the room and switched it off, then, turning, stooped to kiss her. She stirred, opening sleepy eyes.

'I didn't hear you come in,' she said, struggling into a more upright position.

'Nor anything else, by the look of you!' he teased, seating himself beside her and loosening his tie.

'How did the dinner go?'

'As well as can be expected, with a crowd of dry and dusty barristers! But guess who was also at the restaurant?'

'Tom Cruise?' she asked facetiously.

'Not quite. Your father, with a lady I've never seen before.'

'The crafty old devil! What was she like?'

'Quite attractive, actually. Smartly dressed.'

'Which would fit half the population of London! Did he see you?'

'No; I'd no wish to embarrass him, so I kept my distance.'

'Why should he be embarrassed? He's not a monk. And at least then we'd have known who she was.'

'Does it matter?' Oliver asked lazily, running a finger round the neckline of her dressing gown. 'Next time we see him, it'll probably be someone else.'

She wriggled under his caress. 'I'll phone him tomorrow and tell him he was spotted.'

'Just as you wish. In the meantime, as you might have noticed, I have other things on my mind.' He bent forward and kissed the space he'd made above her collar. 'So how about concentrating for now on this old man?'

'With the greatest of pleasure!' she said.

At much the same time, Jonathan and Vicky were half-watching the late film on TV. He had waited till the boys were in bed and they were having supper before telling her the full story of his trip to Manchester, and as he'd anticipated, she'd been very shaken by it.

'Are you *sure* no one knows your connection?' she asked more than once.

'As sure as I can be, love. Anyway, without the blasted memory stick, we're no threat to anyone.'

'You say "we", but it's really just you, isn't it? It wasn't Steve she approached.'

'But he was there when we met. He's involved, though admittedly not as much as I am.'

She considered for a moment. 'So, since you've no proof, you'll forget the whole thing?' Her eyes pleaded with him.

'Honey, you know me better than that!' He tried to make a joke of it. 'I'm a newspaper man!'

'So what *are* you planning? You might as well tell me.'

'Nothing drastic. But Maddy's going to book herself into one of the health farms for a weekend's pampering.'

'A weekend's snooping, you mean.'

'Obviously, she'll see what she can find out.'

'And Steve's happy with that?'

'Not exactly happy, but resigned. It's the only option open to us.'

She'd leaned over the table, putting her hand on his. 'Jonathan, I've only just got you back. I don't want to lose you.'

'Darling girl, you're not going to! Heavens, this isn't Chicago!'

'Someone still got killed. Someone you knew. That's bad enough for me.'

Now, giving up all pretence of watching television, he put an arm round her. 'Don't worry, darling,' he said softly. 'It'll be all right, I promise.'

'I hope to God you're right,' she said.

That weekend, London basked in an Indian summer. On the Saturday, Lewis and Anna took the train to Kew, where they spent an enjoyable day wandering round the gardens and lunched in the Orangery Restaurant. By unspoken agreement, the traumas of Manchester were not mentioned, though Anna found herself casting surreptitious glances at the newspaper billboards they passed. Surely by now the police had tracked down the killer?

'I meant to tell you,' Lewis said at one point. 'I had a phone call from Wendy the other day. She wanted to know if we'd kept in touch.'

Anna smiled. 'How are they?'

'Fine. I think they're planning to invite us over some time. Would you like to go?'

'Certainly. I'd love to see them again.'

'Good; I'll arrange it, then.'

'When we were in South Africa, she mentioned Mandelyns' thirtieth anniversary. Is that Mandelyns Court, which you referred to earlier?'

'Yes, it was the first one I purchased. Then, when I took over Woodcot and Foxfield, I re-branded them with the Mandelyns tag – Mandelyns Woodcot Grange and Mandelyns Foxfield Hall – to form a Group.'

'And Mandelyns Mandelyns Court?'

He returned her smile. 'Hardly; publicly that's known as Mandelyns Beechford, the nearest town, but "in house", as it were, we refer to it as Beechford.'

'Simpler, certainly. What form is the celebration taking?'

'Anniversary dinner and overnight stay for friends of the Group, by way of a thank-you – politicians, actors, big business, you name it, as well as heads of the catering and advertising firms we use, and so on. Just over a hundred in all. It's been a year in the planning, and most of the invitations have already gone out.' His face clouded. 'I just hope to God what happened at Manchester won't put a spoke in the wheel.'

'Surely it'll all be settled by then. When is this weekend?'

'The twentieth and twenty-first of November – just five weeks away.' He turned to her suddenly. 'Will you come, Anna? It would make all the difference to me.'

'Good heavens, why me? I've had nothing whatever to do with Mandelyns!'

'But you have with me!'

'But I wouldn't know anyone. I'd be completely out of my depth.'

'You'd know Wendy and George, and I can invite your son and daughter, too.'

'But—'

'Don't you see? It would be the ideal way for us all to meet. They needn't know about our relationship, just that we met in South Africa and I'm inviting you, as a friend, and them to keep you company. It's the perfect solution!' He looked at her doubtful face. 'No need to make a decision now; think it over, and you can give me their addresses later.'

South Africa! Anna thought. How long ago it all seemed – Harry and Susan, and Edda the tour manager; Table Mountain and Durban and the game parks. And losing her way in the dark, she thought before she could stop herself, and inadvertently overhearing Lewis's phone call. She gave a little shudder.

'Not cold, surely?' he asked.

'No, just someone walking over my grave.'

'Don't say that!' His voice was sharp, and at her startled glance, he gave a little laugh. 'Sorry, but that's a bit close to home at the moment.'

'No, *I'm* sorry. It was a thoughtless thing to say.'

Lewis took her arm. 'We haven't been in the Palm House yet,' he said, leading her in its direction; and, the unwelcome topic safely sidestepped, they resumed their pleasurable tour.

It had all been wonderful, Anna reflected on the train home. Lewis's love-making had been as exciting and fulfilling as she remembered, his conversation as stimulating. He'd suggested they meet the following weekend, but she'd reluctantly had to decline. It would be half-term, and Tamsin would be home. She saw little enough of her granddaughter, and intended to be available for any suggested outings.

Regarding the anniversary, she'd promised to consider the invitation, though she'd held back on Jon and Sophie's addresses, as a safeguard against changing her mind.

'You could, of course, always tell them about us in advance,' he suggested. 'That would work even better.'

But she'd shaken her head at that. 'It'd be too soon after my husband's anniversary; we must wait a decent interval before springing it on them.'

And mention of Miles had resurrected all the latent feelings of guilt she'd been trying to suppress. In her family's eyes, a holiday romance would have been betrayal enough, less than a year after his death; continuing it would surely be unforgivable.

'Bring me up to speed on this one, Jim,' DI Fanshawe instructed. He'd been on leave the previous week and had returned on Monday morning to find a full-scale murder investigation under way.

Pringle outlined the basic facts. 'Odds are it's one of the group,' he finished, 'but the problem is proving it. Too bad we had to let them go; cracks might have emerged under further questioning, but we'd nothing to hold them on.'

'They're from a health farm, you said?'

'That's right, Mandelyns. Never heard of it myself. The head poncho, Masters, is a plausible devil. Too smooth by half. By the look of him, he's used to saying, "Jump!" and everyone jumps. Well, not this baby.'

Fanshawe permitted himself a smile. 'Leaving aside your north/south biases, Jim, was he able to account for his movements?'

'No, that's the devil of it: none of them could. They were off the radar from the time they left the dining room till they met for the day's jaunt some forty minutes later. Any one of them could have nipped to her room, done the deed, and been back in time, looking innocent as the day. Forensics say they wouldn't have had any blood on them; there was just the one clean wound, and the girl's clothing soaked up most of it.'

'So who else was in this group?'

'Well, there's the son, Cameron Masters. The deceased was his PA. Intense kind of guy – seemed severely shaken. He was the one who received the text.'

'It did exist, then?'

'Too right; I saw it myself on his mobile, timed at 09.10.'

'What did it say, exactly?'

Pringle looked down at his notes. '"Please excuse me from today's visit. I do not feel well. Elise."'

'Brief and to the point. Question is, did the victim send it?'

'She could have, in which case the timing pretty well exonerates them. It certainly came from her mobile, which is missing. On the other hand, if she *didn't* send it, the killer knew who to send it to, which points straight back at her colleagues.'

'A delaying tactic?'

'Possibly.' He consulted his notes again. 'Then there's the MD, Michael Chadwick. He was in a fair old state, I can tell you – sweat pouring off him, and he contradicted himself a couple of times. Big bloke, in his forties. Wouldn't have had any difficulty picking her up and chucking her in the bath.'

Fanshawe stirred. 'Could a woman have done it?'

'The official opinion is yes – no great strength required, and marks on the carpet indicate the body was dragged to the bathroom – which could be in Chadwick's favour.'

'Strikes me there's no obvious motive for any of them,' Fanshawe said disgustedly. 'What about the women, then?'

Pringle shrugged. 'Could be jealousy; du Pré was a good twenty years younger than either of them and a damn sight prettier. Preferential treatment, perhaps? Or a grudge could have been building up, and something happened to tip the balance.' He glanced back at his notes. 'Masters' PA was the calmest of the lot, but as we know, still waters run deep. Name of Yvonne Standish, divorced, in her fifties. Pleasant manner, seemed anxious to help, but gave little away.'

'Think she was up to it?'

'If sufficiently motivated, yes. She'd a determined air about her.'

'And the other?'

'Chadwick's PA, Tina Martin – married, late forties. Tall, well-built. Tearful under questioning, but confirmed everything the others had said.'

'Hm.' Fanshawe thought for a moment. 'But the last to see du Pré alive was the hotel receptionist?'

'Yep. She was on the morning shift, so this only emerged the next day, when she came back on duty. She says du Pré gave her a package to post, which the group insist they knew nothing about.'

'Hm. Who was it addressed to?'

Pringle snorted. 'She didn't look, did she? Put it under the counter because someone was waiting to check out, and then forgot about it. She didn't drop it in the mailbag till some time later. But she swears it had been handed in soon after she came on duty at eight thirty, so if du Pré went upstairs after leaving the dining room, she must have come straight down again. Which gives us two scenarios: either she was intending to go on the trip and came down early so no one would see her posting it – which raises interesting questions. Or she really *was* ill, and made a special trip downstairs – equally interesting, since she must have thought it important, for her to make the effort. But in either case, we're faced with the same question: did she meet her killer on the way back to her room?'

'It's one possibility. CCTV no help?'

Pringle shook his head in disgust. 'Haven't got any, have they? Say it would be an infringement of their guests' privacy.'

Fanshawe swore under his breath. 'So what are the other options?'

'Well, it turns out he could have let himself in. The hotel say du Pré was issued with two key cards for the double room – standard practice – and only one was found on her. Failing that, she let him in herself because she knew him. Or she didn't know him, and he forced his way in, which would be unlikely if it were a common or garden thief. If that *had* been the case, you'd look for a sexual assault, but that proved negative.'

'What was taken from the room?'

Pringle shrugged. 'The safe was open, but we don't know there'd been anything in it, and she was still wearing her jewellery. The only item known to be missing is her mobile.'

'Handbag?'

'Had been opened – possibly to remove the mobile – then kicked under the bed, but her wallet was still inside.'

'At least we have the murder weapon – also found under the bed I gather?'

Pringle nodded with satisfaction. 'Complete with her DNA, though wiped of fingerprints. Forensics confirmed it was a fruit knife belonging to the hotel; it had been on the table with a bowl of fruit, compliments of the management. Bet they scrap that courtesy. So, since the killer didn't bring the weapon with him, it could have been unpremeditated.'

'When was she found?'

'Not till five thirty, when the chambermaid turned down the bed and checked the towels. Davis reckons that by then, she'd been dead between seven and nine hours.'

Fanshawe drummed his fingers on the desk. 'So what's the present state of play?'

'Well, the guests weren't allowed out of the hotel till they'd been interviewed and had their details taken – a popular move, as you'll appreciate. Ditto all the staff. Net result: zilch. Several people had noticed the group, because they sat together for their evening meals, but no one paid them much attention, and not a single person admits to seeing the victim on Friday morning, even though she came down to breakfast and again, later, to the reception desk. Convenient memory lapse, if you ask me.'

'No sinister men lurking in the corridors?'

'Afraid not, but it's no use asking about strangers in a hotel.' Pringle glanced at his watch. 'The parents' flight is due in an hour. I've arranged for a car to meet them.'

'Well, at least I had my holiday,' Fanshawe said resignedly. 'OK, we'd better call a press conference for this afternoon. A bit of publicity won't do any harm at this stage.'

*   *   *

'How's my handsome son, this bright Monday morning?'

Cameron sighed. 'Hello, Mother.'

'You don't sound overjoyed to hear me!'

'I'm sorry. I've a lot on my mind at the moment.'

'All the more reason to take me to lunch! It'll help you relax, and it's weeks since I've seen you.'

'Really, Mother, it's not a good time just now—'

'You have to eat, darling. Today, you can eat with me.'

It was never any use trying to deflect her. 'Very well, but I can't spare the time to come to London.'

'No matter, the mountain will come to Mahomet. Twelve thirty at the Stag?'

It was the hotel just down the road.

'Very well. I'll see you there.'

'And try to work up some enthusiasm!' she said.

Myrtle Page was fifty-seven, but could have passed for ten years younger. Her modelling career had taught her how to care for her skin, her hair, and her figure, lessons that had stood her in good stead over the years. Another legacy was her taste for flamboyant dressing, and she still made an entrance wherever she went.

She was seated at a table in the restaurant when Cameron arrived.

'Darling!' He bent to greet her, and she kissed the air in return. 'I've ordered a bottle of Chablis.'

'I hope you enjoy it, but as you know, I don't drink at lunchtime.'

She pouted, then studied him more closely. 'You look pretty rough, sweetie, if I may say so. I could pack for a week in the bags under your eyes. Anything wrong?'

'Just the small matter of my PA being murdered, and Father and I chief suspects.'

She stared at him with round blue eyes. 'Is this some sort of joke?'

'I wish it were.'

'But tell me more. Whatever happened?'

'It was in the papers – you must have seen it. She was stabbed in a Manchester hotel.'

Myrtle's brows drew together. 'I did see something, but there was nothing to connect it with you. What on earth were you doing in *Manchester*?' She made it sound like Outer Mongolia.

'Vetting a possible purchase. God knows if it will come off now.'

'But your names weren't mentioned, surely?'

'Not initially, but now the cat's well and truly out of the bag. I'm surprised you haven't seen it.'

She shrugged. 'You know me, darling; I'm not interested in the news – too depressing.'

The waiter approached with the wine, and Cameron covered his glass. Myrtle performed the tasting routine, nodding her approval. They sat in silence while her glass was filled and the bottle placed in an ice bucket. As the waiter moved away, the impact of what he'd said suddenly registered.

'*Your* PA, did you say? Not that little French girl?'

'Elise, yes.'

'But that's terrible, darling! God, how—'

He held up a palm. 'I'm not going to discuss it, Mother. If you want the details, read the papers.' He straightened. 'So – how's Damien?'

Damien Jessop, Myrtle's latest husband, was, at forty, only three years older than Cameron, who disliked him intensely. But his ploy had worked; his mother brightened.

'Oh, didn't I tell you? He's landed a part in this new soap everyone's talking about. Not one of the major characters, but he's going to work on developing it. He says it has potential.'

With only the occasional prod, the subject of Damien and his doings lasted them through the meal. Only as they were leaving did Myrtle obliquely refer to the murder again.

'Does Lyddie know? About . . . you know?'

'She must do. I haven't spoken to her, but she's probably contacted Father.'

Myrtle nodded. 'I think we should check, though, so she's prepared. Would you like me to speak to her, darling? You've enough on your plate.'

'Whatever you think best,' Cameron said.

Mike Chadwick lay immobile, staring through the darkness at the invisible ceiling, his mind a churning maelstrom. The local police had descended on Beechford that morning – as if they'd not had enough grilling in Manchester! – and it had been a mammoth task trying to conceal their presence from the guests.

The murder itself was, of course, public knowledge, thanks to TV and the press, and they'd had a couple of cancellations. For the most part, though, there was a feverish air of excitement about the place that sickened him. Ghouls! he thought viciously. They'd feel very differently if they were personally involved.

Personally involved. The words echoed in his head as his thoughts veered off at a tangent; involved in the sort of events that until this week he'd only read about, never dreaming they could touch him. God! he thought, in an agony of indecision, should he, after all, keep it to himself? How, otherwise, could he protect Karen and the family?

He moved convulsively, and his wife stirred at his side. How would she react, if he told her? For that matter, how would everyone else react, if it became public? He'd wondered briefly if Tina suspected something; he'd caught her looking at him a little oddly that morning. God, he *had* to pull himself together, or he'd be a candidate for a heart attack

Inch by inch, he moved to the edge of the bed, lowered his feet to the floor and slowly, cautiously, stood upright. Karen stirred again, murmuring in her sleep, and he tucked the duvet round her shoulders, hoping she wouldn't register his absence. His dressing gown hung on the back of the door. He reached for it, let himself quietly out of the room, and went barefoot down the stairs in search of a glass of whisky.

NINE

It came on the Tuesday morning. How the devil could it have taken so long? By mule train? A more realistic guess was that no one at the paper had bothered to check the mail on Saturday, and it had only surfaced in the post room yesterday.

Jonathan tore open the padded envelope and pulled out the USB device, closing his fingers convulsively round it.

'Is that it?'

He turned. Vicky was in the kitchen doorway. Behind her, the boys were scraping their cereal bowls.

'Yes – at long last. I'd given up hope.'

'*I* was hoping it would never come,' she said quietly.

'There's nothing to worry about, love, really. At least it will give us something to go on, and I promise I'll be careful.'

Though impatient to see its contents, it made sense to run it through with Steve, and Jonathan speed-dialled him. 'I've got it!' he said triumphantly.

A moment's pause, then an incredulous 'Honestly?'

'Honestly. Where are you?'

'Just finishing breakfast.'

'Shall I come straight up to the flat, so we can go through it?'

'Absolutely. I'll be waiting with bated breath.'

The train journey seemed slower than usual, and Jonathan couldn't settle to his paper. How much would be revealed, and would it point to who might have wanted to kill Elise? He should shortly know.

Steve had his laptop ready and coffee on the stove, and as soon as they were seated side by side he inserted the memory stick into the USB port. Immediately, they were presented with a selection of folders to open, folders entitled Woodcot, Foxfield and Beechford – which they'd never heard of, but which was presumably the third Mandelyns resort – another under the name of Selby & Braddock Inc. ('The manufacturers?' Steve hazarded), and the names of several newspapers, including, they noted wryly, *UK Today*.

'Write-ups of the deaths, no doubt,' Jonathan said. 'She must have photocopied those separately. So – where do we start?'

'How about Foxfield? That's where Elise was based, and where that actress went.'

They clicked on the appropriate folder and were given the option of a number of files, one of which was labelled Maria Lang. They read it in silence. It gave the actress's real name, her address and date of birth, the dates on which she'd visited Mandelyns, a note of her allergies and preferences, and the treatments she had received, followed by an assessment of the results. Ms Lang had run the gamut, her last treatment, *Mandelyna*, having been given in June. At the foot of the card, a manuscript entry had been added without comment: *Date of death: 5th July 2010*.

They sat back and looked at each other.

'Close,' Steve commented. 'Let's see what the papers had to say.'

There were obituaries from all the nationals. Most contented themselves with reporting that she had died 'suddenly' or 'unexpectedly', but a couple of later ones suggested a viral infection.

'Which it might well have been,' Jonathan said. 'Or not, as the case might be.'

'You do realize we've no option but to pass this on to the police?' Steve said. 'It could be crucial evidence in a murder enquiry.'

Jonathan stared at him disbelievingly. 'You're not saying that after all this—?'

'No, mate, I'm not saying we don't look into it ourselves. First, we'll download it to our own computer, then send the drive to Manchester like honest citizens. *Anonymous* honest citizens. And, having performed our civic duty, we'll be free to do our own thing.'

Jonathan nodded. 'You're right, of course. OK, well let's see what else we've got.'

A separate file listed all the clients who'd received *Mandelyna* from its inception that spring, over sixty in all, and, as Elise had told them, another four names were followed by a date of death. Three were women prominent in their fields – a public-school headmistress, a judge, a member of parliament – which, of course, was why their deaths had been widely reported and first come to Elise's notice. But her suspicions had led her to burrow further, and she'd come across a fourth – a Mrs Emily Broadbent.

Jonathan stared at the name for a full minute, trying to link two widely differing associations. Then he said in a strangled voice, 'My God!'

Steve turned to him, frowning. 'What is it? You look as if you've seen a ghost.'

'The name of one, anyway. I *knew* her, Steve – Emily Broadbent. Not well, but my sister did. She always called her Aunt Em.'

Angus poured wine into Sophie's glass and his own, then sat down at the table. 'Have you heard how Imogen is?' he asked, taking the plate his wife passed him.

'Not since the funeral. Why?'

'Just that it was such a traumatic time for her – all the upset of her aunt's death, and then, on top of it, Daisy bunking off school and having to be sent back kicking and screaming, meta-phorically at least. It was a lot to cope with.'

Sophie said lightly, 'Imo always has to have a crisis in her life.'

He raised an eyebrow. 'Not a very sympathetic remark, darling.'

'Well, she does rather thrive on them – as long as there's someone's hand to hold, usually mine.'

'All the same, it might be a kindness to give her a ring.'

Sophie helped herself to vegetables. 'We'll be seeing her on Thursday, don't forget.'

Angus frowned. 'Will . . .? Oh, of course! Roger's birthday do.'

'So you can set your mind at rest then, can't you? Frankly, I'm more concerned at the moment with what I'm going to do with Tamsin and her friend during half-term next week. I really can't afford to take time off, with the countdown to Christmas starting.'

'You can work from home, can't you? You say ninety per cent

of your time is spent dealing with emails, and as long as someone's in the house—'

'Yes, but what I *can't* do is be at their beck and call to drive
them around. They'll just have to amuse themselves.'

'How long will they be here?'

'Friday evening till a week on Sunday.'

'There'll be something suitable at the cinemas – there always
is, at half-term. And they're old enough to go to matinees by
themselves, aren't they, at thirteen?'

'Provided it really *is* suitable. It's hard to judge girls' ages
these days, and the cinemas don't check as thoroughly as they
should.'

'They'll probably be happy enough up in her room, watching
DVDs or playing on the computer.'

'But they ought to be outside, especially if the weather's good.'

Angus lapsed into silence. All his suggestions having been
met with objections, it seemed wiser not to offer more.

On Wednesday morning, Lewis phoned.

'Just a thought,' he said, 'but I have to be in your neck of the
woods tomorrow, and I wondered if, since we won't be meeting
at the weekend, I might perhaps call on you after my meeting?'

A dozen thoughts collided in Anna's head: would the neighbours see him? What would they think? Was he – a lurch of the
stomach – expecting to spend the night? But almost immediately
she rebelled. Was she going to spend the rest of her life afraid
of twitching curtains?

'That would be lovely, Lewis,' she said. There was a slight
pause, and she added diffidently, 'Will you be able to . . .?'

'Stay the night?' he finished, a smile in his voice. 'If I'm
invited!'

'Then I'm inviting you. What time will you arrive?'

'About six thirty? If it would be easier, we could go out to eat?'

'I wouldn't hear of it. You've not sampled my cooking yet!'

'A treat in store!'

A thought struck her. 'Do you know where I live?'

'Of course I do. I ascertained that before leaving South Africa!'

She laughed. 'See you tomorrow, then.'

*   *   *

'You don't really like it, do you?'

'Of course I do.' Even to his own ears, Roger's voice lacked conviction.

'Are you sure? It looked so nice in the shop, I thought—'

'Really, it's a lovely sweater, it's just . . .'

'What?'

'Not a colour I usually wear,' he said lamely. *And it's a polo neck, whereas I prefer V.* 'Anyway, it's no big deal; I can take it back, can't I, swap it for another, like you did that handbag last Christmas?'

'I so wanted it to be perfect,' Imogen said shakily.

Roger's patience snapped. 'All right, forget it. It's lovely – the right size, a nice weight, everything, and to prove it, I'll wear it tonight. OK? Now, I really have to go.' And, picking up his briefcase, he thankfully left the house.

Imogen burst into tears.

Her day went from bad to worse. The butcher had forgotten to order the gammon she'd requested, her cleaner rang to say she had toothache and wouldn't be in today, and the lemon mousse hadn't set. By seven o'clock, when the guests were due to arrive, her nerves were in shreds.

Roger had returned from work and set about putting out the drinks. He was wearing the new sweater, and she had to admit it didn't suit him. The high neck looked as though it were choking him, and the taupe that she'd thought so smart in the shop drained the colour from his face. Oh, *God*! She wished she could just go to bed and pull the duvet over her head.

Jonathan looked about him, wondering how he could introduce the subject of Emily Broadbent and Mandelyns without putting a damper on the evening. Better not approach Imogen directly; she looked a little fraught, and Roger, his other option, was busy seeing to the drinks. For lack of alternatives, he moved over to his sister.

'Is Imogen over her aunt's death, do you think?' he asked in a low voice.

'For heaven's sake, what is this?' Sophie exclaimed. 'First Angus, now you! She's coping, as we all have to in such circumstances.'

Jonathan stared at her in surprise. 'Actually, it's her aunt I wanted to ask about. Did you ever hear the cause of death?'

Sophie, slightly mollified, frowned. 'Why do you want to know?'

'It's just that I heard it came out of the blue. Soon after her birthday, wasn't it?'

'That's right. Imo said she was looking better than she had for years. Uncle Ted had treated her to a weekend at Mandelyns as an early birthday present, and they joked it had made her look ten years younger.'

Bingo! 'Did she have some special treatment, then?'

'God, Jonathan, I don't know the details. I should think we'd all look ten years younger after a weekend of pampering.'

Before he could repeat his question as to the cause of death, Roger's brother came to join them, and the opportunity was lost. Could he, dare he, approach the husband? Jonathan wondered. Sophie would have the address. Still, he couldn't pursue it now. Shelving the problem for the moment, he joined in the general conversation.

They were twelve in all – herself and Roger, Sophie and Angus, Jonathan and Vicky, Roger's brother Douglas, his wife Sarah, and two sets of neighbours. So far, things weren't going too badly. The meal was a buffet, spread out on the dining room table, and to Imogen's relief it looked suitably tempting. The replacement ham, parboiled then baked with honey, was an acceptable substitute for the gammon, the chicken kebabs were proving popular, and she'd been complimented on the imaginative salads.

The mousse, having stubbornly remained runny, had spent the last hour in the freezer. Imogen could only hope the emergency treatment had worked. She took a quick sip of wine, opened the freezer door, and lifted it out. Exactly what happened next, she could never remember. One moment the glass bowl, sending shocks of cold to her fingers, was firmly in her grasp. The next, it had slipped free and smashed to the ground, splashing yellow mousse over her dress, the units, and a large portion of the floor.

For several seconds she stood immobile, staring at the wreckage. Then she bent and distractedly started picking out the larger shards of glass before, abandoning the task, she burst into tears for the second time that day.

Head in hands, she didn't see Angus come into the kitchen, and the first indication of his presence was his quick exclamation of concern.

'Oh, Imogen, no!'

She heard him lay down the plates he'd brought in and, avoiding the mess on the floor, move round the kitchen towards her.

'Look, don't worry, honestly. Is there another pudding?'

Incapable of speech, Imogen continued to sob.

To his relief, Angus saw a Pavlova, crisp and perfect, on the counter, though admittedly they'd be hard pressed to get twelve servings from it. Alongside it, though, was a bowl of fruit, presumably not intended for this evening.

'We can take the fruit through as well, and there's cheese already on the table. With the Pavlova, that'll be fine, honestly. I'll clear this up. Please don't cry; it's not the end of the world.'

She felt his hand on her arm and blindly, unthinkingly, turned towards him, burying her face in his chest. Tentatively, his arms came up to hold her.

'It's been such a horrible day!' she sobbed. 'Roger hates the sweater I bought him, and there wasn't any gammon, and the mousse—' But thoughts of the mousse brought on another torrent of tears, and she shuddered to a halt.

'We all have days like that,' Angus said soothingly. 'It's just bad luck today happened to be one of them. But the food's marvellous, Imo, really. Everyone's enjoying it, and they've eaten so much, they won't even miss the mousse!'

Dear, kind Angus! Roger would have blamed her for breaking the bowl.

He handed her a handkerchief, and she dabbed at her face, looking up at him with swimming eyes. Moved by her misery, he bent to kiss her forehead, but in the same moment she raised her head, and his mouth landed clumsily on hers. As though released by a spring, her arms flew round his neck, and before either of them fully realized what was happening, they were engaged in a full-blown kiss.

The door swished open, and a voice said, 'Is there anything—?'

Sophie's voice.

They broke apart, turning startled faces towards her. Across the room, the three of them stared at each other. Then Sophie turned on her heel and went out again.

'Oh God!' Imogen whispered. 'Go after her, Angus! Don't let her think . . .'

Swearing fluently under his breath, Angus hesitated. He glanced back at Imogen and the mess on the floor. He'd promised to help her clear up, but first, as she said, he must straighten things with Sophie.

'I'll be right back,' he said, and hurried from the room, looking quickly round the hall before glancing into both the sitting and dining rooms. 'Anyone seen Sophie?'

'She went outside,' Sarah, who was sitting on the stairs, informed him. 'Said she wanted something from the car.'

Angus strode to the front door, opening it to the furious revving of an engine, followed by the sound of a car scorching away. His car.

He ran to the gate, in time to see its tail lights disappearing round the corner. Hell and damnation, she'd left him stranded! How the devil was he going to get home? God, she couldn't really have thought . . . But what would *he* have thought, had their positions been reversed? If he'd come across her in Roger's arms?

A cold wind moved over him, making him shiver. He groaned, wiping his hand across his face. She might at least have let him explain. But explain what? He could hardly deny they'd been kissing. God help him, he'd even enjoyed it.

He glanced back at the house. Since he'd pulled the door shut behind him, he now had the indignity of having to ring the bell to be readmitted. And what was he supposed to tell everyone? Oh, *why* had he happened to go into the kitchen at that crucial moment?

Shivering, worried and miserable, Angus walked back up the path.

For the first time in months, Anna felt entirely happy. The evening had been perfect, especially as, at least for the moment, she'd succeeded in burying her guilt. Lewis had arrived with roses and a bottle of Margaux, and he'd been most appreciative of the meal, which, admittedly, had been delicious. Now they were relaxing on the sofa, his arm round her shoulders, listening to a CD of the Three Tenors. And tonight still lay ahead. Anna hoped super-stitiously that she wouldn't have to pay for such happiness.

A hope that was not to be granted. At one moment they were alone in the lamplight; the next, the sitting room door had burst open and Sophie erupted into the room.

She stopped short on seeing them, and they in turn froze, gazing back at her.

'Who the *hell's* that?' she demanded, her voice rising.

'Sophie!' Disengaging herself, Anna quickly stood up. 'That's hardly the way to greet my guest! This is Lewis Masters, a friend I met on holiday. My daughter, Sophie,' she added to Lewis.

He had also risen, and now went towards Sophie, smiling, his hand outstretched. She ignored him, her eyes fixed on her mother.

'My *God*!' She put both hands to her head, gripping her scalp. 'What's *happened* to everyone?'

Anna hurried to her, gently lowered her hands, and held them. 'What's the matter, darling? Has something happened?'

'I was hoping for a bed for the night,' Sophie said shakily, 'but—'

'Of *course* you can have a bed. You don't have to ask. But – where's Angus?'

Sophie's mouth tightened. 'That's . . . immaterial.'

Anna threw Lewis an anguished glance, and he smoothly took up his cue.

'Look, I can see I'm not needed here, so I'll be on my way. Thanks for the meal, Anna; I'll phone you in the morning. Nice to have met you, Sophie.'

He moved past them into the hall, took his coat from the stand and his briefcase from the foot of the stairs, and let himself out of the house.

Anna wrenched her thoughts from him and led her daughter to the sofa where, minutes earlier, she'd been so close to Lewis. 'Tell me what happened,' she said.

'Oh, I'll tell you what happened!' Sophie's voice was brittle. 'First, I walk into a room and find my husband kissing my best friend. Then I walk into another and find my mother kissing a strange man.' She gave a choked laugh. 'It's almost funny: twice in an hour, two sets of guilty faces, with almost identical expressions.'

'We weren't kissing,' Anna said weakly.

'You would have been, any minute.'

'And he's not a strange man. As I explained, we met in South Africa.'

Sophie stared at her with sudden, horrified, understanding. 'You're having an affair!'

'*No*! Well . . .'

Sophie sprang up. 'My God!' she cried again. 'Jon and I send you on holiday to get over Dad's death—'

Anna was also on her feet. 'Stop it!' she demanded. 'Stop it right there!'

They stood staring at each other, both breathing heavily. Then Sophie's anger seemed to evaporate, and she said tonelessly, 'I'm sorry. I just . . . don't know what to think. One minute, everything was fine; the next, the ground seemed to give way beneath me, and nothing was certain any more.'

Anna understood only too well; a similar analogy had struck her in South Africa. Aching with sympathy, she went to pour them both a brandy. 'Tell me about Angus,' she invited.

Biting her lip, Sophie slowly sat down again. 'We were at Roger's birthday party. I went into the kitchen, to see if I could help, and found Angus and Imo in a passionate embrace.'

'Oh, darling. Surely—'

'So I walked out of the house and drove straight here. I . . . didn't know where else to go.'

Anna pulled her into her arms and held her close, feeling her trembling. 'There has to be an explanation. Both of them adore you.'

'And perhaps each other.'

'That's nonsense. Had you and Angus had a row?'

Sophie shook her head. 'He did ask very solicitously after Imo the other day – whether she'd got over Aunt Em's death.'

'Nothing suspicious in that, surely?'

Sophie pulled gently away and reached for her brandy glass. 'My first drink of the evening. I was on the wagon, because I was going to drive home – Angus handed me the car keys when we arrived.' She gave a half-smile. 'I bet he regrets that now.'

Anna hadn't taken in the implications. 'You just abandoned him?'

'I did.'

'Well – what will he do? How will he get home?'

'There are trains,' Sophie said.

Anna sipped her own drink. 'And what do you propose to do in the morning?'

'Go home, as soon as he's left for work.'

'Then what?'

'Nothing dramatic. Apart from anything else, Tamsin will be home tomorrow, with her friend Florence. But I'll expect an explanation, and it had better be a good one.'

'Has he tried to contact you?'

'Probably. I switched off my mobile. Anyway –' Sophie met her mother's eye – 'it's your turn now. Tell me about lover boy.'

It was not an evening Angus wanted to remember. Back inside the house, he'd found Sarah and Vicky cleaning the floor, and the Pavlova and bowl of fruit on the dining table. Imogen, seemingly composed, sent him one swift, questioning glance, and he shook his head. Thereafter she kept out of his way.

He announced, as casually as he could manage, that Sophie was suffering from one of her migraines and had asked to be excused.

'Was she fit to drive home?' Vicky asked worriedly. 'Shouldn't—?'

'She insisted I stay. She'd always rather be alone when they strike. So if you and Jon could drop me off at the station . . .?'

'Oh – of course: no car. Or would you rather stay the night?'

'Thanks, but no. I must get back to Sophie, satisfy myself she's OK.'

Given the choice, he'd have left at once, anxious to speak to her before she'd exaggerated the scene out of all proportion; but he couldn't expect Jon and Vicky to leave early to suit him, and it was almost eleven when they pulled up at the station.

'I'll phone in the morning to see how she is,' Vicky said, and Angus could only hope Sophie would pick up her cue.

The train to London was half empty. A few solitary passengers were dotted about, some sleeping, some reading, some simply staring out of the window into the darkness. He'd been trying Sophie's mobile on and off for the last hour, but it was permanently on voicemail. Obviously, she had no intention of speaking to him. He spent the journey rehearsing the best way to explain what had happened.

At Charing Cross he had to queue for a taxi, and when, half an hour later, it stopped at his gate, he was alarmed to see the house in darkness. Even if she'd gone to bed, she might at least have left the hall light on.

Fresh panic hit him when he reached their bedroom. The bed hadn't been touched since it was made that morning. Sophie was not at home. Frantically, he again tried her mobile, again she was unreachable. Where the hell was she?

At Anna's? Now that he thought of it, that seemed the obvious solution; her house was only a twenty-minute drive from Roger and Imogen's. However, it was now well past midnight and far too late to phone. And if by any chance Sophie *wasn't* there, there was no sense in alarming Anna.

He spent a restless night, continually reliving those crucial minutes in the kitchen with Imogen. The fact that, after his botched platonic kiss, it had been she who'd prolonged it, was no excuse. She was on edge, unhappy, not knowing what she was doing. It had been up to him to put her gently aside and defuse the situation, and he was unable to explain why he had not.

Thank God Sophie's car was in the garage; at least he'd be able to get to work in the morning. On that single positive note, Angus finally fell asleep.

TEN

Incredibly, Roger was totally unaware of the traumas of the evening. He'd taken Sophie's abrupt departure at face value and, instead of the reprimand she'd expected, had even sympathized with Imogen over the crystal bowl, a wedding present.

'These things happen,' he said philosophically.

Furthermore, they made love, Imogen clinging to him with a passionate mix of love and guilt that both surprised and delighted him.

'I must have more birthdays!' he joked, stroking her bare shoulder and unaware of held-back tears.

'I'm sorry about the sweater,' she murmured unsteadily. 'You can't take it back now you've worn it, but I'll buy another and you can choose it yourself.' She'd have given him a factory-full, to appease her guilt.

He laughed. 'Nonsense, I was an ungrateful brute, and I'm sorry. The sweater's fine, but I must say, this is the best present yet!'

And he started to kiss her again.

When he eventually fell asleep, she prepared to endure the long hours of darkness, her mind a whirlpool. What would Angus think of her, behaving like that, let alone compromising him with Sophie? And what of Sophie herself? She'd certainly never speak to her again! Sophie, who was her best friend, who had stood by her so often when she was in trouble: what a way to repay her! But, oh God, please don't let either of them tell Roger! Don't let them tell *anybody*!

Why had she clung to Angus like that? Yes, she'd always liked him – even fancied him a little – but that wasn't the reason. It was just that he was kind and understanding, and *there*, just when she needed reassurance. And anyway, she remembered with a little shiver, he *had* kissed her back; did that make it better or worse?

What should she do? Apologize to them both, or pretend it had never happened?

And having reached that unresolved point, Imogen unexpectedly fell asleep.

Neither Anna nor Sophie had slept well, and both were heavy-eyed
at breakfast.

'Can we pretend last night never happened?' Anna asked with
a wry smile, pouring coffee.

'I wish we could.'

'I'm sure things will work out. Perhaps Imogen was upset –
you know how emotional she can be – and he was just . . .
comforting her?'

Sophie frowned, remembering. 'I think there was something
on the floor,' she said. 'A mess of some sort, and a broken bowl.'

'There you are, then!'

'Ma, what I saw went way beyond comforting.'

Anna sighed. 'And about Lewis . . .'

Sophie tensed, and Anna leaned forward, reaching for her
hand. 'Darling, it sounds trite, but *no one* will *ever* replace Daddy.
I *know* this happened too soon – I'm ashamed that it has – but
it might be the only chance I have of not spending the rest of
my life alone.'

'You're *not* alone!' Sophie said fiercely.

'You know what I mean. Believe me, I'd have given anything
to delay this for a year or so.'

'When were you going to tell us?'

'Certainly not before Daddy's anniversary. But another reason
for not saying anything is that I didn't know *what* to say. There's
no guarantee anything will come of it; it might all have fizzled
out by Christmas, in which case it would have been pointless to
upset you.'

'But you want it to go on?'

Anna shook her head. 'I honestly don't know, Sophie.
Sometimes I do, sometimes I don't.'

'Is he serious?'

'Again, I don't know.'

'Has he mentioned marriage?'

Anna smiled. 'Talk about role reversal! No, he hasn't, but I've
rather cut him off any time he hints at the future.' She paused.
'Will you tell Jonathan?'

'Would you rather I didn't?'

'I leave it to you. I wouldn't want him to find out later that you knew.'

Sophie nodded, stirring her coffee. 'Has . . . Lewis . . . got family?'

'Yes, a son, a daughter and an ex-wife.'

'Has he said anything to them?'

'I've no idea, but I did ask him to keep it between the two of us.'

Sophie glanced at her watch and stood up. 'I don't know why I'm quizzing you; I've worries enough of my own, not the least being I feel ridiculous eating breakfast in a cocktail dress. It's time I was going; I've things to prepare for Tamsin and Florence's arrival.' She paused. 'How about coming for the weekend? I know you want to see Tamsin, and your being there would help smooth things between Angus and me.'

'Mightn't it get in the way of your sorting it out?'

Sophie shook her head. 'Please come. Unless, of course . . .?'

'Lewis? No, I'd already told him I'm not free this weekend. But won't Florence be in the guest room?'

'She's using the futon in Tamsin's room. In time for tomorrow's lunch, then?'

'If you're sure,' Anna capitulated.

After she'd gone, Anna phoned Beatrice. 'Just wondering how you're getting on. Is the cast off?'

'It is indeed, thank heaven. I still have to be careful, though.'

'Are you able to drive?'

'Yes, but the automatic's a bonus. Why? Do you want us to set off for Monte Carlo?'

Anna laughed. 'Not quite. But I was wondering if you're free to come and spend the day with me? I'm in need of wise counsel.'

'Love, I can't. We've a Bowling Club Dinner this evening, and it's all systems go. Can the counsel be dispensed over the phone?'

'Not really, it's too complicated.'

'Tomorrow, then?'

'I can't, Bea; I'm spending the weekend with Sophie and Angus. Tamsin's home for half-term.'

'That'll be fun. Give her my love.' She paused. 'How urgent is this need for counselling?'

'I suppose it'll keep.'

'How long will you be at Sophie's?'

'Till Monday morning, I should think.'

'Then come straight on here. Monday's a quiet day, thank God.'

'Thanks, Bea; that'll be great.'

'Until then, I'm afraid you'll have to rely on your worry beads! Must go – the butcher's at the door. See you!' And she rang off.

Anna had no sooner replaced the phone, than it began to ring.

'Have you still got company?' asked a clipped voice.

'Oh, Lewis, hello! No, she's just gone. I'm so sorry about all that! It was the most appalling timing!'

'Indeed it was, though I should be the one to apologize, for having compromised home ground. Much safer to stick to London.' He paused. 'Did she explain why she arrived out of the blue?'

'A row with her husband. She came looking for comfort, poor darling, and got more than she bargained for. I can understand her reaction, but that doesn't excuse it, and I know she'd want me to apologize.'

'At least the invitation won't come as a surprise, if you allow me to send it.' He paused, and when she made no comment, added, 'Did she calm down later?'

'A bit. She wants me to spend the weekend with them, to see Tamsin.'

'Then you'll have a more enjoyable time than I shall; it seems I'll be entertaining the police for at least part of it.'

'Oh dear! Have they still not found the killer?'

'Presumably not, but there's been a development, they tell me, unspecified over the phone. Whatever it is, it necessitates further interviewing. Think of me, when you're reading bedtime stories.'

Anna smiled. 'We're a little past that, but I'll certainly be thinking of you.'

'And I of you, my love. I'll be in touch.'

Sophie was still answering neither her mobile nor the landline, and Angus had no idea whether or not she'd returned home. He couldn't believe she'd stay away, especially with half-term upon them – but suppose she did? Suppose she met Tamsin and Florence, as arranged, and spirited them off somewhere?

He shrugged away the thought, telling himself he was being ridiculous, but it lingered at the back of his mind, and it wasn't until he arrived home at six thirty to find lights on that he was able to dispel it.

He'd also agonized over whether or not to take flowers, but such a cliché of sexual misdemeanour seemed best avoided. Accordingly, he was empty-handed when, heart in mouth, he let himself into the house.

'Dad!' Tamsin came running down the hall and into his arms, nearly knocking him over with the exuberance of her embrace.

'Hi, sweetie! Good to have you home!' His eyes moved to the girl behind her. 'And this must be Florence?'

'Yes, she's in my dorm.' Tamsin turned. 'Florence, meet my dad.'

The girl came shyly forward. 'Hello, Mr Craig.'

'Hello, Florence, and welcome! It's good to have you here.' He glanced down the empty hall. 'Where's Mum?'

'In the kitchen. Dad, Florence has her own horse!'

'Lucky girl!' Angus said non-committally and, with a smile at both of them, made his way towards the closed door.

Sophie was at the sink peeling potatoes and did not turn as he came in. He went over to her, put his arms round her, and kissed the back of her neck, feeling her quiver.

'I missed you,' he said.

'Really?'

'Yes, really. Darling, you must have realized it wasn't what it looked like.'

'There didn't seem much room for misunderstanding.'

Belatedly, he wondered if she'd spoken to Imogen. Unlikely, he felt. Any attempts to reach her from that quarter would have been met with the same stone wall he'd encountered.

'Did you go to your mother?'

'Yes. Standard procedure in the circumstances.'

'Sophie—'

She raised her voice to talk over him. 'She's coming for the weekend, by the way. She wants to see Tamsin.'

There was a moment's silence.

'We need to talk,' he said miserably.

'Indeed we do, but now is not the time. I'm preparing dinner, and the girls might come in at any minute. So could you make yourself useful by checking the radiator in the dining room and bringing me a G&T?'

'Of course.'

An armed truce, then. He supposed, resignedly, it was all he could expect.

So this, thought Maddy Peel, was the famous Mandelyns Foxfield.

She had turned off the main road and driven up a long, winding drive bordered by trees in their autumn colours of crimson and gold. As she rounded a bend, a deer ran across the road in front of her, causing her to jam on the brakes. How the other half live! she thought.

The main building was Georgian, its ambience that of a country house. Now, having been weighed and measured, and filled in a medical questionnaire, she was standing in her bedroom, looking in awe at the thick, springy carpet, the ivory-coloured furniture, the gold-plated fittings in the en suite. Luxury indeed!

Since the purpose of her visit wasn't weight loss, there were thankfully no diet restrictions, though alcohol was restricted to a glass of wine at dinner.

'The dress code for dinner is smart casual,' she'd been told, 'but during the day, most people wear the towelling robes provided. No point in having to keep dressing and undressing between massages, saunas, and so on.'

So here she was, and after the week she'd had, she could murder a vodka and tonic. Ah well, she wasn't here to enjoy herself – or at least, not *only* to enjoy herself. People who had stayed here – perhaps in this very room – had subsequently died, and it was as well to remember that.

With a suppressed shiver, she started to unpack her case.

Saturday morning. Jonathan stretched luxuriously. The sound of the television from below indicated that his sons were up and about. In a few minutes he'd get up himself and bring Vicky breakfast in bed. But there was no hurry. He turned over, pulling the pillow into his neck, and was closing his eyes when a tentative voice came from the doorway.

'Are you awake, Daddy?'

'No,' said Jonathan firmly.

There was a giggle, a patter of bare feet, and, reluctantly opening his eyes, he observed his elder son, hair tousled and clad in pyjamas, standing hopefully beside him.

'Go away, Tom. It's still early.'

'Can I have my pocket money?'

Jonathan groaned. 'Not now, for heaven's sake! You're not even dressed, and the shops aren't open yet.'

'But I want to see how much I have.'

'Well, you know how much I'll be giving you and how much you've got already. Just add them together. You can do sums, can't you?'

'Not *that* sum,' Tom said. 'I want it in my *hand*, then I'll know if I can buy another dinosaur.'

'Look, I'll be getting up soon. Go down and watch CBeebies with Tim.'

'*Please,* Daddy!'

Jonathan sighed. 'All right, bring me my wallet. It's on the chest of drawers.'

As Tom reached up for it, he manoeuvred himself into a sitting position, trying not to disturb Vicky, who'd resolutely kept her eyes closed throughout this exchange.

'What's this, Daddy?'

On his way back to the bed, Tom had flipped the wallet open and pulled something from one of the slots.

'Hey, you don't qualify for any notes! Put—' Jonathan broke off, a wave of heat sluicing over him. Because it was not a note Tom had extracted, but a white plastic card. A key card. For a wild moment, he thought he was going to vomit.

Then Vicky was saying calmly, 'That's Daddy's room key from the Manchester hotel. He must have forgotten to hand it in when he left.'

'It doesn't look like a key,' Tom said doubtfully.

'Give it to me.' Jonathan almost snatched it from his son's hand. 'And the wallet.'

Tom, abashed, handed it over, and, avoiding his eyes,

Jonathan unzipped the coin section and extracted a fifty-pence piece.

'Satisfied? Now, go downstairs and play with your brother.'

'Thank you, Daddy,' Tom said meekly, and trotted out of the room.

There was a brief silence. Then Vicky said, 'It wasn't *your* room key, was it?'

Jonathan shook his head. 'God, I'd forgotten all about it. If anyone had found that on me . . .'

Vicky slid her arm round him. 'And just who would be likely to do that? Other, that is, from your family?'

'What the hell am I going to do with it, Vic? I can't send it back. The police must know it's missing; they'll assume the killer has it!'

'Then they'll be wrong, won't they? As to what to do with it, you're going to cut it into very small pieces and drop it in the bin bag. Now, are you going to make me a cup of tea, or what?'

At breakfast, Maddy avoided the pleasant-looking girl she'd normally have joined and instead approached a table where a blonde woman in her fifties was already seated.

She paused with her tray. 'Is anyone sitting here?'

The woman looked faintly surprised. 'No, feel free.'

Maddy unloaded her orange juice, muesli and yogurt, smiling determinedly. 'I'm Maddy, by the way.'

'Good morning, Maddy. I'm Gina.'

'This is great, isn't it?'

Gina smiled. 'Your first visit?'

'Yes – a treat from my boyfriend.'

'The right kind of boyfriend to have!'

'Have you been before?'

'Oh yes, I'm a regular. My firm sends all its executives to Mandelyns at least once a year, to help us unwind.'

'The right kind of firm to work for!'

Gina laughed. 'Touché. Have you booked any treatments yet?'

'A massage at ten and a facial at eleven thirty.'

'Good start.'

'Actually, I'm rather at a loss what to go for – what they all do, I mean.'

Gina sipped her herbal tea. 'Well, you can ignore the rejuven-
ating ones!'

Maddy's heart flipped. Was it going to be this easy? 'Which
are they?'

'Their names are pretty explicit. *Jeunesse, Shangri La,
Persephone . . .*'

'Someone told me there was a new one everyone was raving
about.'

'There are always new ones. That's what keeps us coming
back.'

'But this one was special. It's supposed to have spectacular
results.'

'Aren't they all?' Gina drawled.

Better not to pursue the subject, Maddy decided; she mustn't
appear too interested. 'I'll have to have another look at the
brochure,' she said.

Angus had taken the girls swimming, and Sophie was alone in
the house, preparing a beef casserole for that evening. With her
husband temporarily out of the way, her thoughts had reverted to
her mother and the extraordinary revelations of Thursday evening.

Normally, she'd have talked this over with Angus, anxious for
his level-headed opinion to help her put it in perspective. But
she was in no mood for favouring Angus with confidences, and,
since she was desperate to discuss it with someone, Jonathan
was her obvious choice. In fact, she decided suddenly, she'd
phone him now, before they went out for the day.

It was Vicky who answered. 'Oh, Sophie, how are you? Has
the migraine gone? I tried phoning several times, but couldn't
get through. Did you get my messages?'

Expecting them to have been Angus trying to reach her, Sophie
hadn't replayed them. Migraine? Must have been his explanation
for her departure. 'I'm fine now, thanks. Is Jonathan around, by
any chance?'

'Yes, of course. I'll get him for you.'

A minute. Then: 'Hi, sis. Head OK?'

'Yes, thanks. Look, Jon, can you talk for a minute?'

'That sounds serious.'

'It is, quite.'

'Hang on, I'll take this to the study.' There was a pause, then: 'OK, shoot. What's up?'

Not having planned how to break the news, Sophie came straight out with it. 'Ma's got a boyfriend.'

There was a stunned silence. Then: 'Say again?'

'Ma's got a boyfriend. I've just found out. She met him on holiday.'

'But – but that *can't* be right! I mean, she and Dad – God, it's not a year yet!'

'I know. She's consumed with guilt.'

'But who the hell is he?'

'Lewis Master or Masters or something.'

A faint bell chimed in Jonathan's memory, but Sophie was hurrying on.

'I . . . called in on Thursday on my way home, to see if she'd any Ibuprofen. And – he was there. They were both shattered to see me, I can tell you.'

'I bet! What's he like?'

'What does it matter what he's *like*?' Sophie snapped. 'He exists; isn't that enough?'

'But did you like him?'

'I didn't have the chance to find out. He beat a hasty retreat, but I'm pretty sure he'd been intending to spend the night.'

'Ye gods! What does Angus think?'

'I . . . haven't told him yet.'

'Well, there's not a lot we can do about it, is there? To put it mildly, they're both adults. What does he do, do you know?'

'Retired, I should think. He's a bit older than Ma, by the look of him.'

'God, Sophie, I don't know what to think. It never entered my head she'd even *want* anyone else, especially so soon. I mean, she and Dad were so – so *right* together.'

'The trouble is, they're not together any more.' She paused. 'If it had been after a decent interval, I'd have been glad for her. But I'm finding it hard at the moment.'

'You and me both!' Jonathan said feelingly.

'Actually, she's coming for the weekend, to see Tamsin. She'll be here in a couple of hours.'

'Will you refer to it?'

'I probably won't get the chance. Tamsin's brought a friend home, and there's not likely to be much privacy. Quite honestly I'm grateful for that, because I don't know what to say. I'd like to give her my blessing, but . . . I can't.'

'You think it's serious, then?'

'God knows. She was evasive when I asked her. The trouble is . . . I *love* her, Jon! I *want* her to be happy, but just – not like this!'

'Does she know you're telling me about it?'

'She left it up to me, so it won't come as a surprise. Look, I must go. I haven't made a start on lunch yet.'

'Can I tell Vicky?'

'If you want, but obviously no one else. I'll let you know if I find out any more.'

'OK. Well – good luck!'

Sophie disconnected and went slowly back to the kitchen.

Maddy was enjoying herself. She was lying prone on a treatment bed, her face in a hole to assist her breathing, while firm hands kneaded all the tension out of her. The masseuse, who'd introduced herself as Sally, was young, bright, and, Maddy was glad to find, chatty.

Choosing her moment, Maddy remarked casually, 'Is there some kind of survey going on? I saw two official-looking men in suits on my way here. With everyone else in robes, they stood out like a sore thumb!'

The busy hands paused fractionally.

'I thought for a moment they were going to question me!' Maddy prompted.

'Actually . . .' Sally paused for so long, Maddy despaired of her continuing. Then she said carefully, 'They were probably policemen.'

Bull's-eye! 'My goodness!' Maddy kept her voice light. 'What are they doing here?'

'We're not supposed to talk about it,' Sally admitted belatedly.

'But . . .?'

'But . . . something awful happened, up in Manchester. You probably read about it.'

'Oh, of course – the girl in the hotel. Heavens, you don't mean she came from here?'

'Yes; she was the PA of one of the owners – a French girl.'

'What was she doing in Manchester, then?'

'They'd gone up on business, Mr Masters, Mr Cameron, the MD, and their three PAs.'

No wonder the police were sniffing around, Maddy thought. 'Did you know her?'

'Only by sight. Being in admin, she didn't have anything to do with the spa.'

'And they still don't know who killed her, or why?'

'It seems not. We were all interviewed earlier in the week – it was quite scary – but in the last day or two, the police have come back with more questions, and we don't know why. It's . . . unsettling.'

'I'm sure it is.' As instructed, Maddy rolled over on to her back, and the towel was strategically rearranged. 'Normally, though,' she added artlessly, 'it must be very interesting working here. You have a lot of celebrities, don't you?'

Sally brightened, relieved at the change of topic. 'Yes, you never know who you're going to find on your couch!'

'Didn't Maria Lang come here? I used to love her films.'

'That's right – a lovely lady. She was one of our regulars, we were so upset when she died. Her career hadn't been going too well – she was quite frank about it – and she was determined to build it up again, so she was delighted that the treatments were making such a difference. She looked years younger and was really hopeful of landing a part in the new James Bond film.' Sally sighed. 'But you never know what's round the corner, do you?'

'Indeed you don't,' Maddy agreed.

Lewis stared unbelievingly at the computer screen, his face white with anger.

One of the policemen leant forward to switch it off, and the screen went blank.

'Any comments, Mr Masters?'

'Only that this is an appalling breach of confidentiality. I can't begin to imagine how you got hold of it.'

'It was sent to Greater Manchester police, sir. Anonymously.'

Lewis frowned. '*Manchester*? Why on earth—' He broke off, suddenly seeing this interview in a totally different light. 'You're surely not suggesting this has any bearing on Miss du Pré's death?'

'Quite a coincidence, though, wouldn't you say? Two instances of your Group being brought to our attention in as many weeks? Would the young lady have had access to these records?'

'No, she would not. They're password-protected.' Lewis drew a deep breath. 'But that apart, exactly what is supposed to be deduced from all this?' He waved a dismissive hand at the blank screen. 'That a few women who visited this resort have unfortunately died? Hardly an earth-shattering revelation, I'd have thought.'

'On the contrary, sir. Whoever compiled it seems to have believed there was a connection. They came to you – you gave them some kind of treatment – they died.'

Lewis said icily, 'Unfortunately, people die all the time, Inspector. I might point out that nearly a hundred clients have undergone this particular treatment. The fact that a handful later passed away is unfortunate, but totally unrelated.'

The policeman toyed with his pen. 'This treatment you speak of – it has been fully tested, I take it?'

'Of *course* it has! We have our reputation to consider, and so do our manufacturers. No product is used until strenuous tests have been undertaken over many months.'

'On humans as well as animals?'

'Most definitely. If the treatment had been at fault, many others would have been affected.'

The detective considered, pursing his lips. 'We'll be needing samples, sir, to run more tests under laboratory conditions. From the other two resorts, as well.'

'You're more than welcome.'

'And we'll have to ask you to withhold the treatment until the tests have been completed.'

Lewis strove to control his temper. 'Then for my part, *I* shall ask for a full and public exoneration, once you have conducted them. I've no intention of allowing a permanent slur to remain on the Group.' He paused. 'But to come back to Miss du Pré, there's surely no way you can link this infringement with her death?'

'That's still open to debate, sir, but various angles are being investigated.'

With which, Lewis had to be content.

Maddy stood hesitantly in the corridor leading from the spa to the lobby. It was the lull between the routines of the day and dinner, and few people were about. During the last twenty-four hours she'd worked out the layout of the rooms on the ground floor and had on several occasions seen a member of staff go through a door off this corridor. Furthermore, from some strategic positioning, she'd been able to catch a glimpse of a desk inside.

Where there was a desk, she reasoned, there were likely to be filing cabinets. The question was, could she slip into the room unnoticed? No light showed under the door – a good sign – and to avoid showing one herself, she'd stuffed a torch into the pocket of her robe.

Heart in mouth, she approached the door and had reached for the knob when a voice behind her said, 'Can I help you?'

Maddy jumped and spun round, to see one of the girls in powder-blue smiling pleasantly at her.

'Oh, sorry,' she stammered. 'I . . . seem to have lost my way. I was . . . looking for the loo.'

'First on your right down the passage,' the girl said, and Maddy had no choice but to turn in the indicated direction, her heart hammering against her ribs. Thank *God* she hadn't come a minute later, to find her inside with her torch on, perhaps at a filing cabinet. *Be careful!* Steve had warned.

Having waited in the washroom an appropriate time, Maddy made her way back to her room, still unnerved by her experience and regretfully accepting that she'd lost her appetite for any further sleuthing. She'd let Steve and Jonathan down, she thought, furious with herself; this expensive weekend had been all for nothing.

As soon as the police had left, Lewis phoned Cameron.

'Yes, Father, I know,' his son cut in before he could speak. 'They've been here, too. Much good may it do them.'

'You heard they're suspending the treatment?'

'I suppose they've no choice, in the circumstances.'

'God, Cameron, this is what you phoned me about in South Africa. I thought you'd scotched it, once and for all.'

'And I did, where Elise was concerned; it seems she wasn't the only one with doubts. What's worrying is that if this gets into the public domain, the relatives of the dead women will get wind of it and might even, God forbid, try suing us.'

'Let's not anticipate trouble. At the moment, our top priority is to find out who's responsible for this malicious nonsense.'

'Oh, I agree, but it won't be easy. Of the handful who had the password, there's not one I wouldn't trust completely.'

'No one's been sacked lately? There's no one with a possible grievance?'

'No, the police asked that. It's a total mystery, but I can't for the life of me see why they're linking this with Elise. She'd nothing remotely to do with the treatment.'

'Could be the sender's taking advantage of our being in the news to cause further trouble. That would explain why the disc or whatever was sent to Manchester.'

'Possible, I suppose. Incidentally, the police let slip that her parents are over and want to take her back to France with them, poor devils.'

'Will they release the body?'

'Search me. Depends if they've carried out all the examinations they need.'

'The girl was stabbed! What else do they need?' Lewis ran a hand over his face. 'I'm getting too old for this, Cameron.'

'Well, at least we know there's no substance to all this nonsense. There's absolutely nothing wrong with the treatment, and sooner or later the police will have to admit it. As to Elise's death . . .'

'It was a robbery gone wrong,' Lewis said positively. 'There's no other explanation. When he found he'd killed her, he panicked and fled. I just wish to hell they'd hurry up and arrest someone, and life can get back to normal.'

ELEVEN

'How did it go?' Anxiety was strident in Steve's voice.

'From your point of view,' Maddy confessed, 'it was a dead loss. I certainly didn't earn my keep.'

'You didn't find out anything?'

'Not much, I'm afraid. I did ask my masseuse—'

'Oh, you had one of those, did you? Perhaps I should go there myself!'

'—but she only knew the girl by sight. Apparently, six of them had gone to Manchester on business – the two owners, the MD and their PAs. What's more interesting, though, is that the police were there.'

'At Foxfield?' His tone sharpened. 'Did they speak to you?'

'No, but the point is they'd already interviewed everyone, so why did they go back?'

'Probably because we sent the memory stick to Manchester. That would have set the cat among the pigeons.'

'You might have told me!' Maddy said indignantly.

'No matter. The main thing is that no one suspected you of snooping.'

She didn't speak, and he added urgently, 'They didn't, did they?'

'I don't think so.' She gave a little shiver, remembering. 'I *was* caught with my hand on an office door, but I said I was looking for the loo.'

'God, Maddy, that sounds risky! Are you sure they weren't suspicious?'

'Pretty sure. The girl gave me an odd look, that's all, but after that, I didn't dare probe any further. I'm so sorry, Steve. I feel I should refund the cost.'

'Nonsense. You enjoyed the weekend, though, overall?'

'Oh, it was great! All that mollycoddling made you feel really special. And the food was excellent! I was expecting to exist on rabbit food, but far from it. If you weren't on a diet it was haute cuisine – *healthy* haute cuisine, of course!'

'Hard on those who *were* on a diet!'

'Their tables were screened off, so they didn't see what they were missing. But I definitely feel the better for it – leaner and altogether fitter.' She gave a little laugh. 'I suppose you wouldn't like one of the other resorts investigating *next* weekend? I might have better luck there!'

'Finances certainly wouldn't stretch to that! So when am I going to see this new, fitter you?'

'Tomorrow evening?'

'I can hardly wait!'

Steve reported Maddy's findings, such as they were, on Monday morning.

'She couldn't discover much about the treatment, but she did learn who'd been up in Manchester – the two owners, the MD and their three PAs – just the six of them.'

'And then there were five. Presumably, they all have alibis?'

'God knows; the three men certainly wouldn't have wanted that information passed on.'

'But they didn't know the memory stick existed, did they? She'd already posted it by the time whoever it was caught up with her.'

'True, though I suppose they might have found out and taken revenge. But to return to Foxfield, an interesting fact is that the police were back there.'

'Ah!' Jonathan said. 'So said memory stick made them sit up and take notice. We'd better start on our interviews, then, or they'll pip us to the post.'

'We'll need a convincing spiel.'

'Articles on women who've contributed to the community?'

'Something along those lines, yes.'

'But that wouldn't cover Emily Broadbent,' Jonathan said reflectively. 'She was just an ordinary housewife.'

'Then you'll have to make use of your family connection.'

'Which will need careful handling.'

'Well, I leave it to you. You make a start on her, I'll take Mrs Justice Holbrook.'

Anna had gone home, and as Sophie carried her sheets down to the utility room, she admitted to herself that the visit hadn't been an unqualified success. Part of the trouble, certainly, was the underlying tension with Angus, but overshadowing even that was her inability to accept the idea of 'Lewis'. She had wished, uselessly, that she could discuss it with Angus, but first there was the other matter to be resolved, and she'd wept alone in the privacy of her bathroom for the betrayal, as she saw it, of her father.

Coming back to Angus and Imogen, though, she accepted, as she poured in the detergent, that she'd never seriously believed there was anything between them. Hurt pride had made her want to punish him, but she'd succeeded in also punishing herself. She'd been wrong to let it drag on like this, and the longer it lasted, the more likely Tamsin was to notice signs of friction. Tonight, she promised herself, she would put an end to it.

'I have to say, I did wonder,' Beatrice remarked.

'Wonder what?' Anna was immediately on the defensive.

'Whether there was more to that enigmatic man than you were prepared to admit. I did ask, if you remember, when you showed me the photos.'

'I know; I was tempted to tell you then, but Bea, I was so ashamed. I still am.'

'Love, these things happen.'

'But how could it, when I'm still crying for Miles? And – oh God, it's his anniversary in two weeks! How can I face the family? They'll think I'm such a hypocrite!'

Beatrice didn't reply for a moment. 'Will Sophie have told anyone?'

'I don't know. She and Angus are in the middle of a spat, but she might well have phoned Jonathan. Why?'

'I was just wondering if it might clear the air if you brought the whole thing into the open. Introduce the family to Lewis, meet his.'

'Actually, that's what he suggested. They're having a big party next month, and he wants to invite us all. I was considering it, but Thursday night changed everything. This last weekend was fraught enough; Sophie hasn't forgiven me, I know, though she tried to hide it. Bea, what am I going to do?'

'Ride it out, love. That's all you *can* do. Now, since I'm no longer a one-armed bandit, I've rustled up something rather special for lunch. I hope you enjoy it.'

Jonathan had spent much of the weekend brooding over Sophie's revelations about their mother, which had placed him in a quandary. Anna must guess Sophie had told him; what would she expect him to do? Phone her straight away? Go to see her? And if he did neither, would she think he was deliberately avoiding her?

As he sat doodling at his desk, considering how best to approach Emily Broadbent's death, a perfect solution occurred to him. He'd ask Ma about it! He hadn't got far with Sophie when he'd broached the subject and was chary of upsetting Imogen by a direct approach. But his mother would know, and it would provide an excuse for contacting her.

Before he lost courage, he reached for the phone and, with quickened heartbeat, awaited her voice. But it was the answerphone that clicked in, and he swore softly. Without hope, he dialled her mobile, which was, as he'd expected, switched off. Where the hell was she? Still on the way home from Sophie's? There was nothing for it but to curb his impatience and try again later.

When Angus arrived home that evening and cautiously opened the kitchen door, Sophie came to meet him and, to his delighted surprise, reached up to kiss him. His arms closed round her.

'Does this mean I'm forgiven?' he asked.

'It means I'm sorry for not giving you the chance to explain.'

'Honestly, darling, it was—'

She laid a finger on his lips. 'Later. For the moment, it's enough that we're friends again.'

He kissed her again, and behind them, Tamsin's laughing voice said, 'Sorry to interrupt, but Mel's on the phone. She's invited me and Florence to a party tomorrow – the skating rink first, then back for a meal. We can go, can't we?'

'I don't see why not,' Sophie replied, and, with a considerably lighter heart, she returned to her cooking.

'Hello, Ma.'

'Jonathan! How lovely to hear from you!'

'How are you?'

'Fine, thanks. And you? Enjoying being back in the bosom of the family?'

'It's great. Can't think why I didn't do it months ago.' He hesitated. 'Ma, this might sound an odd question, but did you ever learn the cause of Imogen's aunt's death?'

She sounded surprised, as though it wasn't the question she was expecting. 'A congenital heart defect, apparently – a ticking bomb that could have gone off at any time. Why are you asking?'

'It's to do with a series of articles,' he said, purposely vague.

'I hope you're not going to upset her husband?'

'No, I promise to be tactful.'

A congenital heart defect. For the first time, Jonathan wondered how all these doctors and pathologists who'd given causes of death would react to the suggestion that they'd been mistaken. Not well, he was willing to bet.

Anna waited a moment, then, when he still didn't speak, forced herself to ask, 'Have you spoken to Sophie in the last few days?'

He bit his lip. *Here we go!* 'I have, yes.'

'And what was your reaction?'

'God, Ma, I honestly don't know.'

'Shock? Anger? Disgust?'

'Some of that, I suppose.'

'I'm so sorry, Jon. I'd give anything for it not to have happened.'

He said with difficulty, 'I want you to be happy, of course . . .'

'But not yet?'

'Something like that.'

'Sophie met Lewis,' Anna said reflectively. 'What did she say about him?'

'Nothing, really, except that he shot off when she arrived.'

'Beatrice suggested it might help if you all met, but—'

'*Beatrice* knows?'

'Only as of today. I went to her straight from Sophie's. I had to speak to someone, Jon, and she's the closest friend I have.'

'And she suggested we play Happy Families? God! How she could imagine—'

'She was only trying to help. She blames herself for missing out on South Africa and feels responsible for what's happened. Whereas *I* still feel guilty about going without her. Anyway, I've thought of the perfect Christmas present to make up for it: a weekend voucher to Mandelyns!'

Jonathan, whose attention had wandered, came to with a start. '*What* did you say?'

'That she feels responsible—'

'No, about a Christmas present?'

'I'm going to give her a voucher to Mandelyns. Why?'

'Ma, you can't! Really, you mustn't!'

'What do you mean, I can't? Whatever's the matter with you, Jon?'

'Please! I can't explain, but whatever you do, don't let her go to Mandelyns!'

'What possible reason—?'

'Emily Broadbent went there.'

Anna sounded bewildered. 'Did she? How is that relevant? Look, perhaps I should explain—'

'Sorry, Ma, I must go. Just take my word for it. Any other health farm, just not Mandelyns.'

'Jonathan, you're being—'

'Bye, Ma.' Jonathan cut the connection and sat back, breathing quickly. He hadn't handled that well, but it had taken him completely by surprise. He prayed she wouldn't phone straight back, demanding an explanation, but as the minutes stretched out he breathed more easily. If the worst came to the worst, he'd have to tell her their suspicions, but it was a risky business. As Steve had commented, if word got out that they'd been spreading rumours, they could be taken to court. God, as if life wasn't complicated enough!

Pushing back his chair, he went to help with his sons' baths.

'She didn't know what she was doing,' Angus finished. 'She was stressed out, the disaster with the mousse was the last straw, and she just snapped.'

They were lying in bed, his arm round her shoulders.

'You weren't exactly pushing her away,' Sophie reminded him.

'To be honest, I was in shock; it had come so completely out of the blue. But really, sweetheart, it had no more meaning for either of us than a New Year kiss. Don't hold it against her;

she was in need of instant comfort, and I happened to be there. That was all.'

In fact, Sophie's next meeting with Imogen was sooner than she'd either expected or wanted.

As they pulled into the ice rink car park the next afternoon, a familiar Focus slid into place behind them.

'Oh God!' Tamsin said theatrically. 'I'd forgotten Mel knew Dire Daisy!'

'*How* does she?' Sophie asked, feeling her heart sink. 'They don't live near each other.'

'She's at Mel's school,' Tamsin said, picking up her duffle bag. 'Still, we should be able to avoid her.'

'Who's Dire Daisy?' asked Florence with interest.

'The daughter of friends of ours,' Sophie said quickly, fore-stalling a less acceptable description. 'And don't call her that, Tamsin; it's not very nice. You needn't spend much time with her, but you owe it to Mel to be polite.'

A snort was her only reply.

'I'll pick you up from the house at eight o'clock,' Sophie called after her as the two girls set off across the car park, and a hand was raised in acknowledgement.

She risked another look in the mirror, only to meet Imogen's eyes staring straight at her. With a sigh, Sophie got out of the car, walked to the one behind, and opened the passenger door. 'May I?' she asked.

'Oh yes, please!'

Sophie slid inside and shut the door. They both started to speak at once:

'I've been wanting to ring you, but—'

'Angus explained what happened—'

They broke off with awkward smiles. Then Imogen said quickly, 'Sophie, I'm so desperately sorry! Is he absolutely furious with me? I couldn't blame him.'

'Of course he's not. He was just . . . taken by surprise, that's all.'

'I made such an utter fool of myself – I don't know how I'll be able to face him! But it must have given you *completely* the wrong impression, when you—'

'It's all right, Imo. I told you he explained.'

'And when you left immediately after,' Imogen continued, as though she hadn't spoken, 'I was frantic! I was sure everyone would ask why, but they seemed to accept the migraine.'

'Quick thinking on my husband's part,' Sophie commented wryly.

'He . . . won't say anything to Roger, will he?'

'Of course he won't! Whatever do you take him for? Look, Imo, it caused a bit of awkwardness, nothing more than that, so let's put the whole thing behind us.' She leant over and kissed her friend's cheek, and Imogen gave her a hard, relieved hug.

'Thanks so much, Sophie. I couldn't bear it if anything came between us.' She gave a little smile. 'It's bad enough with our daughters! I'm afraid Daisy wasn't best pleased to see Tamsin just now.'

'The feeling was mutual. Don't worry, they'll grow out of it. In the meantime, with the girls taken care of, we've a free afternoon ahead of us, so let's enjoy it. How about a spot of retail therapy, since you're up in town, followed by a thoroughly wicked cream tea?'

'I can't think of anything better!' said Imogen.

Anna was perplexed by Jonathan's reaction to the voucher, until she remembered the press had identified the Manchester hotel victim as an employee of Mandelyns. But surely any bad publicity resulting from it would be over long before Christmas? For Lewis's sake, she certainly hoped so.

On the Wednesday morning, Wendy Salter phoned. 'You've probably forgotten all about us by now!' she began.

'Of course I haven't! Apart from anything else, you feature in quite a lot of my photos.'

'Sounds ominous! Well, if you remember, I threatened to invite you to lunch, once we were back in the old routine, so I'm now carrying out that threat. We'd love to see you again.'

'That would be great, Wendy, thanks.'

'I gather you're still seeing Lewis?'

Anna said carefully, 'From time to time, yes.'

'I'm so glad. Poor love, he's in need of a bit of TLC at the moment, what with all this murder hoo-ha.'

'Yes, it's been . . . terrible.'

'I'm hoping lunch will provide a welcome break. Now, you're in Westbridge, aren't you, and, as you know, we're in Richmond. It shouldn't take you more than half an hour or so, should it? Have you got satnav?'

'No, but I have your address. I'll download directions from the net.'

'Fine. I checked with Lewis first, because he always has so much on, but he could make either Tuesday or Wednesday next week, if that's OK with you?'

'Wednesday would be fine, thank you.'

'A week today, then – super! We'll really look forward to seeing you. About twelve thirty?'

On one of his regular visits to Foxfield, Lewis had spent the morning in its boardroom, discussing marketing. When the meeting broke up, he'd strolled through the grounds to Cameron's bungalow, where they were now awaiting their lunch.

Normally, Cameron ate in the main building, but at present the atmosphere over there was heavy with unease and suspicion, and he was glad to escape it.

Not that it was much better here; he and his father had exchanged barely a word for the last ten minutes. He cast around for some way to lighten the atmosphere. 'I hear you were spotted in London recently, with a lady on your arm.'

Lewis looked up with a frown. 'Spotted by whom?'

'Oliver, actually. Lyddie told me.'

'I'm surprised he thought it worth reporting.'

'Oh, come on, Father! I'm trying to make conversation here! Who was she?'

They were interrupted by a knock at the door, and Cameron opened it to take receipt of two covered trays, each bearing a steak and kidney pie, baked potato, carrots and broccoli, and a plate of cheese and biscuits. The next few minutes were taken up with transferring them to the ready-laid table, where an opened bottle of wine raised Lewis's eyebrow.

'I know the lunchtime rule,' Cameron said quickly, 'but I felt we could both do with it.' They seated themselves, and he poured the wine. 'So come on, then, spill the beans: who is she?'

'If you must know, someone I met on holiday.'

'And you've kept in touch? That's not like you!'

Lewis, making a start on his lunch, didn't reply, and Cameron pressed, 'Name?'

'Anna. Anna Farrell.'

About to pick up his cutlery, Cameron paused. 'Farrell?'

'Yes, why?'

'The name seems to ring a bell.'

'You could be thinking of her son; he's a journalist. Sometimes writes for the nationals, I believe.'

'That must be it,' Cameron said.

The interviews for the hypothetical articles were not going well. Comparing notes, it was clear that although the respective families were more than willing to detail their loved ones' life histories and achievements, they had never for a moment questioned the causes of their deaths.

'I've come up with congenital heart defect and purulent meningitis,' Jonathan said gloomily. 'What about you?'

'Pre-existing cerebral aneurysm, and anaphylactic shock, allegedly after eating peanuts.'

'Not, one assumes, at Mandelyns?'

Steve shook his head. 'Which only leaves the actress. It's a damn sight harder to approach her family, but the papers hinted at a virus.'

'Don't forget Elise said these symptoms could be reactions to the treatment.'

'But how, exactly, do we prove it? Anyway, the police have a lot more resources than we do. Since we did our duty and sent them the memory stick, we might as well retire gracefully and leave them to it.'

'But it was *our* story!' Jonathan demurred.

Steve shrugged. 'Win some, lose some. We'd do better to move on and concentrate on old Perceval and his factory. Might be less newsworthy, but at least it will provide our bread and butter.'

Pringle pushed the plastic-covered letter across the desk. 'What do you make of this, Trevor?'

DS Smith reached for it, reading the large-font, bold print:

Ask journalist Jonathan Farrell why he met murder victim Elise du Pré in his hotel room the night before she was killed.

He looked up quickly, his eyes brightening. 'There is a God! First bloody lead we've had! Fits in with what the parents said, and all.'

'About a lover? Seems to, first confirmation we've had – if you can call an anonymous letter confirmation.' He sighed. 'Time was when we could at least get *some* handle on these poison pen affairs: the newspaper the words had been cut from, handwriting analysis, typewriter with a faulty key. But with these bloody computers, it's a different ball game.'

'So what's the first move?' Smith asked eagerly.

'We check the local hotels, see if anyone of that name was in town that night. It should at least give us something to go on.'

'About time, and all,' Smith said feelingly.

Friday evening, thank God, Jonathan thought. It hadn't been an auspicious week. He was closing down his computer, when there was a tentative tap on the study door. 'Yes?' he called. 'Come in.'

Tom's head, wide-eyed, appeared round the door frame. 'Mummy says please could you come downstairs. There's two policemen waiting to speak to you.'

Jonathan stared at him, his heart setting up an uncomfortably accelerated beat. 'Policemen? Are you sure?'

'Mummy said they are, but they're not wearing helmets.'

'Thanks, Tom. Tell them I'll be right down.'

Tom nodded and withdrew, and Jonathan rose slowly to his feet, his mind racing. Could they have traced the memory stick to him? No, no possible way. Nor, even more importantly, could they tie him to Elise. So what the hell did they want? A parking ticket? Speeding fine? Neither of those necessitated home visits.

Bracing himself, he went downstairs. Vicky was waiting for him in the hall, her face frightened. She didn't speak, just nodded towards the sitting room. Jonathan nodded back, briefly touched her hand, and went in and closed the door.

Two men turned to face him. Plain clothes; he'd feared as much.

'Sorry to disturb you, sir. DS Newton and DC Pennington, Westbridge CID.' They held up warrant cards, and Jonathan nodded.

'How can I help you?' He waved a hand towards the sofa, and both men sat down. Jonathan seated himself on an upright chair facing them, vainly hoping the height might give him an advantage.

'Just a few questions, sir, if you wouldn't mind.' The older man's Kentish accent was misleadingly reassuring. 'I take it you have no objection to our conversation being taped?'

'Of course not,' Jonathan said from a dry mouth, watching as a small recorder was set up on the coffee table.

The DC gave the time, place and names of those present, and sat back.

Newton began the interview. 'Could you confirm, sir, that you spent the night of Wednesday the thirteenth of October at the Commodore Hotel in Manchester?'

Jonathan felt the colour draining from his face. Useless to deny it – somehow, they must have proof. He moistened his lips. 'That's right; my colleague and I were up there on business.'

'And could you also confirm that, during that evening, you entertained a young lady by the name of Elise du Pré in your room?'

The room tilted. This couldn't be happening. Blindly, instinctively, he went on the offensive. 'If you're insinuating what I think you are,' he blustered, 'I most emphatically deny it!'

The detective was unperturbed. 'Then I'll put it another way, sir. Did the young lady in question *visit* you in your room?'

There was a long pause, while Jonathan wondered frantically what to say. The two men sat patiently at their ease, making no attempt to hurry him. Eventually, he cleared his throat. 'She did pop in, yes, but my colleague will confirm he was there the whole time. I assure you—'

'This colleague's name and address?'

Jonathan supplied them. He must warn Steve he'd be contacted.

'What was the purpose of her visit?'

Jonathan took a deep breath. If he was to dispel suspicion of an affair with Elise, it seemed he'd no option but to admit to the memory stick – and God knew where that would lead.

Newton spoke into the continuing silence. 'I'm sure you're aware, sir, that the young lady was unfortunately murdered the following day.' He paused. 'By person or persons unknown.'

Sickly, Jonathan nodded.

'Well, sir?'

He straightened in his chair. 'We're journalists, Sergeant, and she'd asked for our help. She was . . . worried about a matter at work and wanted us to look into it.'

'The matter being?'

In for a penny, Jonathan thought. 'It concerned a treatment that was given at the resorts where she worked. She discovered several women had died after receiving it.'

Newton pursed his lips. 'The resorts are in the southern counties, I believe?'

Jonathan nodded.

'Where you, obviously, are also based. So why should the meeting take place in Manchester?'

'We were up there on business, as I explained, and so was she. She had some . . . evidence to hand over and felt it might be safer than meeting nearer home.'

'Evidence?'

'She'd copied the clients' records on to a memory stick.'

Jonathan looked intently from one man to the other, but neither betrayed prior knowledge. Which didn't mean they didn't know exactly what he was talking about.

'And she handed this device to you that evening?'

Stick to the truth. 'No, she only *told* us about it; she posted it to us the next day. Then sadly, as you say, she was killed, and when we'd had time to study it, we realized the information it contained might have some bearing on her death. So we sent it to the Manchester police.'

'Very public-spirited of you. Did you see Miss du Pré again the next day?'

This time, he *had* to lie. 'No.' *Not alive, anyway.*

'How did you spend that Thursday, sir?'

'We'd a nine o'clock appointment with the gentleman we'd arranged to interview.'

Again, name and address were called for.

'And after that?'

'We caught the two thirty flight home.'

There was a silence, and Jonathan prayed they wouldn't probe further.

Pennington leaned forward. 'How well did you know this young lady, sir?'

'Not well at all. As I explained—'

'But you'd met her prior to Manchester?'

'Only once. She was nervous of being seen talking to the press.'

'And when you'd seen this memory stick, did you or your colleague take any steps to verify her suspicions?'

'We made a few enquiries, but we felt the police would have more resources to look into it.'

'Indeed.'

Another silence, then, to Jonathan's overwhelming relief, Newton nodded to his companion and both men stood up.

'Very well, sir. That's all for the moment, but we may need to speak to you again. Your statement will be typed out, and perhaps you'd call in at the station on Monday to sign it. In the meantime, thank you for your time, and have a good weekend.'

Incapable of replying, Jonathan saw them to the front door. As it closed behind them, Vicky came quickly into the hall.

'Jonathan!'

He caught her to him, burying his face in her hair. 'It's all right, darling. At least, I think it is.'

'What did they want?'

'They somehow got hold of my name in connection with Elise. God knows how.'

She pulled back, staring into his face with horror. 'They don't think *you* killed her?'

'Sh!' Jonathan looked anxiously up the stairs, but there was no sign of the boys. 'I don't think so,' he said quietly. 'I answered their questions as honestly as I could.' *With one exception.*

'But suppose—?'

'Let's not suppose anything,' Jonathan said firmly. 'I'm going to pour myself a large whisky, and you might like to join me. After which, we can look forward to a happy family weekend. All right?'

For a moment longer she stared into his tense face. Then she gave an obedient little smile.

'All right,' she said.

TWELVE

By the time they met on Monday, Steve had also been interviewed.

'Thanks for the warning,' he said feelingly. 'They must have known you'd contact me, but there was nothing they could do about it. I suppose they were hoping I'd contradict something you said.'

'I hope to God you didn't.'

'There wasn't much scope to. Everything you told them was correct, you just left out finding her.'

'Quite an omission, though!'

Steve smiled crookedly. 'True.'

'There's no way they could prove I was in her room, is there?' Jonathan asked, suddenly anxious.

Steve shrugged. 'Who knows? I still can't imagine how they knew we'd seen her.'

'Exactly! That's what's been bugging me! How could they possibly have got hold of my name?'

'Unless,' Steve said slowly, 'the murderer told them.'

Jonathan stared at him. 'Would you care to explain that remark?'

'It just occurred to me; according to press reports, the only thing known to be missing is her mobile. Why would her killer take that?'

'You tell me.'

'To check on who she'd been in touch with?'

Jonathan stiffened apprehensively.

'See what I'm getting at?' Steve went on, more eagerly as his theory gained ground. 'If he had her mobile, he could have seen your text, giving her the room number. And you'd also have been on her list of contacts, wouldn't you?' He gave a short laugh. 'Not had any heavy breathers on the line, have you?'

'No, thank—' Jonathan broke off, coldness washing over him.

'Wait a minute, though; there was one call – I thought it was a wrong number.'

'What did they say?' Steve asked sharply.

'Nothing. I—'

'They just hung up?'

'Yes, when I – oh God, when I said my name.'

'Did you dial one-four-seven-one?'

'No, it was early morning and I was half-asleep. I just wrote it off as a wrong number.'

Seeing the look on his face, Steve said quickly, 'Well, don't worry, it still might have been.'

'But it fits too neatly, doesn't it?' Jonathan's voice was bitter. 'I must have seemed the perfect scapegoat.'

'Which,' Steve said thoughtfully, 'seems to rule out the burglar theory. For a start, any thief making a run for it would have snatched up something more valuable. According to the papers she was wearing jewellery, and her handbag was there for the taking.'

'If it *was* a burglar, it would mean we weren't responsible for her death.'

'I appreciate that, but the more I think about it, the less likely it seems: time of day, committing murder, only the mobile taken – none of these fit the profile, let alone taking the trouble to check you out.'

'So we're back to the memory stick.'

'Possibly. But don't forget she'd already posted it, so how would he know about it?'

'She was always afraid someone would get on to her. Perhaps someone did.'

'If so, it must have been one of those with her, or at least someone from Mandelyns; no one else would gain by trying to suppress it. Still, why are we wasting time on this? We passed it to the police; let them deal with it, and we can get back to Perceval. Have you got those figures he gave us?'

'We're back to square one on the tip-off,' Pringle reported to DI Fanshawe later that morning. 'Farrell might have had it off that evening – though his colleague backed his story – but there's no way he could have killed her. He has a watertight alibi for the time of death.'

'In the form of what?'

'Business appointment. They were at Percevals the other side of town from just before nine till eleven fifteen. The firm confirmed it. She was long dead by then.'

Fanshawe sighed. 'Back to the drawing board, then. How are Surrey and Berkshire doing with the resorts?'

'Interviewing's continuing, but there's a lot of staff to get through. They're concentrating on those who give treatments.'

'No more women turned up dead?'

'No, the count remains at five, and though we're discreetly checking, all seem above board. I reckon we're flogging a dead horse here, sir.'

'A whole stable of them, by the sound of it. How are the tests going?'

'Slowly, as always, but nothing suspicious so far.'

'Could something have been added *after* it left the manufacturers? By someone at the resort, for instance?'

'With what aim?'

'To expedite the effects? Instant improvement? God knows; I'm not well up in these things.'

'Well, if so, the boys down there will root it out, but frankly, if all the deaths were natural, so what? No harm seems to have come of it.'

Wendy and George lived in a mock-Georgian house on the outskirts of Richmond, and its immaculate paintwork and graceful lines looked their best in the thick autumn sunshine. The lawn in front of it was as smooth as velvet, and the flower beds, crammed with dahlias, chrysanthemums and a few late roses, were a riot of colour.

The gates stood open, so Anna drove in, parking behind a car already there – Lewis's, presumably. All three of them came out to greet her, Lewis's kiss on the cheek no more and no less effusive than those of their hosts.

'How lovely, to be all together again!' Wendy exclaimed. 'I can't believe it's only a month since we flew home! It seems another world!'

Lewis looked tired, Anna thought anxiously. She'd not seen him since Sophie interrupted their evening together, and the grooves on his face seemed deeper, his eyes more sunken. This ongoing investigation must be very wearing. However, he seemed determined to put his worries behind him, and, while drinks were served, he amused them with the story of a pop star – name discreetly withheld – who had spectacularly blotted his copybook during a weekend at Woodcot.

Lunch was served in the conservatory overlooking the back garden, the open doors letting in both the unseasonable warmth and the scent from the autumn clematis growing just outside. It consisted of a delectable salmon and prawn flan with avocado and watercress salad, followed by summer pudding and cream.

Towards the end of the meal, George, having boasted about his grandson's prowess on the football field, enquired after Anna's grandchildren.

'Tamsin was home last week for half-term,' she said. 'She's thirteen, and my daughter was horrified when she appeared one morning wearing heavy purple eyeshadow. Sophie blames the friend who was staying with her and made them both wash it off before allowing them out of the front door.'

'I bet that went down well!' said Wendy with a laugh. 'I remember my mother catching me at much the same age, trying on her lipsticks.'

'Oh, we all experimented,' Anna agreed, 'which is well and good around the house, but at that age not to be encouraged outdoors.'

Wendy glanced at Lewis. 'Sorry about this grandparental chat!' she apologized.

'Don't mention it. There are compensations. Remember what you said to me, George, when young Daniel was born?'

George shook his head a little apprehensively.

'That while delighted to be a grandfather, you were less pleased to be married to a grandmother!'

'Charming!' Wendy exclaimed, with mock indignation. 'But how are your two? Any sign of wedding bells?'

'No, though these days that doesn't rule out progeny.'

'True. Lydia and Oliver are pretty solid, I know, but what about Cameron? Didn't you say there was a girl on the scene?'

'There's been a girl on the scene, as you put it, since he was sixteen, but none of them has come to anything. At thirty-seven, I'm beginning to despair of him.'

'What's the latest one like?'

'Alice? I've never met her. My son tends to compartmentalize his life.'

'But they've been together for a while now, surely?'

'"Together" mightn't be the best description. She doesn't live with him; Cameron still enjoys the bachelor life in his bungalow at Foxfield.' He stirred his coffee thoughtfully. 'Between ourselves, I suspect that she's married, and to someone well known. In other words, it would cause a scandal if their relationship became public.'

'Intriguing, but not exactly promising.' Wendy glanced round the table. 'Now, if everyone's finished, we thought you might like to see the video we shot in South Africa. Or have you had more than enough of your own photos?'

'I'd love to see it!' Anna said. 'Moving pictures are far more evocative, and the ones I took were a disaster. I kept just missing what I was trying to photograph!'

'Right, you brought it on yourself! Let's go through to the sitting room.'

The next hour or so was spent reliving their holiday. George had been an enthusiastic photographer, and any number of occasions that Anna had forgotten were brought back to mind, along with many of their fellow holidaymakers – Bill and Prue, young Tony, and, of course, Edda, with her selection of colourful skirts. In a general view of the group at Kruger, Wendy pointed out Anna and Lewis in the background, throwing crumbs to the blue starlings.

However, it was the animals rather than his companions on which George had concentrated, and there were splendid shots of giraffes, lions and elephants, as well as all the less imposing but equally intriguing creatures they'd seen along the way. The final pictures were of the farewell dinner in Pretoria, laughing faces round the table. After which, Anna remembered, Lewis had come to her room. She glanced at him, saw he was watching her, and they exchanged a smile; obviously, their thoughts had been running on the same lines.

It was only when they were leaving that George brought up the subject that had been at the back of all their minds. 'Sorry about this trouble you're having, old man,' he said gruffly. 'It must be hellish, having the police on your back like that.'

'I've had happier experiences,' Lewis said tightly. 'They're round every corner at the moment, though God knows what they're looking for.'

A murderer, probably, Anna thought with a shudder.

'I hope it won't interfere with the celebrations,' Wendy said.

'I don't intend to let it.'

'That's the spirit!' She turned to Anna. 'You'll be there, of course?'

Anna flushed. 'I haven't decided yet; it's difficult, with the family.'

'God, what an infernal mess it all is!' George exclaimed. 'Aren't the police making any progress at all?'

'Not that I can see,' Lewis answered. 'They've pursued the odd false lead, but it hasn't got them anywhere.'

'Oh?'

But he ignored the implied question, and they moved outside. Thanks and goodbyes were exchanged, and Lewis, holding Anna's car door for her, murmured, 'I'll phone you tomorrow.'

Then she was on her way home, but memories of the video and the day's lively conversation were overshadowed in her mind by that last exchange. How much longer would this cloud be hanging over Lewis? And what would be the eventual outcome?

Police are continuing to question staff at the three Mandelyns Health Resorts concerning the murder of an employee in a Manchester hotel three weeks ago. Lewis Masters, co-owner of the Group . . .

Jonathan read the paragraph again before the full impact hit him. Even then, he couldn't absorb it. Lewis Masters? Wasn't that the name of Ma's admirer? God, it *couldn't* be! A potential murderer, going out with his mother?

Oblivious of the chatter around him, he raced through the rest of the report: investigations continuing in Manchester, liaison between police forces, no new leads. But . . . Lewis Masters! He couldn't get his head round it.

There was no way he could use his mobile on the train; what he had to say was highly confidential, not to say slanderous. He

would, in any case, be seeing Steve shortly, but they were meeting
Brian Perceval, Keith's son, and this couldn't be discussed in
front of a third party. Only then did he realize that Steve wouldn't,
in any case, understand his panic. To him, Masters was simply
the owner of the Group; he knew nothing of his involvement
with Anna Farrell – and nor, for that matter, did Vicky, since
Jonathan hadn't been able to bring himself to tell her.

In fact, he realized bleakly, no one beside himself was aware
of the full implications. But, hell, he had to talk to *someone*!

He stared at the newspaper till the print blurred before his
eyes. Not Steve, then, nor Vicky. Which left Sophie. He recalled
the stirring of memory when she'd first mentioned Masters' name.
He hadn't nailed it at the time, and apparently neither had she.
Knowing nothing of the memory stick and its implications, nor,
he assumed, Masters' connection with Mandelyns, she'd be bliss-
fully ignorant of the fact that the man in the news was their
mother's lover. He wondered uneasily if he'd be able to enlighten
her without revealing his own part in the drama.

Around him, people were beginning to stand up, and he realized belatedly that they were approaching Charing Cross.
Hurriedly folding his newspaper, he also headed for the door.

Sophie was surprised by her brother's call. She was engrossed
in a new design for a jumper and resented being disturbed.

'Can't it wait?' she asked, with a touch of impatience.

'No, it can't. Look, Steve and I are meeting someone for lunch.
Can I come on to you afterwards? Are you at home?'

'No, I'm in the workshop, and fairly busy, actually.'

'This won't take long, but I have to speak to you.'

She sighed. 'All right, if you must. About three?'

'Bless you, sis,' he said, and rang off.

Sophie frowned briefly, then dismissed the exchange and
returned to her design.

Sophie's business premises consisted of two large rooms, one
for knitting, one for stock and packaging, and a smaller one that
served as her studio, where, in relative peace, she worked on her
designs. The whole was fronted by a boutique offering potential
customers a chance to see the finished garments, which did

enough business to justify its opening from eleven to four three days a week, staffed by a couple of students.

'So what's so urgent that it's brought you all the way out here?' she asked, three hours later. She and Jonathan were in the minute kitchenette off the workroom, waiting for the kettle to boil. On his way through, he'd been intrigued by the six knitting machines, three of which were currently not in use.

'If you only employ three women, why do you need six machines?' he asked now.

'Because they're for different things,' she replied. 'One does ribbing, for instance, which you can't do on an ordinary machine. One's for more chunky garments, and one's a standard gauge for fine knitting. And don't forget I also run machine-knitting workshops, where people come to learn.'

'I never realized it was so complicated,' Jonathan admitted, watching her pour boiling water into the mugs. 'What a clever girl you are!'

'Enough of the compliments; I want to know why you're interrupting my muse.'

'First, though, that pale blue cashmere in the window . . .'

'Yes?'

'What size is it?'

'Brother dear, you should know by now it's available in *any* size. That's the whole point of designer knitwear: you choose the colour and style, and it's made to your measurements. Why?'

'I was thinking of getting it – or one like it – for Vicky, for Christmas.'

Sophie fished out the tea bags, added milk, and set the mugs on a tray. 'Fine, but we can discuss all that later; we've not had Bonfire Night yet. So, for the *third* time – what's on your mind?'

He followed her into the studio, seating himself opposite her. He'd been rehearsing his opening sentences off and on all day and was still not entirely happy with them. But time had run out, and he had to take the plunge.

He took the mug she handed him with a nod of thanks. 'I presume you've heard of the murder of that girl up in Manchester?'

Sophie set down her own mug with an angry little thump. 'For God's sake, Jonathan, stop changing the subject! I've got work to do, even if you haven't.'

'*Listen*, Sophie – just listen. You know the case I mean? It's been in all the papers.'

'When have I time to read the papers?'

'And on TV. The girl in the hotel room.'

'I did hear something,' she admitted grudgingly. 'So what?'

'She worked for the Mandelyns Group.' He watched her, but there was no flicker of recognition. 'Which is owned,' he continued deliberately, 'by one Lewis Masters. Does *that* name ring a bell?'

Her eyes widened. 'You don't mean—?'

'Oh, but I do. Lewis Masters, currently "courting" our mother, if that's the word, is co-owner of Mandelyns, and he and the girl were up in Manchester on business, with a few others. Sophie, they were all staying at the same hotel!'

Her eyes hadn't left his face, but a hand went to her throat. 'You're surely not telling me—'

'I'm telling you that he's been interviewed several times by the police. He *could* have done it, Soph. So, for that matter, could any of them.'

'But . . . for God's sake, why would he? I mean . . .'

'He might have had a motive.' Jonathan took a deep breath. 'I happen to know the dead girl suspected a treatment they'd been using had resulted in deaths.'

There was a brief silence, then she said, '*How* do you "happen to know"?' He watched her making connections. 'Just a minute . . . She was French, wasn't she, the victim? Jon, she wasn't the mysterious girl you told us about, at dinner that night? The one who kept arranging to meet you, then not turning up?'

Jonathan bit his lip. He'd forgotten that conversation. 'Actually, yes, she was.'

'So you did meet eventually?'

He nodded.

'And you think that's why she was killed? Because she told you about it? Then you're in danger, too! You must go to the police!'

'Don't worry,' he lied quickly, 'no one knows she told me.' He'd no intention of admitting he'd already been interviewed by the police.

'How long have you known about this?'

'Well, I knew, of course, what Elise suspected, but it was only today I realized who Masters was, just before I phoned you.'

She picked up her mug, holding it in both hands, and sipped slowly at her tea.

'Do you think Ma knows?' she asked after a minute.

'I think she must do.'

'Well, she obviously doesn't suspect him, or she wouldn't—'

'Sophie, she's *in love* with him!' Jonathan said savagely.

She looked at him for a moment, then laid one hand, hot from the mug, over his. 'I know, Jon,' she said softly.

He brushed his free hand across his eyes. 'Sorry. It's just with Dad's anniversary coming up next week . . .'

'I know,' she said again. Then, tentatively, 'What are we going to do? Have you thought?'

'No; is some special ritual involved?'

'I don't think so. We could go to church, I suppose, or visit his grave . . .' Her voice tailed off uncertainly.

'I'm not at all sure, in the circumstances, that I want to spend it with Ma.' He made a dismissive gesture. 'Anyway, we can think about it over the weekend. In the meantime, I'm sorry to have sprung this other business on you, but I thought you should know.' He smiled ruefully. 'On reflection, though, perhaps you'd rather I'd kept it to myself.'

'Of course not.' She paused. 'Have you told Vicky?'

'About Ma? No.'

'I've not told Angus, either. He's always been so fond of her, I didn't want to – shatter his illusions.'

'Are yours shattered?' Jonathan asked quietly.

'Let's just say shaken. Of *course* she should have another chance of happiness, but . . .'

'Yes.' Jonathan drank his tea. He added wryly, 'Sorry; all this will have scuppered your muse completely.'

She nodded. 'And by the time I've managed to retrieve it, it will probably be going-home time. In which case, I shall cut my losses, leave early, and cook an extra-special supper for my husband.'

They stood up.

'Thanks for telling me, Jon. You'll keep me in the loop, won't you?'

'Of course.'

They walked in silence back through the workroom into the shop.

'And come back to me about the cashmere,' Sophie added. 'I'm sure Vicky would love it, though I say so myself!'

She unlocked the door, and they gave each other a longer than usual hug.

'Take care,' she said.

'You too.'

And, turning up his collar against the cool breeze, he set off towards the tube station.

At first, Lydia Masters wasn't paying attention. The swaying of the tube was making her sleepy; it had been a long day, and she was finding it hard to concentrate on her paperback. Then, penetrating her tiredness, she caught the word *Mandelyns* and looked up sharply.

It was a woman opposite who'd spoken, raising her voice against the rattle of the train, but Lydia's view of her was obstructed by the straphangers swaying between them.

'Three weeks, and they've still not arrested anyone,' she went on.

'Can't think what's stopping them,' sniffed her friend. 'It was the old bloke, wasn't it? Stands to reason.'

Lydia stiffened, her heartbeat accelerating.

'How do you make that out?' the first woman enquired.

'Well, it's the old story, isn't it? Too much to drink, more than likely, and reckoned he was in with a chance. She wasn't having any, he lost his temper, and bingo!'

Lydia gripped her book convulsively as rage swept over her. How many in the crowded carriage could hear this vitriol?

The first woman was speaking again. 'Same could apply to the other men – more likely, I'd have thought. That one's old enough to be her father.'

Her friend snorted. 'Since when has that stopped them? No, my money's on him. He was the boss, wasn't he? Didn't think she'd dare refuse him.'

They were approaching Lydia's stop. Before she lost her nerve, she stood up and, unceremoniously pushing aside the man blocking her view, glared down at the women.

'I hope you realize that what you've been saying is gross

slander,' she said clearly, her voice ringing as the train slowed down. 'You've not a shred of evidence to back it up. It's as well for you that my partner's not with me; he's a barrister, and he'd know how to deal with you!'

And, leaving them staring after her open-mouthed, she pushed her way through the throng and out on to the crowded platform, only realizing she was crying when someone touched her arm and asked if she was all right.

Half an hour later, Oliver's arms around her, she was still shaking.

'I know you couldn't really have done anything,' she admitted. 'But I was so furious, I wanted to put the fear of God into them.'

'And I'm sure you did, my love. You can be very fierce when roused!'

'I suppose I overreacted, but it seemed so unfair that they could slander Dad like that and get away with it.'

'They probably didn't mean any harm,' he said reasonably. 'It was just gossip, whiling away the journey.'

'There speaks the defence barrister!' Lydia scoffed, moving away from him.

'Well, it's a thin line between freedom of speech and defamation of character, but if it's any comfort, no one there would have known him, so it wouldn't have meant anything. What's more, they'd have forgotten it within five minutes – except, perhaps, the women whose throats you went for!'

'But is that really what people think, Oliver? That's what frightened me; I hadn't realized they might be saying that all over the country. And about Cameron, too. It's just so . . . horrible!'

'I know it is, my love, but all we can do is sit tight, let the police get on with it, and hope it won't go on much longer.'

'Easier said than done,' she said.

THIRTEEN

When he got home that evening, Jonathan lost no time in Googling Lewis Masters. Within minutes, he learned that he'd been born in Saffron Walden, Essex, and educated at Shrewsbury School and Brasenose College, Oxford. He married the model Myrtle Page in 1972, and they had a son, Cameron Lewis, born June 1973, and a daughter, Lydia Mary, born April 1980. The marriage was dissolved in 1990.

In 1977 he opened his first health club in Dovercourt, Essex. Several others followed in neighbouring counties, and in 1980 he purchased Mandelyns Court in Surrey and developed it as a residential health farm. In the years that followed, he went on to purchase Woodcot Grange in Hampshire (1989) and Foxfield Hall in Berkshire (1991), re-branding both with the Mandelyns name.

There was more, but Jonathan felt he had the essentials. What interested him most was Lewis's marriage to Myrtle Page. She'd been a big name in the past and was still hitting the headlines in *UK Today*, though usually for the wrong reasons. What was clear was that she still liked the limelight – and no doubt would respond favourably to any request for an interview. Which could be interesting.

He was still pondering this when a new message flashed up on his screen, and he saw, with mixed feelings, that it was from his mother. He clicked on it, to find it addressed jointly to himself and Sophie.

Darlings, it began. *I hope you will understand if I say that I'd like to spend Dad's anniversary quietly by myself this year. Bless you both for all the love and support you've given me over the past months, and please believe me when I say I love and grieve for him as much as I ever did. Nothing will ever change that. All love, Ma.*

Her ears must have been burning, Jonathan thought. He read

it through again before deleting it, then wondered if he should have sent a reply. Well, he'd think about that tomorrow. In the meantime, it was one less problem to worry about.

Sophie phoned him later that evening. 'You got the email?'

'Yes. I must say it was a relief.'

'Me too. But Jon, I think we should be together, don't you? Angus can't take time off, unfortunately, but if Vicky would like to join us, she'd be very welcome.'

'I'll ask. The kids will be at school, so there wouldn't be a problem there. What have you in mind?'

'Just taking flowers to the grave, and perhaps a quiet lunch after.'

'Fine by me. Let me know what train you're on, and I can meet you, either with or without Vic.'

He was about to disconnect when her voice stopped him. 'Jon – I've just thought: suppose Ma's there, too?'

'I don't think she will be. She'd have guessed we might go, and she did say she wants to be alone. But if she *is* there, it's no big deal.'

They left it at that.

Imogen pulled her scarf more tightly round her neck. It was a cold, misty evening, and while the bonfire warmed their faces, their backs felt the chill. She was holding firmly on to Jack's hand, much to his indignation, but the damp wood was spitting, and hot ash and sparks were flying in all directions.

Stalls selling hot dogs, sausages and baked potatoes were doing a roaring trade, there were polystyrene cups of soup to keep the cold out and Yorkshire parkin and toffee apples for the asking. Imogen was glad they'd opted for a public display rather than hold their own; it was much less trouble, and there was a happy, social atmosphere. Meanwhile, on top of his pyre, poor Guy Fawkes gradually disintegrated, each further slide into the flames greeted with shrieks of triumph. Once he was gone, the fireworks would begin.

She glanced at her parents, their faces lit by the firelight. Her mother's still had a sad expression in repose, and Imogen reached instinctively for her hand.

Pat Selby returned the pressure. 'I meant to ask you,' she said. 'Did you know Jonathan called on Uncle Ted?'

Imogen turned sharply. 'No? Why was that? He hardly knew either of them.'

'That's what I thought. What's even stranger is that, according to Ted, he seemed interested in Em's visit to Mandelyns.'

Imogen frowned. 'What possible interest could it be of his?'

Pat lifted her shoulders. 'Journalists, like God, move in mysterious ways.'

'But he must have given *some* reason for calling?'

'Not really, just mentioned vaguely that he was doing a series of articles. He was trying to be tactful, Ted said, but it didn't stop him asking a lot of questions about the cause of her death.'

'What bloody cheek!' Imogen exploded.

'Language, Timothy!' Roger rejoined them, armed with a savoury-smelling carrier bag. 'Now, who ordered what?' He began handing out the food. 'The hot dog's for Jack, I think. Pasties for . . . Les and Pat, hamburgers for us, and a bag of chips to share. Use the paper napkins to hold them – they're pretty hot.'

As they started to eat, he turned back to Imogen. 'What were you being so indignant about?'

'Jonathan Farrell going to interview Uncle Ted.'

Roger raised an eyebrow. 'He must be following up some line or other.'

'About Aunt *Em*?'

'All will be revealed, no doubt.'

There was a shout as the first of the fireworks soared into the sky, scattering stars of red and blue and silver and gold. Imogen said no more, but she still felt mutinous. Next week, she knew, was the anniversary of Miles Farrell's death; how would Jonathan like it, if she went prying into its causes?

Jack tugged suddenly at her coat. 'Mummy, *look!*' he yelled, and, abandoning her introspection, she turned to see a succession of rockets filling the night sky with magic. As Roger had said, all would doubtless be revealed, but nonetheless, given the chance, she'd find out if Sophie knew anything about it.

*   *   *

There were cards from Sophie and Angus, and Jonathan and Vicky, and a home-made one from the boys, in which Tom had written laboriously, 'Dear Granny, we're thinking of you and Grandpa.'

Anna's eyes filled again with tears. She'd already received a text from Tamsin, presumably at Sophie's instigation. Did she really deserve her family's sympathy? At least she'd spared Jon and Sophie embarrassment by opting to be alone, but now the prospect of the long day ahead filled her with dread. How should she spend it? She couldn't simply wallow in guilt and grief or she'd be a nervous wreck; nor could she bear to go near the church. She'd visit the grave later in the week, when the day itself wasn't so poignant.

She could drive into the country and go for a walk. But the day was misty and uninviting, with the threat of rain – not guaranteed to alleviate grief.

One thing, however, she'd determined in advance: she would not, positively not, think about Lewis. The visit to Wendy and George had brought home to her how worried he was about the ongoing investigation and the threat it might pose to the planned celebrations. Consequently, when, as promised, he'd phoned the next day, she'd accepted the invitation, at least on her own behalf.

'I'll just be one of the guests, though, won't I?' she'd asked anxiously. 'I mean, there won't be anything to suggest we're—?'

'Don't worry, my darling, this is principally a business do; there's no question of your being hauled up to the top table or anything. I'll arrange for you to sit with Wendy and George, and I promise not to single you out in any way.'

The embossed card had arrived on Saturday, and she'd put it in a desk drawer until today was safely over.

Now, she stood in the sitting room, looking at the sympathy cards arrayed alongside Miles's photograph. She could get out the albums, relive happier days, but they would only make her cry again. How *did* people cope with anniversaries? Most, she reminded herself, would at least be spared the added guilt.

A ring at the doorbell startled her. The post had already been; who else could be calling? Glancing in the mirror to check her eyes, she went to the door and opened it to find Beatrice on the step with a sheaf of flowers.

'Oh, Bea!' she said, the tears starting again.

Beatrice took her arm and led her gently back inside, laid the flowers on the hall table, and put her arms round her. 'I don't usually have such an unfortunate effect on people!' she observed, patting Anna's shoulder, and she gave a choked little laugh. 'If you'd rather I didn't stay, fine, but I reckoned perhaps a non-family face might be welcome.'

'You're so right!' Anna admitted, drying her eyes. 'I was feeling very sorry for myself, and I'm not sure I have the right to.'

'Of course you have,' Beatrice said briskly. 'You've lost your husband, whom you loved dearly, and, one way or another, you've had a pretty traumatic year. But I'm not here to ladle out sympathy. By the look of you, you've done enough grieving for the present, so I suggest we drive out somewhere, have a pub lunch, and, weather permitting, a short walk. And if you want to talk about Miles, or Lewis for that matter, or would rather not, either would be fine with me. How does that sound?'

'Perfect. I can't thank you enough.'

'I don't want thanks, Anna. Now, let's put these flowers in water before *they* start wilting as well!'

Beatrice's bracing company was just the tonic Anna needed, and she found herself able to talk quite freely about Miles, even about the day he died.

'It was such a shock,' she remembered. 'One minute he was fine and looking forward to his game of golf. The next, there was a knock at the door to say he was dead. It was . . . unbelievable.'

She looked across the pub table at her friend. 'God, Bea, I miss him so much! So how, in the name of heaven, could I have become involved with Lewis?'

'Perhaps you needed more comfort than I or the kids could give you,' Beatrice suggested.

'Sex, you mean?' Anna demanded bluntly.

'Perhaps.' Bea's voice was calm. 'Or, put more sympathetically, physical comfort as well as emotional. Look, you promised to be faithful to Miles *till death did you part*, right?'

Anna nodded.

'So – were you unfaithful while he was alive?'

Anna looked shocked. 'Of *course* not!'

'Then why the hell are you beating yourself up like this? There's even a school of thought that says finding someone else within a year is proof of how much you loved your partner, though I confess I'm not entirely convinced.'

'Sounds like a cop-out to me.'

Beatrice laughed. 'That's more like the Anna I know!'

'You're right. Which shows I'm ready to stop wallowing and hear all about your plans. Have you any exciting bookings lined up, important people or events you're catering for?' She gave a little laugh. 'I sincerely hope Mandelyns' thirty-year bash isn't one of them?'

'No, I haven't been thus honoured, you can relax on that front. But I have one or two engagements which sound promising.'

And, emotional issues temporarily shelved, they settled down to discuss more pleasurable and less hazardous subjects.

At another pub ten miles west of them, Sophie and Jonathan sat in subdued silence. Vicky, having committed to hearing Year Two read in the school library, had been unable to join them.

It had started to rain as they arrived at the church, intensifying the sadness both were feeling as they walked through the cemetery to their father's grave and read the inscription on the headstone. In front of it was a flower bed, where, in the early days, Anna had planted small annuals and low-growing shrubs. Some were still in bloom, but others looked bedraggled and forlorn in the wet earth.

They'd held an umbrella over each other as first one, then the other, placed the flowers they had brought in the stone container provided for the purpose.

'Ought we to check there's enough water in it?' Sophie had asked.

Jonathan looked up at the leaden sky. 'If there isn't, there soon will be!'

'All the same, I think I'll get a watering can and top it up. The rain mightn't penetrate the foliage.'

Their offerings having been provided for, they'd stood for a moment in silence, heads bowed. Then Sophie's hand crept into her brother's, and, together, they had turned away and made their way back to the car.

Jonathan glanced out of the pub window. The rain was heavier now, providing no incentive to move.

'Would you like coffee?' he asked.

Sophie looked up. 'Yes, please.' Her fingers played with the cutlery in front of her. 'I wonder how Ma's bearing up. I hope she's OK.'

'She will be.'

'Don't be too hard on her, Jon.'

'I didn't think I was being.'

The waitress approached to remove their plates, and they ordered coffee.

When she'd moved away, Sophie said, 'You don't really think Lewis had anything to do with the girl's death, do you?'

He shrugged. 'If she was a danger to his beloved Mandelyns . . .'

Sophie considered the point, neither conceding nor opposing it. 'It must have come as a terrific shock, a girl you knew being murdered. How did you hear about it?'

Jonathan stared at her, his mind whirling. Coming completely out of the blue, this was a question he'd not prepared for.

'TV or radio, or not till you read it in the paper?' She looked at him questioningly, and he moistened his lips.

'I . . . don't remember.'

'Oh, come on, Jon, you must! It's not every day someone you know is murdered!'

He gazed at her helplessly, panic clogging his brain.

Sophie frowned. 'What's the matter? Why are you looking at me like that?'

'One latte, one espresso,' said a voice above them, and they made space for their cups.

Her frown deepened. 'Where were you that day? With Steve, or working from home?'

Oh, what the hell? he thought wearily. She knew half of it, she might as well know the rest.

'Actually, I was in Manchester,' he said and, above her startled exclamation, added tonelessly, 'In fact, I was the one who found her.'

*   *   *

Yvonne Standish turned into the drive of the neat little semi on the outskirts of Beechford, using her remote to open the garage door. Its purpose was invalidated, however, since, yet again, Kathy hadn't collapsed the buggy, which meant she had to get out in the rain to move it so the car would fit in the garage. One more irritant to add to her general feeling of depression.

Or perhaps not so general, since it was firmly rooted in the long-drawn-out police enquiry, and the increasing effect it was having on Lewis. Her heart ached to see the deeper lines etched on his face, the bags under his eyes, and though she yearned to offer comfort, there was little she could do.

'Hello?' she called, closing the front door and hanging her wet raincoat on the hook.

'In the kitchen,' came her daughter's voice.

Yvonne pushed open the door, to be greeted by the sight of nine-month-old Rose in her high chair, her mouth liberally covered in the orange-coloured mixture Kathy was trying to spoon into it.

'Hi,' Kathy said, without turning, but Rose treated her to a wide, toothless smile.

'You didn't collapse the buggy,' Yvonne said, striving to keep the annoyance out of her voice.

'Well, I was soaked through – I'd forgotten to take a brolly – and I wanted to get Rose indoors before she caught cold.'

An inadequate excuse, Yvonne thought, since the baby was always wrapped up to her eyebrows, but in the interests of harmony, she let it drop. The truth was that, despite her efforts over the years, she and Kathy had never been close. Punctilious and responsible by nature, Yvonne had always been irritated by her daughter's fecklessness, and now they were again living under the same roof, they continued to rub each other the wrong way. In her mother's opinion, Kathy thought only of herself, doing as little as possible around the house and several times failing to hand over the agreed sum for her keep.

A year ago, she'd been living with her boyfriend in a flat in Guildford, but soon after she became pregnant he moved out, and there was no way Kathy's wages as a hairdresser could cover his share of the rent. Yvonne had been ready enough to step in and offer accommodation till she could find somewhere cheaper, but Kathy had made no attempt to do so.

Was she being selfish, she wondered, in wanting her little house to herself? After the stresses of the day at Mandelyns, she longed for time alone, to listen to the radio or watch television, to eat when and what she wanted. But now the TV was permanently tuned to Kathy's choice of programmes, and suggested alternatives caused an evening of sulks. She never cooked supper, and she loaded or emptied the dishwasher only under protest.

Yvonne came to a sudden decision. Enough was enough; she would take matters into her own hands and find somewhere near both the hairdressers where Kathy worked and the nursery where she parked the baby. If necessary, she would offer a loan, repayable over a reasonable amount of time. Given space, they'd both recover their equilibrium, and Yvonne would make a point of babysitting at least once a week, giving Kathy a chance to meet her friends and herself the opportunity to be with her granddaughter.

Feeling marginally more cheerful, she took the ready-prepared casserole out of the fridge and was lighting the oven when the doorbell rang. Kathy, though she'd now finished with the baby, made no move to answer it, so Yvonne did so and was startled to see Tina Martin on the step, a huge umbrella sheltering her from the rain.

Yvonne's heart plummeted. 'What is it?' she asked quickly. 'Has something happened?'

'No, no. I've just been to the supermarket, and since I was in your area, I hoped we might have a quick word?'

A 'quick word' could have been exchanged at any time during the day, but Yvonne smiled agreement, waited while Tina propped the dripping umbrella in the porch, and ushered her inside.

'If you'd like to take your coat off and go into the lounge,' she said, 'I'll pop the supper in the oven, then pour us both a drink. Or—?' She broke off, realizing Tina would be driving.

'A small one would be fine, and very welcome.'

She met Kathy at the kitchen door, Rose in her arms. 'Who was it?' she asked.

'A friend from work. I don't think she'll stay long, but it would help if you could see to the vegetables.'

'I'm going to bath Rose.'

'Before you go up? It would only take . . .' But her daughter had disappeared up the stairs.

Counting to ten, Yvonne put the dish in the oven, took wine from the fridge and glasses from the cupboard, and went back to the lounge. Tina had removed her coat and draped it over a chair.

'I hope this isn't inconvenient?' she said belatedly.

'No, it's fine. What was it you wanted to discuss?'

'Oh, I just thought that, as fellow suspects, we might compare notes.'

Yvonne, about to hand over her glass, paused. 'Suspects?'

'Well, let's face it, we are, aren't we? All of us? We were on the scene, and any one of us could have done it. No wonder the police are lingering.'

Yvonne moistened her lips. 'And exactly what would have been our motive?'

Tina shrugged. 'I can't speak for the men, but as far as we're concerned, she was a stuck-up little so-and-so, wasn't she? Thought she was better than the rest of us, when in reality she'd the morals of an alley cat.'

'*What*?'

'Well, perhaps that's a bit strong, but she must have been handing out her favours. I mean, it's pretty obvious, isn't it, that she met someone up there, either by arrangement or pickup?'

That, Yvonne remembered, had been the suggestion put forward by Mike and seconded by Tina, up in Manchester. Why, she wondered, was she repeating it now?

'That must have been what happened,' Tina was hurrying on, 'because the only alternative is that it was one of us.' She took a quick sip of her drink. 'Do you think the police are making any headway?'

'We've no way of knowing, have we? I only hope they're off the premises before the twentieth. But Tina, I can't believe you've come out of your way on a wet evening, just to go over it all again! If it's worrying you so much, why didn't you bring it up during the day?'

'Because there's no privacy there at the moment. I've the feeling everyone's trying to hear what you're saying.' Another gulp of wine. 'Also, I'm very worried about Mike. This is really getting him down.'

'Lewis too,' Yvonne said quietly. 'And no doubt Cameron, though we don't see as much of him.'

Tina nodded abstractedly. 'I know it's ghastly for everyone, but honestly, Mike's going to have a stroke or something if he goes on like this.' She paused. 'Strictly *entre nous*, I found a bottle of whisky in his desk drawer.'

'That's not good, certainly.'

'No. I was wondering—' She broke off, started to say something, then seemed to change her mind. 'Look,' she said quickly, 'I'm holding you up – I must go.'

She finished her wine in one draught, caught up her coat, and shrugged it on as she hurried to the front door. But as they reached it, she turned back to Yvonne.

'Who do *you* think did it?' she challenged.

'I don't know, Tina, but if I were you, I should stop trying to second-guess the police and let them get on with it. They'll nail someone eventually.'

Tina shuddered. 'It makes you wonder, though, doesn't it?'

Yvonne could only agree that it did.

The next morning, Sophie was still reeling from Jonathan's disclosure, and her anxiety on his behalf had trebled. When, with only passing interest, she'd first read about the murder, she couldn't in her wildest dreams have imagined that not only was one of the suspects involved with her mother, but her own brother had found the body. Come to that, she *still* couldn't believe it; it was bizarre, unreal.

Also, the burden of Jon's secret weighed heavily on her. Suppose she made some slip that gave him away? He'd assured her that his alibi cleared him of the murder, but he could surely be charged with withholding information, failing to report a dead body, tampering with the crime scene, and any number of other misdemeanours. Worst of all, she daren't share this new knowledge with Angus, yet another secret she was keeping from him. In the space of a few weeks, her world had changed, and not for the better.

Her mind still occupied, she reached automatically for her ringing mobile and flipped it open to see Imogen was calling. 'Hi, Imo,' she said.

'Hi yourself. How are things?'

'Muddling along. Thanks for the card, by the way.'

'I was thinking of you all. How did it go?'

'We just took some flowers to the grave and had a quiet lunch together.' She knew Imogen would take it that her mother was included, which was all to the good. There was no acceptable explanation as to why she hadn't been.

'I was wondering,' Imogen was continuing tentatively, 'if you know why Jonathan went to see Uncle Ted the other day?'

Jon and his memory stick crusade! Why hadn't he warned her? 'Did he?' she prevaricated. 'I didn't know.'

'For some reason, he was interested that Aunt Em had been to Mandelyns.'

Thankfully, Sophie seized on her cue. 'That'll be it, then; I saw in the paper that they've an anniversary coming up. He's probably doing an article on them.'

'Oh.' Imogen sounded only half convinced.

'How is Uncle Ted?' Sophie asked quickly. 'I've been meaning to phone him.'

'He's gradually finding his feet, but I know he'd be pleased to hear from you.'

'I'll give him a ring later.'

'I'm coming up to town next week,' Imogen went on, 'to start Christmas shopping. Any chance of meeting for lunch?'

'Of course. Let me know when, and I'll book a table. The restaurants are packed this time of year.'

'See you, then. Bye.'

'Bye,' echoed Sophie. Was there anything else her brother hadn't told her about?

Yvonne was also less at ease than she'd been the day before, having spent a restless night mulling over Tina's visit and abrupt departure. She'd not found a plausible explanation for either. What had she been hoping to confirm or ascertain? And had she succeeded?

Any one of us could have done it, she'd said. Suppose, Yvonne thought suddenly, Tina had been testing her, attempting to judge if she was under suspicion herself?

Having never entertained the idea, she tried to consider it

dispassionately, on the basis that, as Tina had pointed out, they were all suspects. The motive she'd put forward – basically jealousy – was thin in the extreme, but could have been a screen for something deeper.

With a gesture of impatience, Yvonne abandoned the exercise and returned to her work.

The post had already arrived when Jonathan reached the kitchen on Wednesday morning, and Vicky was holding a large white card in her hand. She was reading it as he came in.

'What do you make of this?' she asked, passing it across.

Jonathan glanced at it, and froze. *The company of Mr and Mrs Jonathan Farrell is requested at the Thirtieth Anniversary Celebration* . . .

Oh, *God*! He looked up, meeting Vicky's bewildered gaze.

'How did they get hold of our names?' she asked anxiously. 'Does it mean they know about the memory stick? Jonathan, I don't like it! They even have our address! They—'

'Whoa!' He held up a hand, rapidly searching for the best explanation. Because there was no way he was going to miss this opportunity. 'I'm sure it's nothing sinister, love. I meant to tell you, apparently Ma met the owner of Mandelyns in South Africa. Talk about coincidence! No doubt he sent invites to everyone in the group, and since she hasn't a partner, he kindly included us, and probably Sophie and Angus, to keep her company.'

Vicky looked doubtful. 'But he doesn't even know us!'

'It's not a private party, Vic, more a publicity exercise.'

'This came with it.' She handed over another card, headed *Programme of Events.*

In order to obtain maximum enjoyment from the occasion, he read, *overnight accommodation is offered with the compliments of the management.* The events themselves were listed as Afternoon Tea from 3 p.m. to 5 p.m., Champagne Reception at 7 p.m. and Gala Dinner at 7.45. At the foot were the discreet words *Black Tie* and *RSVP by 13th November.*

'Wow!' Jonathan exclaimed. 'They're certainly pushing the boat out! You can bet all the great and the good will be there, celebs and the lot. Better take your autograph book!'

'You mean we should go?'

'For pity's sake, why not? Chances like this don't come up every day.'

'But it might be a trap! You could be walking straight into the lion's den!'

'Vicky, believe me. There's no way they could know I've any connection with the memory stick – they mightn't even know it exists.'

'But it's very short notice – next week, for heaven's sake – and we have to reply straight away.'

They'd delayed posting it till after Dad's anniversary, Jonathan surmised. Better not comment on that. He glanced back at the card. 'Overnight accommodation – that's a treat in itself! If it's anything like where Maddy stayed, it'll be extremely plush. Honestly, sweetie, all you need worry about is finding a babysitter.'

'And buying something to wear,' Vicky said. 'I haven't anything remotely suitable.'

Jonathan laughed, relief surging through him. Potential crisis successfully averted. 'I should have seen that coming!' he said.

FOURTEEN

Anna sat staring into her coffee cup. By now, Sophie and Jonathan would have received their invitations. There was no knowing how they'd react, but after her conversations with Beatrice, she'd accepted that since both of them now knew about Lewis, further secrecy was pointless. In fact, a social occasion with a lot of other people present might be the ideal way to smooth over difficulties.

Consequently, when Lewis phoned yesterday, she'd given him their addresses. Now, all she could do was hope they'd accept. Apart from more serious considerations, she'd welcome their support; she hadn't met Lewis's family, who would all be there – possibly including his ex-wife.

With a twinge of doubt, Anna hoped she was doing the right thing.

'You lucky devil!' Steve said. 'How the hell did you wangle that?'

'A sheer fluke! It turns out Lewis Masters was on safari with Ma, and he's lashed out invitations to all and sundry. So there we have it – champagne reception, overnight accommodation in the lap of luxury . . . and a legitimate chance to snoop round Mandelyns. Can't be bad.'

'You're surely not still harping on about that treatment?'

'No, I think we have to accept Elise was off-beam there, but if that wasn't the motive for her death, what was? And before you remind me, I know it's in the hands of the police now, but we *were* in at the beginning, and I can't help feeling somehow responsible. So I figured I might track down the ex-wife and, with luck, learn some home truths about her husband and son. They're two of the chief suspects, after all.'

'Seems a bit of a long shot.'

Steve didn't know, of course, that, far from a casual acquaintance, this potential murderer now loomed large in his mother's life.

'Anyway,' Jonathan continued, 'I'll see what I come up with. And failing all else, I'll get a first-hand experience of Mandelyns.'

'Maddy will be green with envy; I made a rod for my own back, letting her go to Foxfield.'

Jonathan laughed. 'Never mind, I'll give you a blow by blow account, and perhaps you'll decide to go there for your honeymoon!'

As it happened, Jonathan was finding it harder than he'd expected to track down Myrtle Page. He'd tried a succession of websites; but although most listed photographs, potted biographies, and appearances on magazines covers and advertisements (including Mandelyns' Lasting Youth products), none gave contact details. In the end, he phoned a friend at the paper, who, several hours later, came back with a phone number.

'Strictly unofficial,' he was warned, 'but this person has been used before as an intermediary. It's worth a try.'

It was a woman who answered, an elderly, fruity voice that merely gave her number.

'Ms Irving?' Jonathan began.

'To whom am I speaking?'

'My name is Jonathan Farrell; I do occasional work for *UK Today.*'

'Ah – a journalist!'

'For my sins. I've been trying to get in touch with Myrtle Page and was told you might be able to help me?'

'And why should you want to contact her?'

'I'm hoping to do an article on models of the seventies,' Jonathan improvised.

'Whom have you spoken to so far?'

An astute old bird! 'Actually, no one,' he confessed. 'I . . . wanted to start at the top.'

A low laugh. 'Myrtle might be susceptible to flattery, young man, but I'm a tougher nut to crack. I'll need more than that.'

'Well, I know, of course, that she was married to Lewis Masters of Mandelyns, and that the Group have a thirtieth anniversary coming up. I thought it would be interesting to hear about the growth of the resorts from her perspective.'

'Rather than from the horse's mouth?'

'If you're referring to Lewis Masters, I hope to speak to him as well.'

'I see. Well, I'll pass on your request for an interview and see if she's amenable. Have you a contact number?'

'Of course.' Jonathan supplied it. 'I'd be extremely grateful if you could put in a good word for me,' he added.

'You can certainly turn on the charm, can't you, Mr Farrell? I shouldn't mind being interviewed by you myself! Very well, I'll come back to you with Myrtle's answer.'

And she rang off before he could thank her. Intrigued, he Googled Geraldine Irving, to discover she'd been a minor actress in the sixties and seventies. He swore softly, chiding himself for not having checked on her before and hoping his obvious ignorance wouldn't count against him.

Back at Foxfield on his fortnightly visit, Lewis made a point of calling on Bob Jeffries, the general manager.

'What's the position on a new PA for my son?' he asked him.

'Actually, we've only just begun advertising,' Jeffries replied. 'It seemed a little . . . heartless to do so earlier, but since the investigation's dragging on, we felt we should make a start. Once we've whittled them down, Cameron will see the shortlist, but in the meantime Louise Braithwaite is doing the necessary.'

'Tell me, Bob, what's the general mood here? It's where the girl was based, after all.'

Jeffries shrugged. 'She didn't appear to have any close friends. Everyone's shocked and upset, of course, but that's probably as far as it goes. The police have been trying to find out if there was any bad feeling, but as far as I know they've not come up with anything.' He glanced at Lewis's brooding face. 'How are things at Beechford?'

'Much the same – having to sidestep the police at every turn.'

'What about preparations for the dinner? Is that going all right?'

'I believe so; I'm told most of the replies are in now. We'll be closed all next week, of course, when preparations move into the final stages.' He picked up his briefcase. 'Is Cameron around?'

'No, he's at Woodcot today.'

Lewis nodded. 'I'll catch up with him later. Goodbye, then,

Bob. I look forward to seeing you and your wife on the twentieth.'

'We're looking forward to it, too.'

Lewis took the lift down. Towelling-robed figures were hurrying across the hall in twos and threes, while another group stood chatting in front of the large open fire. One or two glanced at him as he passed, but he was barely aware of them.

Looking forward, he thought as he opened his car door, didn't necessarily translate as looking forward *with pleasure*. It was a bitter pill that what he'd anticipated for so long as a culmination of success and achievement should now be overshadowed by a murder enquiry. Surely to heaven the police would crack it soon! If he'd been given to praying, he'd have sent up a plea that it should be before next Friday.

Yvonne turned from the coffee machine and saw Tina sitting at a table by herself, a magazine open in front of her. On impulse, she went to join her.

Tina looked up with a start and forced a smile. 'Caught skiving! I was checking on recipes; the in-laws are coming to dinner at the weekend.'

Yvonne smiled and sat down opposite. 'Tina, could I ask you something?'

Tension flared in her face, but she said lightly, 'No harm in asking!'

'Just before you left the other evening, I had the impression you were about to say something. Was I right?'

Tina flushed unbecomingly, the colour spreading up from her neck to cover her entire face. 'No, I . . . don't think so.'

'Something that perhaps you thought better of saying?' Yvonne persisted.

A quick shake of the head, but Tina wasn't meeting her eyes.

Yvonne waited; and eventually she looked up.

'All right, then, but you won't like it.'

'Try me.'

Tina took a quick drink of coffee. 'I'm sure it didn't mean anything, anyway. It was just . . . that morning, before we left for Chester . . .'

Yvonne felt goose pimples on her arms. 'Yes?'

'I was on the same floor as Elise, and as I got out of the lift after breakfast, I was almost sure I saw Lewis, disappearing round a corner. I didn't think anything of it at the time; I just turned in the other direction, towards my own room.'

Yvonne felt suddenly encased in ice. 'But later, you *did* think something of it?'

Tina moistened her lips. 'Well, his room wasn't on that floor.'

There was a long silence, while Yvonne's blood drummed in her ears. 'Have you mentioned this to anyone?' she asked at last, surprised at the steadiness of her voice.

Tina shook her head.

'No one at all?'

'No. At first, what with the shock and everything, I forgot about it. Then, later . . . well, I assumed the police would have checked and must have cleared him. Anyway, I couldn't be a hundred per cent sure it was him, and if it *hadn't* been, I wouldn't have been exactly popular, shopping him to the police.'

Another silence. Then Tina said fearfully, 'What are you going to do?'

'It's your story, Tina. It's up to you, not me.'

'You think I should tell the police, even at this late stage?'

'It's entirely up to you,' Yvonne repeated. She stood up, leaving her coffee untouched. 'Thank you for telling me,' she said, and walked quickly back to her office.

Jonathan was at his desk when the call came, and he answered it automatically, his mind still on the screen in front of him.

'Jonathan Farrell?' asked a low, husky voice, and instantly it had his full attention.

'Speaking.'

'Myrtle Page. I'm told you'd like to do an interview?'

'I should indeed, Ms Page, if you're agreeable.'

'Oh, I'm always agreeable to publicity,' the voice drawled. 'But I gather this is principally to do with Mandelyns?'

'Not principally, no; what I'd like to discuss is your career – how you got started, how you rose to the top of your profession, and how much you consider the world of modelling has changed.'

'Good answer!' came the reply. 'Geraldine said you knew the right buttons to press!'

'I assure you—'

'Only teasing, Mr Farrell, pressing buttons in my turn. Don't deny me that pleasure!'

Jonathan, nonplussed, waited.

'Will you have a photographer with you?'

'I . . . thought it would be less formal without one,' he replied, never having contemplated it.

'Fine; I only asked so that I'd know how much warpaint to put on. Very well, Mr Jonathan Farrell: how would tomorrow afternoon suit you?'

'Very well indeed!' he said with alacrity. This was proving much easier than he'd feared.

'Two thirty then, at number five, King's Gate Mews, Kensington.'

'I look forward to it.'

As she rang off, he sat back in his chair, pushing his fingers through his hair. Since this was coming off sooner than expected, he hadn't yet prepared what to ask her. Obviously, she wanted to concentrate on her career, which was fair enough, if a little old hat from his viewpoint. But he was fairly sure she could be persuaded to discuss her ex-husband and his venture. According to her biography, she was now married to an actor some seventeen years her junior. Jonathan hoped he wouldn't be on the scene tomorrow.

Not having been in any hurry to return to Beechford, Lewis called in at Woodcot on his way home, making a circular tour of it and missing his son by half an hour. Of the three resorts, this had been the least affected by the investigation, since none of its personnel had been up in Manchester. As a result, there was a noticeably more relaxed atmosphere among the staff, serving only to emphasize the strain on the other two.

'I've a good mind to camp here for the next week or two!' Lewis joked to the general manager. 'It's not too pleasant at either Beechford or Foxfield at the moment. Too many boys in blue.'

'It must be hellish,' Stuart Daly sympathized. 'Are they no further on?'

'I wouldn't know, since they don't confide in me, but we live in hope.'

'I only met Elise a couple of times, when she called here with Cameron. She was an attractive little thing.'

Yes, Lewis thought, she was; the ensuing frustration and anxiety of the investigation had obscured the personal angle that should have been at its core – the tragic death of a young woman. He remembered with shame his outburst in his hotel room, the day of her death.

'You're right,' he said soberly. 'And the inconvenience is a small price to pay, if it uncovers who killed her. We owe her that, at least.'

It was after seven when he arrived back at Mandelyns Court, and he was about to take the lift direct to his flat, when he heard his name called, and turned to see Yvonne hurrying in through the front door.

'Good heavens!' he exclaimed. 'I thought you'd be long gone! Is something wrong?'

'No,' she replied a little breathlessly. 'Or at least, not exactly.' She paused. 'I was hoping to have a word with you, but when it got to seven, I thought you must have gone on somewhere for the evening. I'd just reached my car when I saw you drive in.'

'And whatever it is can't wait till tomorrow?'

She half-smiled. 'Not if I'm to get any sleep!'

'Then you'd better come up to the flat and tell me about it.'

The express lift carried them to the top floor, where Lewis threw his briefcase on to a chair, switched on a couple of lamps and drew the curtains. 'Not that anyone can see in,' he commented, 'but I dislike a black rectangle in the middle of the wall. Take your coat off. Can I get you a drink of anything? I presume you won't have alcohol?'

'Not before driving in the dark, thanks, but straight tonic would be fine.'

He poured her a glass, and a whisky for himself, before sitting back in one of the large armchairs.

'You look tired,' Yvonne said apologetically. 'Look, I'm sorry – I should have waited till tomorrow after all. I'll . . . just drink this and leave you in peace.'

'Oh no you won't, not after arousing my interest. So tell me: what is it?'

She swirled the sparkling drink round her glass. 'I so wish I didn't have to do this.'

Lewis frowned. 'Now you're really beginning to worry me. Get on with it, for God's sake.'

'Very well. It's just that . . . I had coffee with Tina this morning.'

Lewis waited.

'And she told me something had been worrying her.'

'Yes?' His impatience was increasing.

She said in a rush, 'On the last day, before we left for Chester, she . . . thought she might have seen you near Elise's room.'

There was a palpable silence. She daren't look up, kept her eyes fixed on the bubbles in her glass.

'Oh . . . my . . . God!' Lewis said very slowly.

'Obviously, she was mistaken, but I thought you should . . . know.'

God, why isn't he saying anything? Why isn't he denying it, telling me not to be so bloody silly, that of course he was nowhere near . . .?

When she could bear it no longer, she looked up, to find him staring at her, his face white.

'You're not going to believe this,' he said, his voice strangled, 'but I swear to God I'd forgotten all about it. My mind was on other things, which is why I made the mistake in the first place, and once I got to my room, it went entirely out of my head. *Entirely!*' he repeated forcefully.

Yvonne said with an effort, 'What did?'

'That I mistook my floor. The couple who were in the lift with me got out at the fourth, and I automatically followed them. I was halfway to the room that must have been directly under mine, when I realized my mistake and went back. But God help me, until this minute, I didn't know that was her floor.'

He met her eyes then, and she saw anxiety in them. 'You do believe me?'

'Of *course* I do! I never for a moment thought—'

'Thank you,' he cut in, with a strained smile. 'That's good to know. Should I speak to Tina myself, do you think? Explain?'

'It would probably be better, coming from you.'

'And, of course, I'll also tell the police.'

She made an instinctive movement. 'Is that . . . necessary?'

'Someone else might have seen me.' He frowned. 'Why, don't you think they'd believe me?'

'It's a risk, but if you feel you should . . .'

'I'll sleep on it, but I'll certainly speak to Tina, first thing in the morning. Thanks, Yvonne, for telling me. It can't have been easy.' He smiled. 'I hope that now you'll be able to sleep tonight?'

'Like a baby!' she said.

Jonathan took the tube to Gloucester Road and, following directions he'd taken from the Internet, walked for five minutes before turning off the main road into a maze of squares and terraces leading to King's Gate Mews.

Number five was identical to its neighbours, a three-storey house, the ground floor of which was mostly taken up by a double garage, with a white-painted front door alongside. The upper part of the house was in rosy brick, the first floor having three windows, the centre of which boasted a small, wrought-iron balcony, while three dormer windows punctuated the slated roof. Very nice too, he thought.

The door was opened in response to his ring by a middle-aged woman of Mediterranean appearance.

'My name is Jonathan Farrell,' he said. 'I believe Ms Page is expecting me.'

She nodded and gestured for him to enter. He saw that the house went back farther than he'd thought; there was a kitchen or utility room beyond the hallway, and from where he stood at the foot of the stairs, he could see through its window to a paved terrace beyond.

Again obeying her gesture, he followed the maid, or whatever she was, up the narrow staircase to a large living area. His immediate impression was of luxury – deep-piled carpet, expensive hangings, paintings vibrant against white walls, and deep sofas covered in cream tweed, from one of which Myrtle Page rose gracefully to greet him.

'Thank you, Isabella,' she said and, as the maid returned downstairs, came towards him with outstretched hand. 'Mr Farrell, I presume?'

'Thank you for agreeing to see me.'

Myrtle Page was by any standards a striking woman, and he found it hard to believe she was in her late fifties. Tall and almost painfully thin, she had high cheekbones, slanting eyes of a disconcertingly light blue, and a wealth of red-gold hair that he suspected was no longer natural. She was wearing tight white trousers, a silk tunic in jade green, and a heavy gold chain that hung almost to her waist.

The hand he took was long, the wrist bony, and the fingers liberally bejewelled. Once a model, he thought, always a model. He met her eyes, faintly mocking, and realized that the summing-up had been mutual.

'Please sit down,' she said. 'It's some time since anyone requested an interview. I'm out of practice.'

'I hope you won't mind my recording this?'

'Not in the least.'

He switched on the machine, setting it on the low table between them, and as he did so, she retrieved a silver cigarette case from the shelf beneath.

'And I hope *you* won't mind if I smoke? It soothes my nerves.'

'Of course not.'

'Perhaps you'll join me?' She offered the case, but he declined with a smile, watching as she lit a cigarette, inhaled deeply, and settled back on the sofa opposite him.

'Right, darling; off you go, then.'

And the interview began. Though eager to reach the part of her life that most interested him, it seemed politic to concentrate first on her modelling career. Consequently, the next twenty minutes were spent enlarging on the sketchy details he'd gleaned from his Internet search, culminating in what had proved to be her big break, being picked to model for Delaney.

'Though what I really should have been modelling was maternity clothes!' she added with her throaty laugh, lighting another cigarette. 'Because by then Lewis and I were married. Still, we managed somehow to work round my bumps.'

The opening he'd been waiting for! 'That was before he started his health clubs?' Jonathan asked, rapidly recalling dates.

'Oh yes, at that stage no one had heard of him. He was an accountant when we met, and bored out of his mind, poor love. He'd always hankered after his own business, and he had one or two tries before he hit on the health clubs. Mercifully, they took off in a big way, but for the first years of our marriage I was the main breadwinner.'

'Then, in 1980, he bought Mandelyns Court.'

'Correct; and when they launched their own beauty products – behold!' She lifted both hands, palms uppermost. 'They had a ready-made "face" to advertise them. Which, I may say with all modesty, did them no harm at all.'

'I'm sure.' Jonathan hesitated, unsure how to turn the conversation back to her husband. But again she forestalled him.

'It's appalling luck, all this bad publicity they're getting. The timing could hardly be worse.'

'Yes, indeed.' He paused. It didn't seem likely, but . . . 'Did you know the dead girl?' he asked.

'Not personally, no, though I'd seen her with my son.'

He took a shot in the dark. 'Wasn't she his PA?' Either his or his father's.

Myrtle nodded. 'Later, yes.'

A frisson ran down his spine. 'Later?'

She tilted back her head, blowing out a perfectly formed smoke ring, which she studied for a moment before continuing. 'I suppose that's how she got the job. Not, mind you, that she wouldn't have been good at it – I'm sure she was. Cameron's not one to let sentiment stand in the way of business.'

Jonathan was struggling with this new and somehow alarming angle. 'But you'd seen them together *before* she went to Mandelyns?'

'Oh yes, several months before, at the theatre. They didn't see me, and I never mentioned it – my son's a very private person. He's always had a pretty girl in tow, and I didn't give it a second thought, till I saw her again at Foxfield. I assumed she was a guest, till someone told me she was his PA.'

'You think they were still . . . in a relationship?'

'Well, darling, I'd have said that was the point of the exercise, wouldn't you? I did try a little gentle pumping once – enquired after his love life, and so on. He said his girlfriend's name was Alice, which, on reflection, was probably as close as he could get without spilling the beans.'

Her long fingers were playing with the chain round her neck.

'I'm so desperately sorry for him. He looked dreadful when we met for lunch, but when I tried to comfort him, I was immediately cut off.'

They were interrupted by the sound of footsteps coming up the stairs, and the maid Isabella appeared with a tea tray.

'I always have tea around three o'clock,' Myrtle said as it was laid on the table between them. 'It keeps me going till the sun's over the yardarm! Tea time, followed by G&T time!'

Having unloaded the tray – cups and saucers, silver teapot and milk jug, a saucer of sliced lemon and plate of shortbread – the maid withdrew, and Myrtle, stubbing out her latest cigarette, poured the tea.

'Milk or lemon?' she enquired.

'Milk, please.'

She handed him his cup and saucer and the shortbread, taking a slice of lemon for herself. Jonathan hesitated, unsure whether the interview was suspended during the tea break, though anxious to return to the subject of Cameron and Elise. But his hesitation cost him, because when she spoke, it was at a tangent.

'Anyway, if I probe too deeply into Cameron's affairs, he retaliates with some cutting remark about Damien, my husband. He persists in referring to him as my toy boy.'

Jonathan followed her glance to a silver-framed photograph on the bookcase, experiencing a stab of recognition. Damien Jessop's face was familiar from his many television appearances, but admittedly the boyish grin seemed at odds with the mature, sophisticated woman in front of him.

'No doubt you're married yourself?' Myrtle said suddenly.

'Yes, and two kids to show for it.'

'Pity!' she said enigmatically.

Jonathan flushed and was stumbling after a suitable response when the sound of the doorbell reached them.

Myrtle exclaimed with annoyance, 'Whoever can that be? I'm not expecting anyone, and Damien has his key.'

Voices reached them from below, one of them male, then a single set of footsteps, and a man rounded the corner of the staircase.

'Cameron!' Myrtle exclaimed. 'Hello, darling, we were just talking about you! What a pleasant surprise! Did you ask Isabella for another cup?'

'I can't stay, Mother,' the newcomer said tersely, his eyes on Jonathan. 'I just brought you the vouchers you asked for.'

'This is Jonathan Farrell; I think I mentioned he was coming to interview me. My son Cameron, Jonathan.'

Jonathan rose to his feet. Cameron nodded briefly, and he did the same, taking stock of the man he'd been hearing about. He was very dark, his hair sleek and showing signs of receding at the temples, his eyes deep-set and shadowed.

Before Jonathan could form some kind of greeting, Cameron said abruptly, 'I believe our parents met in South Africa.'

'Really?' Myrtle's voice rose in surprise. 'What a coincidence!'

'Is it, Farrell?' Cameron asked levelly. Then, again before Jonathan could respond: 'Have you met my father?'

'No, I—'

'Nor I your mother. Perhaps we should do a spot of joint investigating.'

'Just a minute,' Myrtle interrupted. 'Are you saying Lewis and Jonathan's mother are seeing each other?'

'Seeing's the least of it!'

She gave a low laugh. 'Well, the old fox! Good luck to him!' She glanced apologetically at Jonathan. 'But we're embarrassing my guest. Darling, do sit down, and—'

'No, really, I have to go.' He came forward and dropped an envelope on to the table. 'I'll be in touch.' His eyes flicked to Jonathan. 'Nice to have met you,' he said, and, turning, ran lightly back down the stairs, leaving the two of them to deal with the bombshell he had tossed between them.

FIFTEEN

'They were *lovers*?' Steve echoed incredulously.

'It would certainly seem so. Which puts a different complexion on things, wouldn't you say?'

'If nothing else, it explains why she was so hesitant to blow the whistle. But you're saying no one knew?'

'Well, it would have made things difficult, wouldn't it? In point of fact, though, it probably doesn't alter anything. I mean, it won't affect alibis and such.'

'Having met him, do you think he could have done it?'

'Any one of them could, as we've said all along.'

'But does being her lover make it more or less likely?'

'We won't know that till we know the motive. If we ever do.'

'Fair enough. So – how was *la belle dame*? Did she eat you for breakfast? Or tea, or whatever it was?'

'No, though if we hadn't been interrupted, who knows?'

Steve laughed. 'Dream on! Did she dig any dirt on hubby?'

'Actually, she seemed quite fond of him. I was surprised; I'd heard it was an acrimonious divorce.'

'Ah well, time heals most things, they say.'

'If you're going all philosophical on me, I'm ringing off!'

'You'll write up the interview, though?'

'Too right I will. She's back in the news, with the Mandelyns anniversary coming up. Memories of the early days, et cetera. I'm glad I got in first.'

'I suppose she'll be at the do next week. She'll be surprised to see you there!'

Or not, Jonathan thought as he ended the call. What he hadn't passed on to Steve was the fact that Myrtle had told Cameron he'd be there. That, Jonathan was sure, had been the real reason he'd called. But why, having made a detour specifically to see him, had he left after only a couple of minutes?

A possible answer struck him: Cameron might have seen his name on the guest list and wanted to be sure of recognizing him at the dinner. But again, why? So they could have a longer, more private conversation? And if so, what about? Not their parents, surely?

He switched on the recorder and replayed the interview. Since he'd hoped to continue it during tea, he hadn't turned it off, and Cameron's arrival was duly recorded, as was the slight awkward-ness following his departure.

'I hope you don't feel I came under false pretences,' he'd said to Myrtle as he left.

'Let's just say under a flag of convenience.'

'I really am a journalist, you know, and I really will write up this interview. It's been a pleasure to meet you.'

'Dear boy!' she'd said and, before he realized her intention, leaned forward and kissed him full on the lips. Jonathan went hot under the collar, remembering. Older woman or not, he could well understand Damien falling under her spell.

Karen Chadwick stood looking at her husband with folded arms.

'How long is this going on?' she demanded.

Mike looked up, startled. 'What?'

'You know damn well what – you moping around the house like a sick parrot!'

'Karen, we're in the middle of a murder enquiry, we have a dinner for a hundred guests coming up, and you ask why I'm worried?'

'But it's something more personal, isn't it? I know you, Mike.' She drew a deep breath, steadily holding his gaze. 'Tell me the truth: did you kill Elise du Pré?'

He gasped. 'Good God! What kind of question is that?'

'A necessary one, in the circumstances. *Something's* eating you up, and I want to know what it is.'

He felt the sweat break out – on his face, in his armpits, on the palms of his hands. But her first question, at least, he could answer.

'I assure you categorically that I did not kill Elise, poor girl. Why the hell should I have done that?'

'Why the hell should anyone? OK, so it's something else. And don't trot out that excuse about the dinner, because it just won't wash. You could organize such things in your sleep.'

Briefly, Mike closed his eyes. 'Don't worry, I'll sort it.'

'But you haven't, have you? It started when you got back from Manchester – which is what made me think of Elise – and I've been waiting all this time for you to discuss it with me, as usual. But you haven't, and now it's eating me up too, and I can't wait any longer. If you think you're sparing me by keeping me in the dark, not knowing's much worse.'

She slipped to her knees in front of him, taking hold of his hands. 'It can't be *that* bad!' she said encouragingly. 'As long as we're all together, nothing—' She broke off as his hands clenched, regarding him with dawning apprehension.

'You've found someone else!' she whispered.

'No! God, no!' He reached for her convulsively, pulling her into his arms.

'But it's something to do with the family? The boys?' Her voice rose. 'Mike, *tell* me, for God's sake!'

Holding her tightly against him so she couldn't see his face, he said, 'It's Paul. No –' as she instinctively jerked – 'he's not hurt. You spoke to him last night, remember? At least, not hurt in that way.'

She pulled back, searching his face. Paul, now sixteen, was their elder son, an exceptionally bright boy. He'd won a scholarship to public school, and, with his flair for languages, had set his heart on a career in the diplomatic service. The world seemed to be his oyster, so what could possibly . . .?

'He's involved in a drugs ring,' Mike said expressionlessly.

'*No!*'

'I'm afraid so, my darling. I caught the first whisper at Simon's concert, the night I got back from Manchester; John Pierce, whose son's also at Ashton, asked if I'd heard the rumours.'

'But . . . if it's just cannabis, lots of young people—'

'It's not just cannabis, it's coke.'

She gasped, her hand going to her mouth. 'But it doesn't mean Paul's involved,' she protested. 'There are over two hundred boys—'

'That's what I hoped, but I was taking no chances. The following day, Sunday, when I said I had to go to Woodcot, I went down to see him, still praying he wasn't involved. We went out for a walk, and as soon as I brought up the subject, there was no mistaking his reaction.'

'What did he say?' Karen whispered, white-lipped.

'At first, he tried to deny it, but when I persisted, he . . . went to pieces. Insisted it was only recreational – all the usual claptrap – and promised faithfully he'd never touch it again.' Mike shrugged hopelessly. 'I might have scared the life out of him, but that's as far as it went. He keeps phoning me at work – for reassurance I suppose, poor kid – but every time I ask if he's stopped using, he admits he hasn't and begs me to hang on, give him more time.'

He looked helplessly at his wife's appalled face. 'Where have we gone wrong, Karen? Where have *I*? I should have known – there must have been signs, and I missed them.'

Karen's voice cracked. 'What will you do?'

'Report him. I have to.'

She stared at him, aghast. 'But Mike, you can't! He'll go to prison! It'll ruin his life!'

'Not as much as if we do nothing. Think about it; Paul says only half a dozen of them are involved, but that's six too many, and if they're not stopped soon they'll become seriously addicted. I've been going out of my mind, wondering what to do for the best. I should have told you – of course I should – but I kept telling myself I could deal with it. I even got as far as writing to his headmaster, giving him the facts as I knew them and imploring him not to reveal his source. The letter was in my briefcase, ready to be posted next day. But I was in such a state that night that I went downstairs and sat at the kitchen table for two hours. And after several glasses of whisky, I tore it up, telling myself that if I sent it, Paul would never forgive me. And nor would you.'

He glanced at her briefly. 'There's also Simon to think of. You know how he looks up to his big brother. If Paul said jump, he would.'

'You're not saying he'd involve *Simon*?' Karen regarded him with horror.

'Who knows what he might do, when he's on a trip? No, I've dithered quite long enough, it's time for positive action. Once next weekend is over, I'll make an appointment to see Crawford. A letter was taking the easy way out – it's better done face-to-face. I'll lay the facts before him, and he can take it from there. He's a sensible chap, and he's got the good of his school to think of. He'll be determined to stamp it out, and fast.' Mike squeezed his wife's hands. 'But we'll have to accept Paul's days at Ashton are over.'

Jonathan and Sophie had agreed, over the phone, to tell their partners about Anna and Lewis, on the grounds that it might come out during the dinner. In neither case was the reaction as censorious as they feared.

'Have you met him?' Angus asked, after his initial surprise.

'Briefly.'

'What's he like?'

'Impossible to say. Ma seems fond of him, and it's apparently reciprocated, but she's been beating herself up over Dad, poor love.'

'It's a compliment to him that she wants to repeat the exercise.'

'You're not . . . shocked? Or disappointed in her?'

'Of course not, why should I be? It'll be great to see her happy again.'

Sophie put her arms round him and rested her cheek against his jacket. 'I do love you,' she said.

Vicky was even more forthright.

'Good for her!' she said.

Jonathan looked at her in surprise. 'That's all you have to say?'

'What more is there? It's great that she has a second chance.' She looked at him consideringly. 'You don't look too pleased about it.'

'He seems a bit . . . enigmatic,' Jonathan hedged.

'Have you met him?'

'No, I—'

'Then how can you possibly know? Not that there's anything wrong with a bit of enigma! Anyway, I have faith in Anna's good taste. I'm sure he's charming.'

It was arranged that Jonathan and Vicky would collect Anna, and they'd drive to Beechford together.

Now the time had arrived, she was assailed with doubts and worries. Would she be introduced to Lewis's family, and if so, in what capacity? She suspected that the high-profile guest list would all either have celebrity status or long-standing connection with the Group. She should have cleared this with Lewis, but was loath to bother him at this stage with such trivialities.

The die was cast, she told herself dramatically, and whatever would be, would be.

Saturday the twentieth of November was crisp with frost and blue of sky, the Surrey countryside bathed in thick sunshine that lit berries and bare branches alike with a touch of gold.

'Got your posh frock?' Jonathan asked humorously.

'Most certainly,' Anna replied.

'Vicky insisted on a complete new wardrobe!'

'Untrue,' Vicky calmly contradicted, from the back seat. 'A new dress, certainly, and shoes and bag to go with it, but that's all.'

'She'll be the belle of the ball!' Jonathan said fondly.

'I'm wearing my bronze satin,' Anna remarked. 'I've had it a while, but I always feel good in it.'

'It's lovely,' Vicky agreed. 'You wore it to the Golf Club dance last year.' *When Miles was with them.* She hurried on, 'It matches your highlights!'

'Thank God all I have to worry about is a black tie!' Jonathan commented. 'And by the looks of it, ladies, we've arrived.'

They'd been driving for several minutes alongside a stone wall, the length of which was now broken by a wrought-iron gate between two pillars. A man in uniform awaited them with a board, and Jonathan wound down his window.

'Good afternoon, sir. Could I have your name, please?'

'Farrell,' Jonathan supplied. 'All three of us.'

The man marked them off on his list. 'Thank you, sir; if you care to continue up the drive, my colleague will explain the parking arrangements.'

'Guarding against gatecrashers,' Vicky commented as another car turned into the gate behind them.

The drive was almost a mile long, bordered on both sides by trees and shrubs strung with fairy lights.

'It's like driving in a grotto!' Anna remarked.

As the house came into sight, a second uniformed figure approached, and again Jonathan stopped.

'If you'll drive to the front door, sir,' he was told, 'your luggage will be unloaded and your car valet-parked.'

In the large, bustling lobby, girls in powder-blue suits and white blouses were greeting guests, handing out keys, and escorting them to their rooms, while porters threaded their way to the lifts with trolleys of luggage.

'Everyone seems to be arriving at once!' Anna commented.

Before conducting them to their rooms, their hostess pointed out the drawing room, where tea would shortly be served. 'There's no hurry,' she assured them, 'just come down when you're ready.'

Anna was relieved to find her room next to Jonathan and Vicky's. 'Give me a knock when you're ready to go down,' she said. 'I wonder if Sophie and Angus have arrived yet.'

The room she found herself in was large and comfortable and had a small balcony overlooking the grounds. A tap on her door heralded the arrival of her suitcase, and she unpacked quickly, relieved to find no creases in the satin dress. She did so hope, for Lewis's sake, that everything would go off well. Perhaps, just for twenty-four hours, his worries could be put on hold.

They did not spot Sophie and Angus during afternoon tea, though with the continually moving throngs of people, it was hardly surprising. The drawing room was a large, pleasant room, where sofas and chairs had been grouped round low tables ready laid with stands of cakes, sandwiches and plates for four people. Soon after they seated themselves, a waitress arrived with two teapots, offering Indian or China tea.

As well as tiny sandwiches with a variety of fillings, there were scones, accompanied by individual dishes of cream and jam, and little iced cakes.

'I bet this isn't the usual fare!' Jonathan joked. 'Think of the calories!'

Anna was keeping an eye open for Lewis, but he was nowhere to be seen. Probably checking last-minute details for the evening, she assumed. However, when, forty minutes later, they'd returned to their rooms, he phoned her.

'Everything OK?' he asked.

'More than OK – fabulous!'

'Excellent. Family all here?'

'I came with Jonathan and his wife. I've not seen the others yet.'

'Your son's a journalist, isn't he? If he'd like to write up the occasion, he's more than welcome. My PA can give him any details he needs – we never turn down the chance of publicity!'

'I'll pass the message on! But Lewis, if anyone asks about my connection with Mandelyns, what should I say?'

'How about we're considering a merger?'

She caught her breath.

'Look,' he went on, 'we'll only manage a couple of words at most this evening, but once all this is over, I think it's time we discussed a few things. Agreed?'

For a heart-stopping moment she hesitated. But she'd already admitted to herself that just as she'd fallen for Miles so quickly, so had she for Lewis. If he now needed an answer from her, she knew what it would be. 'Agreed,' she said.

When they went down for the reception, a very different scene met their eyes. The sound of conversation had floated up the stairs to meet them as throngs of people milled about the foyer, glasses in hands, and Vicky, noting the elegant dresses of the women, was thankful she'd splashed out on a new outfit.

The drawing room was transformed. Such furniture as remained had been pushed against the walls, and a bar was set up at the far end, though it didn't appear to be in service. Through a sudden gap in the crowd, Jonathan caught sight of Myrtle, with the dapper young man who was her husband. She raised her eyebrows at him and blew a kiss. Then the crowd closed again, shutting her off from view.

Waiters and waitresses were moving between the groups with trays of glasses, and as Anna was taking hers, she heard her name called, and turned to see Wendy manoeuvring her way towards her.

'Hello, Wendy! Lovely to see a face I know!'

'Ditto! We're sitting together at dinner, which is great. Have you seen the seating plan? There are several around, but I can tell you we're on table eight.'

'Thanks. May I introduce my son and daughter-in-law, Jonathan and Vicky? Wendy Salter, whom I met in South Africa.'

'I recognize you from the photos!' Vicky said, taking her hand.

'Lovely to meet you. The rest of my family are around somewhere, but you'll see them when we go through.'

'Your daughters are with you?' Anna asked.

'One is, with her husband. The other lives in Brussels.'

'Of course – you told me.'

Their attention was claimed by a burst of static from a microphone, followed by Lewis's voice.

'Ladies and gentlemen . . .' The room fell silent. 'I'd just like to welcome you to Mandelyns Court this evening and say how delighted I am that you're helping us to celebrate our thirty-year anniversary. Everyone here has contributed in some way to the continuing success of the Group, and this is by way of a general and very heartfelt thank you. I hope to have a word with you all individually during the evening, and to this end there'll be a complimentary bar in this room after the meal, which I hope will give everyone the chance to mingle. In the meantime, dinner is now about to be served. Enjoy your meal.'

There was a burst of applause, followed by a slow drift towards the door. As she and Wendy entered the restaurant, Anna saw that each of the round tables seated ten, though when she reached theirs, only nine places were laid. To her relief, Sophie and Angus were already there, and they were soon joined by George, his daughter Joanna and son-in-law Bruce. Searching for her name card, Anna found she was seated between George and Angus.

'I've seen several famous faces,' Sophie informed them as they all sat down. 'Four TV stars and two MPs, as a starter!'

'We looked out for you at tea,' Jonathan told her.

'Actually, we skipped it. Tamsin phoned just as we were leaving, which delayed us a bit, and then we were stuck behind a tractor for about ten miles. The joys of the countryside! This place is fabulous, though, isn't it? You should see our room!'

'Have you been here before?' Vicky asked Wendy.

'Not for a long time, though we did have a weekend at Woodcot a couple of years ago.'

'I know what I'll ask for my next birthday!'

The meal was superb – individual seafood soufflés, followed by roast duckling, a magnificent cheeseboard, and a dessert of *îles flottantes*, soft meringues floating on creamy custard and topped with caramel sauce. Wines were served with each course, and coffee

and liqueurs followed. There was only one toast, proposed by a
thin, dark man whom George identified as Lewis's son Cameron,
and they all stood to drink to: 'Mandelyns – the next thirty years!'

Yvonne, who, with Tina, had been keeping a discreet eye on the
proceedings, breathed a sigh of partial relief as the meal came
to an end. Everything seemed to have gone smoothly, and her
only concern was that Cameron was drinking more than usual;
she hoped no one else had noticed the slight slur in his voice
when he'd proposed the toast. Still, she told herself, it was
understandable; they'd been under a strain for weeks now, and
this was a brief chance to relax.

Tina came up to her. 'Reckon we can escape now and have
our own meal?'

'I think so.'

'You're staying in staff quarters tonight, aren't you?'

'Yes, though I'll probably stick around till most of the guests
have gone up.'

'Good luck, then!' Tina nodded to the crowded drawing room.
'The words "free bar" acted like a magnet – looks as though
they're settling in for the night!'

As the meal ended, the ladies had taken what was euphemistically referred to as a 'comfort break', and on her return, Anna,
who'd been ahead in the queue, hesitated at the entrance to the
restaurant, wondering whether to return to their table. As far as
she could see, George, Bruce and Angus were deep in conversation, but Jonathan glanced up, saw her, and came to join her.

'Enjoy the meal?' he asked.

'Very much. I shan't need to eat for a week!'

'I'm sure you can manage a drink, though, while we "mingle"
as instructed! Sophie's keen to do more celebrity-spotting!'

Anna was about to reply, when a voice behind them drawled,
'So this is Mrs Anna Farrell.'

She turned, taken aback at the tone, and looked into the flushed
face of the man who'd proposed the toast – Lewis's son.

Jonathan said levelly, 'Let me perform the honours: Ma, meet
Cameron Masters; Cameron – as you guessed, my mother, Anna
Farrell.'

Cameron nodded, his dark eyes intent on her face.

'I met your father in South Africa,' Anna faltered, sensing animosity.

'Oh, I know.'

Jonathan said, 'If you'll excuse us, we're just—'

But to her consternation, Cameron Masters caught hold of his arm. 'Just a minute, Farrell, I want a word with you.'

Jonathan flushed. 'Then if you'll just let me reunite my mother with . . .'

But Cameron's grip had tightened, and suddenly his face changed, became somehow threatening. He said in a low voice, 'You were having an affair with her, weren't you?'

Anna gave a shocked gasp, and Jonathan stared at him in stupefaction. '*What* did you say?'

'Oh, don't play the innocent with me! I know! I followed her to your hotel!'

His voice was rising, and Anna, suddenly nervous, glanced anxiously round and, to her relief, saw Lewis moving quickly towards them.

'Cameron? What's going on?'

Cameron's hand fell. 'He was having an affair with Elise,' he said.

Lewis stiffened, his eyes moving rapidly about him. No one was looking their way. 'We'd better go somewhere we can talk,' he said tersely. 'Follow me.'

'What does he mean?' Anna asked urgently as Jonathan took her arm. 'What's he talking about?'

But Jonathan, his face white, only shook his head. Ahead of them, Lewis had opened a door, glanced inside, then waited till the three of them had entered, before closing it behind them. They were in some kind of office, furnished with a desk and chairs.

He turned to his son, his face tense. 'You'd better explain that remark,' he said.

Cameron seemed only too ready to comply, and from his flushed face and increasingly agitated manner, Anna saw fearfully that he was more drunk than she'd realized.

'I could tell, that last day,' he began, 'that she was anxious to get back from Chester, though she denied it. So when we reached the hotel, I hung around to see what she'd do, and sure enough, once everyone was out of sight, she hurried straight out again and made for the taxi rank. I went after her and took the next in line.' He stared accusingly at Jonathan. 'We followed her to the Commodore Hotel.'

Anna turned to Jonathan. 'You were there, in Manchester? You never told me.'

'Go on,' Lewis commanded. Jonathan, watching his face, wondered if he was reaching the same conclusion as himself. Poor bugger, he thought.

Cameron paused, his breathing laboured. 'By the time I'd paid off the taxi,' he continued after a minute, 'she'd disappeared. There was no sign of her in the public rooms, so the only possible explanation was that she'd gone to one of the bedrooms.'

'But why should you think it was Jonathan's?' Anna queried, but again received no answer.

'I was surprised – relieved, I suppose – to see her back for dinner,' Cameron went on, 'and as soon as it was over, I took her aside and asked her where she'd been. She refused to say and cut me short by going upstairs with Tina. Later, I knocked on her door, but she wouldn't open it, and, not wanting to disturb other guests, I had to leave it.'

Lewis reached behind him for a chair. 'I think we'd better sit down,' he said. He turned to his son, who, alone, remained standing. 'What I don't understand is why it mattered if she'd met someone?'

Cameron didn't reply, and it was Jonathan who said flatly, 'Because they were lovers. Had been, since before she went to Mandelyns.'

Lewis's attention switched to him. 'What makes you say that?' he demanded harshly.

'His mother told me.'

Cameron laughed – an ugly sound. 'Good old Mother! Always one to rely on! I wondered why you were sniffing round her.'

'But why make a secret of it?' Lewis demanded, and Anna ached at the hurt in his voice. 'You could have told me, surely? After all, there was no reason why you *shouldn't* have had a relationship. And what about Alice? Ah!' He supplied the answer himself. 'Alice – Elise. Of course.'

'But I *still* don't understand why he suspected Jonathan,' Anna persisted.

'He took her mobile,' Jonathan said.

There was instant, total silence as the implications of his words sank in.

Then Lewis came slowly to his feet, his face a mask. 'My God,' he said softly.

Anna also rose and, hurrying to his side, took his hand, which closed on hers almost convulsively. Jonathan, watching the two of them, felt a constriction in his chest. This, he realized, was the greatest possible test of their feelings for each other.

Lewis's eyes were riveted on his son. 'I think you'd better go on,' he said.

Cameron stared back at him, his eyes brilliant, his face contorted. 'I'm sorry, Father,' he stammered in a choked voice. 'It should never have happened. God damn it, I *loved* her!'

If he expected a response, he didn't get one, and, after a minute that seemed to last for ever, he dug a packet of cigarettes out of his pocket, extracted one, and lit it with shaking hands, inhaling deeply before continuing. 'I didn't sleep that night. I was jealous, angry, frustrated – everything rolled into one. I knew I couldn't get through the day without knowing who she'd been with, so after breakfast I went back to her room and was about to knock, when I saw her coming down the corridor. She stopped when she saw me, but she could tell I wouldn't be put off this time, and we went into her room.'

There was a long silence. Cameron swayed on his feet, and Jonathan, pitying him in spite of everything, pushed one of the chairs towards him and he sank on to it. Tears were now coursing down his cheeks, and he made no attempt to wipe them away.

'She swore she wasn't seeing anyone, though I could tell she was alarmed when I mentioned the Commodore. And when she *still* refused to say who she was visiting, I just . . . lost it. I caught hold of her and started to shake her, shouting at her to tell me the truth.'

There was a long pause, then, slowly, he continued. 'She must have thought I was going to hit her, and God help me, I might have done. The table was just behind us, and the next thing I knew, she had the knife in her hand.'

Anna, only partially understanding, glanced up at Lewis. He seemed to have aged ten years in as many minutes, and her hand tightened on his, offering him what support she could.

'We struggled for a moment or two.' Cameron's voice was ragged. 'Then . . . I'm still not sure what happened, though God knows I've gone over it often enough. One moment we were struggling, the next, one or other of us lost our balance and we fell together. The knife—' He broke off again, this time covering his face with one hand.

Lewis cleared his throat. 'I think we can skip the next bit,' he said, 'but I assume it was you who sent the text?'

His son nodded. 'God, if I could only turn the clock back! I never meant her to get hurt!'

Anna stared from one Masters to the other, unable to take it in. *Lewis's son* had killed that girl? Numbed by the enormity of it, above all fearful for Lewis, she pressed closer and, disengaging his hand, he put his arm round her and pulled her against him.

Jonathan, having expected to be the one to support his mother, realized, with mixed feelings, that he'd been superseded and, even in the macabre circumstances, found he was glad of it. As Cameron appeared to have come to the end of his account, he took up the story.

'Elise texted me to say she'd prefer not to meet in public,' he began, 'so I sent back my room number. Cameron would have seen that, and my name in her list of contacts; he phoned my number later, to check. But she was telling the truth, Cameron: our connection was strictly business.'

Cameron gazed at him with bloodshot eyes. 'So why the hell *did* she meet you?'

'To discuss the memory stick.'

Both Masters stared at him in disbelief.

'*Elise* had the memory stick?' Lewis demanded incredulously.

'Yes; she copied the files because she was convinced one of your products was responsible for some deaths. She'd tried to talk to Cameron about it, but he threatened her with court proceedings, so she contacted me, knowing I did investigative work. But I have to say it took three or four attempts before she could bring herself to tell me. She'd meant to bring the evidence, as she saw it, to my hotel that evening, but you were late back and she hadn't time to go to her room and collect it.'

Jonathan hesitated, realizing thankfully there was no need to mention his own visit the following day. 'So she posted it to me the next morning. She must have been coming back from doing so, when she met Cameron.'

'Which explains the open safe,' Cameron said dully. 'The police kept harping on about that.'

'You shopped me to the police, didn't you?' Jonathan accused. 'But why wait over a week after you'd phoned to check on me?'

Cameron shrugged wearily. 'It was an attempt to deflect them. Once they had the memory stick, they redoubled their efforts at Mandelyns, questioning everyone all over again. I was . . . afraid the truth might come out.'

'Well, luckily for me I had an alibi for the time of death.'

'But Elise wasn't . . . You weren't . . .?'

'No, I swear it.'

Slowly, very slowly, Cameron bent forward until his forehead was resting on the desk in front of him.

Lewis gazed at him for a minute, then, the father in him making way for the businessman, turned to Jonathan and said tightly, 'I trust you realize there was no truth whatsoever in her allegations?'

'I do now.' Jonathan paused. 'The only death the product caused was her own.'

Silence stretched into every corner of the room, broken suddenly by Cameron's harsh sobs.

Gently, Lewis removed his arm from Anna. 'Excuse me, I must speak to my PA.'

He moved across the room, taking out his mobile. 'Yvonne? I must ask you to make my apologies; Cameron and I have been called away urgently, so we won't be returning to the drawing room, nor will we be on hand to see people off tomorrow.'

The PA must have expressed concern, because he continued, 'No, no, we can manage. But I'd be grateful if you'd put a notice on the board outside the restaurant, so everyone will see it when they go in for breakfast. Something to the effect that we apologize for our unavoidable absence, but hope everyone enjoyed their stay and that we'll soon have the pleasure of seeing them again at Mandelyns.'

Her protesting voice reached them in the seconds it took him to switch off.

'Is there anything I can do?' Jonathan asked awkwardly.

Lewis looked down at his son, sprawled across the desk. 'Thank you, no. I'll drive him to the police station. It's quite safe, I've had nothing to drink.' A grotesque smile. 'Too busy keeping an eye on the festivities!'

The sands had shifted again, Anna thought despairingly, and for Lewis, they could well be quicksand. She went to him and put a hand on his arm. 'Shall I come with you?'

Briefly, the hard lines of his face softened. 'No, darling; this is something I must do alone.'

'But you'll . . . phone me?'

'Of course.' He straightened his shoulders and looked from one to the other. 'I know it'll be difficult, but I'd be most grateful if you'd keep this quiet for the moment. It will be public knowledge soon enough, but I'd prefer it not to mar the weekend.'

'Of course,' Jonathan said, for both of them.

'And though this is neither the time nor the place to say so, I want you to know, Jonathan, that I care very deeply for your mother, and if she'll have me, I'll do all in my power to make her happy.'

'Thank you.' It seemed an inadequate reply, but was all he could manage.

Lewis nodded and turned to his son. 'Better get this over,' he said.

Cameron sat back, rubbed his hands over his face, and stumbled to his feet. Then, with his father's hand on his arm, they left the room.

Anna and Jonathan looked at each other.

'It's . . . unbelievable,' she said unsteadily. 'A heartbreaking story. So tragic and so unnecessary.'

'I know.' Jonathan helped her back to her chair, sat down next to her, and took her hand.

'But you knew a lot more about it, all along.' She turned to him, frowning. 'What was that about shopping you to the police?'

'It was a shot in the dark, but it had to be him. As I guessed, he got my name from her mobile, which he must have taken so he could send the text Lewis mentioned. But then he'd have seen *my* text to Elise, which gave him my name and room number, and he passed them, together with the name of the hotel, to the police. Diversionary tactics, as he said. So, of course, they came round, demanding to know what I was doing with Elise in my hotel room, the night before she died.'

Anna clutched his hand. 'My *God*!'

'Fortunately, I was in Manchester on business and had an alibi for the time she died, so it came to nothing.'

'What must Lewis be going through?' Anna whispered. 'I wish there was something I could do.'

'There will be, later. He'll need you in the months ahead.'

She nodded, and for several minutes mother and son sat in silence, deep in their thoughts.

Then Jonathan roused himself. 'The family will be wondering where we are.'

'Yes; we must go back and give nothing away. Quite a tall order!'

'We'll say I had a nosebleed, and you stayed with me till it stopped.'

'You've never had a nosebleed in your life!'

'Seems a good time to start!' He helped her up and put an arm round her. 'It's been one hell of a shock. Are you all right?'

'No,' she answered, 'but I shall be. Once the sands have settled.'

'The sands?'

She gave a small, sad smile. 'No matter. Let's join the family at the bar. I'm more than ready for that drink you mentioned.'

Jonathan bent and kissed her. 'I'm proud of you,' he said. 'And just for the record, when the sands or whatever have settled, I think you two will be very good for each other.'

'Thank you, darling,' she replied. 'So do I!'